BEAUTIFUL
DISASTER

BEAUTIFUL DISASTER

A PRIVILEGE NOVEL

BY

KATE BRIAN

SIMON & SCHUSTER BFYR

New York   London   Toronto   Sydney

alloy**entertainment**

Produced by Alloy Entertainment
151 West 26th Street, New York, NY 10001

SIMON & SCHUSTER BFYR

An imprint of Simon & Schuster Children's Publishing Division
1230 Avenue of the Americas, New York, New York 10020

SIMON & SCHUSTER BFYR is a trademark of Simon & Schuster, Inc.
Designed by Andrea C. Uva
The text of this book was set in Adobe Garamond.
Manufactured in the United States of America
2 4 6 8 10 9 7 5 3 1
Library of Congress Control Number 2009923734
ISBN: 978-1-4169-6760-6

FIRST
EDITION

For Matt: Couldn't have gotten through the last year without you!

NEW FRIENDS

"Hi, I'm Briana Leigh Covington, but you can call me Ana."

Ariana Osgood stood before the trio of girls in the center of the sunlit campus of Atherton-Pryce Hall and held her breath. She felt the weight of this moment in every bone, every muscle, every tendon of her body. The very first moment of her brand-new life.

It seemed as if it had taken forever to get to this place. The stark memories of all she had been through—the months and months locked up at the Brenda T. Trumbull Correctional Facility for Women, the hours spent planning her escape, the days on the road, wending her way west from Virginia to Texas—all of the images and emotions crowded her brain, threatening to overwhelm her. Ariana had risked everything to get here, to earn a new chance at life. She had cheated, stolen, even killed her friend, Briana Leigh Covington, so she could assume the girl's identity and be truly and utterly free. And now she was finally here.

"Did you say 'Briana Leigh Covington'?" the tall, willowy girl asked. As if she had heard the name before. Ariana's heart stopped. Did this girl know Briana Leigh? Ariana had just arrived at this hallowed private school for the ridiculously overprivileged. Just stepped onto this gorgeous, perfectly manicured campus for the very first time. The jig couldn't possibly be up that fast.

"Yes," she said firmly, steadily. Her fingers gripped the handle on her rolling trunk a bit tighter, but not so tightly that anyone would notice. "But I prefer to be called Ana."

The girl's hazel eyes quickly flicked over Ariana's outfit, her tasteful chocolate brown Theory dress and Gucci slingbacks. They assessed her set of Louis Vuitton luggage with a glance, then slid back up to her face, lingering for a moment on her long, auburn hair, which had been dyed to match Briana Leigh's natural hue. Throughout this ever-so-brief process, Ariana grew increasingly warm, but she didn't move. This was a normal and accepted practice among her people. A girl had the right to take a moment to decide upon the value of knowing the stranger standing before her.

"Interesting," the assessor said finally, noncommittally. She glanced at each of her two friends, the impeccably groomed Chinese girl to her right, and the chunky-jewelry-loving blonde to her left. The blonde smiled almost imperceptibly, and the other girl suddenly became very interested in her BlackBerry. Ariana had the uncomfortable feeling that she was being silently mocked right to her face. Something she had done to many an unfortunate girl, but which had never been done to her.

"I'm Brigit Rhygsted," the blond girl piped up, taking a step forward and offering her hand. She had a hint of a Norwegian accent and the healthiest glow Ariana had ever seen. "This is Soomie Ahn and Maria Stanzini."

Ariana shook Brigit's hand and nodded as the other two girls said hello. For the first time in a long time, she had no idea what to say next. What did a person say to the people who might or might not be mocking her? She had no idea, and she detested the feeling. A group of younger girls walked by and called out hellos to the trio, which Maria and the others acknowledged with brief nods and vague smiles. They were paltry greetings that nevertheless elicited proud grins from those upon whom they were bestowed. Clearly, Ariana had chosen wisely. These were the girls whom all the other girls looked up to. The ones who could not be approached without an invitation. But she *had* approached. She had shown that she believed herself to be equal to their stature. That had to count for something.

"What year are you?" Brigit adjusted the strap on her messenger bag, and her colorful plastic bracelets clinked together.

"I'm a junior," Ariana replied. Even though she had been a junior three years ago. Briana Leigh would have been a junior, so a junior she would be. "What y—"

"Really? Us too! Well, me and Soomie. Maria's a senior. What dorm are you in?" Brigit asked.

Ariana hesitated at having been cut off. Also something she hadn't experienced very often. "Cornwall. What about—"

"Where did you transfer from? You have an accent. Are you from the South? Do you have any friends here? A boyfriend, maybe?" Brigit asked, lowering her voice and giving Ariana a conspiratorial look.

Ariana glanced around at the other cliques on the quad, chatting and laughing in the sunshine. *Had* she chosen the right crowd? There was no way she could be friends with someone who asked this many personal questions in the space of fifteen seconds. Across the way, standing on the steps of the chapel, was an olive-skinned girl with thick black hair tumbling in waves down her back, who seemed to be watching Ariana and the others from the corner of her eye while she chatted with a group of handsome guys and perfectly coiffed girls. She, too, looked like a queen bee, just as Maria had from afar. Was it possible that Ariana had aligned herself with the wrong girls? Had she already made such an awful mistake?

"I—"

"Don't let her scare you," Soomie said, sliding her BlackBerry into the pocket of her navy blue blazer. She smoothed her already smooth black hair and lifted her chin slightly, giving Ariana a better look at the perfectly tied knot in her gold and gray striped tie. The collar of her white shirt was so starched the points looked as if they could slice through metal. "There are three things you need to know about Brigit: A) She needs to know everything about everyone; B) she has the memory of an elephant; and C) she makes excellent hot chocolate. Really. It's her thing."

A phone beeped and Maria quickly removed an iPhone from her bag. She read a text, smirked, and returned the phone to another pocket altogether. Ariana's face burned. Soomie had just put *her* phone away, and she couldn't shake the feeling that Soomie had just texted Maria. Were they talking about her right in front of her face?

Brigit, meanwhile, shrugged and smiled happily. Her uniform wasn't quite as impeccably kept as Soomie's. Her tie was a tad loose and her gray blazer hung open over her untucked shirt. "It *is* my thing," she echoed. "What's yours?"

All three of them looked at Ariana with interest. She took a deep breath. She had to stop being so paranoid. She hadn't figured out Soomie and Maria yet, but Brigit's total lack of self-consciousness was kind of sweet and endearing. Maybe even sweet and endearing enough to help her ignore the third degree. If the girl would let her.

"So, where is Cornwall, exactly?" Ariana asked, even though she knew its precise location, due to the fact that she had long since memorized the campus map.

For the last two weeks, Ariana had been holed up at the Philmore Hotel waiting for Briana Leigh's body to be found at the bottom of Lake Page, where Ariana and her former Brenda T. roommate, Kaitlynn Nottingham, had dumped it. In the meantime, she had spent hours perfecting Briana Leigh's signature, memorizing the welcome packet sent by the Atherton-Pryce Hall admissions office, and tying up loose ends—canceling Briana Leigh's phone, which had been stolen by Kaitlynn right after the girl had betrayed Ariana; writing a breakup letter to Briana Leigh's fiancé, Téo; and securing a fake ID for herself, since she knew everyone at APH would have one.

Thanks to all that time with her nose buried in the APH map, Ariana knew that the campus was laid out in a series of circles, extending outward from the fountain, which was at the exact center of the grounds. The inner buildings—tall and stately, constructed of red brick with white columns and ivy-covered entryways—were the classroom buildings, the chapel, the dining hall and student center, and the administrative offices. Just beyond those, forming a wider circle, were the eight dorms—boys' to the north, girls' to the south—all of them three-story colonial-style homes, each with ten dorm rooms, two common-area bathrooms, and a lounge on each floor. The outermost circle was a bit more imprecise and formed by the gymnasium, the athletic fields, the theater, the arts building and the Pryce Building, which stood on the bank of the Potomac, grand and imposing, like a stern grandfather keeping an eye on the grounds. There was also a ninth dorm, Wolcott Hall, which had been built just down the hill from the Pryce Building, high enough to overlook the campus, but not high enough to appear more important than Pryce. In the brochure, it had been described in the same terms as all the other dorms, with the exception of one important adjective: "coed."

Ariana had never heard of a coed dorm on a prep school campus. She was, therefore, intrigued about its existence. But the housing office had not placed her there, and she could find out more about it in time.

"Cornwall's through here." Maria tipped her head to the side toward the surrounding buildings. Her long gold earring just grazed her shoulder as she turned around. Her uniform looked like it had been fished from the bottom of a duffel bag. Wrinkled shirt, frayed blue jacket, tie balled up and shoved into the breast pocket, pleated plaid skirt with a falling hem. And yet, she was the most beautiful and self-possessed of the three. "Follow us."

"We're all in Cornwall too. For now," Soomie offered up as they walked away from the fountain at the center of campus. "It's the oldest dorm on the grounds, which means, of course, that it was a boys' dorm for about two hundred years. Which means it still smells like sweaty socks."

Maria rolled her eyes. "It does not. You just have sensitive nostrils."

"No, *your* olfactory senses have simply been destroyed due to hours in the studio with dozens of perspiring dancers," Soomie shot back.

"Are you saying that *I* smell?" Maria asked, laying her fingers delicately to her chest.

"Oh, no, Ria. You're all roses all the time," Soomie replied with a touch of sarcasm, earning a narrow-eyed look from Maria.

"Maria is a ballerina. It's *her* thing," Brigit explained to Ariana. "What's your thing?"

"You already asked me that," Ariana said.

"I know. But you didn't answer," Brigit replied, her expression openly curious.

Ariana thought back to Easton Academy. To her poetry and her stint as editor of the literary magazine. She had loved writing back then, but she hadn't put pen to paper in over a year. All thanks to Dr. Meloni, her psychiatrist at the Brenda T. He had stolen all her poetry journals and laughed at her work—right in her face. Since then, Ariana had been unable to write a line. The man who was supposed to help her had effectively taken away her one emotional outlet. Her blood began to boil just thinking about it. Thinking about him.

Calm down. It's over. You never have to lay eyes upon that man again, she told herself, taking a deep breath. *And don't forget, your and Kaitlynn's escape got him fired. So there's justice in that, at least.*

Still, thoughts of Kaitlynn brought up a whole *new* wave of unpleasant emotions. Fear, humiliation, the sting of betrayal. Ariana's former best friend was still out there somewhere, and she was the only person who knew Ariana Osgood was still alive—that she had not, in fact, drowned herself in Lake Page and that the body the police had found was not hers. But she took a deep breath and let it go. Kaitlynn had no idea where Ariana was. She couldn't hurt her. Not anymore.

"I think I'm still looking for my thing," Ariana replied calmly.

"Interesting," Soomie said. Ariana blinked. She was very aware of the fact that that was the second time that one word had been used to describe her. Soomie regarded Ariana for a long moment, as if she was trying to glean some sort of information from her face. A tiny knot tightened around Ariana's heart. Then Soomie suddenly looked down at Ariana's feet. "*Love* the shoes, by the way. Gucci?"

"Thanks. And yes. Good eye," Ariana said, impressed. She was always noticing people's footwear as well, and she felt a potential kinship with Soomie. "So, is fashion *your* thing?"

"Not exactly. Details. Details are my thing," Soomie replied, eyeing Ariana coolly.

Ariana smiled. Perhaps Soomie was a kindred spirit.

"Nothing gets past Soomie," Maria added in a pointed tone.

The smile instantly fell away from Ariana's face and the knot around her heart tightened excruciatingly. Was she trying to tell Ariana that she was still being evaluated? Or perhaps it was worse. Perhaps she and Soomie had already figured out somehow that Ariana was hiding something.

Don't let them get to you. Don't let them see you sweat.

"Interesting," Ariana said, throwing their own word back at them. She saw the three girls exchange an amused look and wondered what they were thinking. Were they impressed by her gumption? Annoyed? Surprised? She wished she knew why these girls seemed to be studying her so very intently. She detested the way it made her feel—uncertain, threatened, and suddenly exhausted. Over the past few weeks she had imagined this moment hundreds of times, the moment she would arrive at her new school and begin her new life, but she had never imagined it would be quite this difficult, this confusing, this intimidating.

The three girls took extralong steps, avoiding the Atherton-Pryce Hall crest, which was etched into the stone at the crossing of three walkways. Ariana made sure to go around it with her luggage, having read in the school's history that treading on the crest brought bad luck. She had left all her bad luck behind, along with her old identity, her old friends, her old school.

"Impressive," Maria said, pausing and reaching back to adjust her loose ponytail. Her sleeves rode up a bit, exposing a few faded bruises around the girl's wrists. "How did you know about the crest?"

"I like to be informed," Ariana replied.

"Interesting," Soomie said again.

Ariana's shoulder muscles coiled. She was starting to grow weary of that word.

"So, Ana, what do you think of APH so far?" Brigit asked, glancing over her shoulder as they came around the class building and into the open space in front of the ring of dorms. The grassy area was dotted with shade trees, perfect for studying under in the fall and spring.

"It's a beautiful campus," Ariana said as a warm breeze rustled the leaves overhead. She felt a sudden surge of anticipation. As if anything could happen. So what if these girls were still evaluating her? She was certain they would accept her in time. And if not, maybe they weren't worthy of *her* attention.

This is your *new chance at life,* she told herself. *Don't let anyone else make the rules.*

"I think I'm going to be very happy here."

Happier than she'd been where she had come from. Which wasn't hard, of course. But that unpleasantness was in the past. This was her future.

NOT-IN-THE-KNOW

"He toured North America *and* Europe this summer, and every one of his concerts sold out in under ten minutes," Soomie was saying as Ariana led the small group into her dorm room. "He had to cancel his dates in Asia because people were getting violent waiting on line."

"That's so insane," Brigit said. "I can't even imagine."

"Try imagining how inflated his ego must be," Maria said with a scoff. "He's going to be intolerable."

Ariana was only half tuned in to the conversation. She was too busy checking out her new home. The dorm room was bright and airy, with freshly painted eggshell walls and gleaming maple floors. Two huge windows faced the quad, one over each of the twin beds, filling the room with sunlight. She paused in the center of the room and looked around, noting the large walk-in closets and the antique but well-kept oak furniture. The scent of wood polish filled the air. Not even the faintest hint of sweat sock.

Ariana's roommate had apparently already come and gone. Next to one of the dressers was a pile of colorful luggage, and several garment bags hung in one of the closets. There was a small, cream-colored envelope in the center of the girl's mattress. Ariana turned and saw that she had one as well. The name "Briana Leigh Covington" was handwritten across the front in ornate script.

"What's this?" Ariana asked, picking up the envelope.

"Don't open that!" Maria, Brigit, and Soomie all shouted at the same time. Ariana's heart flew into her throat and her hand went to her chest.

"Why not?" she breathed.

At that moment an impossibly tall, gorgeous, athletic girl with short blond curls walked into the room, looking like a younger Heidi Klum with short hair. She strode over to one of the desks and grabbed the laptop sitting there. Her jeans were extremely tight and she wore a short-sleeved white top with eyelet details around the edges of the sleeves. When she turned around, she looked at Ariana with complete disdain.

"Because, Transfer Girl, you're not supposed to open it until the rally," she said with a thick German accent.

Ariana blinked. This rude giantess was her roommate?

"Hi, Allison," all three girls recited, sounding totally bored. Allison shot them the same look she'd given Ariana and heaved a sigh.

"I'm Ana Covington," Ariana said, offering her hand. "It seems we're going to be roommates."

"Not for long," Allison replied, tucking her laptop under her arm.

A peal of laughter caught Ariana's attention, and she turned to find a newcomer standing in her doorway. It was the queen bee girl from the chapel steps, and up close she was even more beautiful, her eyes a stunning jade green. She had a tiny rhinestone stud in her nose and wore her white blouse with one too many buttons open. Her tie was completely undone, hanging around her neck and dangling suggestively over her chest.

"Don't pay attention to her. She had a long flight," the girl said to Ariana in a friendly way. "I'm Tahira Al Mahmood, and you must be Briana Leigh Covington."

Ariana blinked. Why did everyone seem to be expecting her?

"She calls herself Ana," Allison said in her thick accent.

"Nice. Much more manageable." Tahira stepped into the room, crossed her arms over her chest, and looked around at Maria, Brigit, and Soomie, her expression amused. "Ladies," she said by way of greeting. "Staking claim to the new girl, I see. Weren't you even going to give her a chance to choose for herself?"

"*She* walked up to *us*," Brigit protested.

"Brigit," Soomie scolded. Ariana could only imagine she was calling Brigit out on the immature tone of her statement.

"What do you mean, choose?" Ariana asked. She had the distinct feeling there was some kind of rivalry going on here, and she wanted to make sure she was on the right side.

Allison hugged her laptop to her chest and stood next to Tahira. Tahira opened her mouth to speak, but Soomie got there first.

"Tahira thinks everything is a competition. That's *her* thing," Soomie said.

"Please. I just like to get to know the fresh meat," Tahira said.

"Yeah, so you can chew it up and spit it out," Brigit mumbled.

"Very mature, Norway," Tahira shot back. She looked Ariana up and down. "When you get bored of the vanilla brigade over here, we're right across the way, having a lot more fun." She pointed blithely at the open door of the dorm room on the other side of the hall, where a few girls were gathered on the beds, gabbing and chatting. A huge pink diamond sparkled on the ring finger of her right hand. "You look like a smart girl. I trust you'll choose wisely."

Then she turned and walked back to her own room, followed by Allison, who silently closed the door behind them.

"Here we go, ladies!" Allison shouted out in the hall. "Pictures from my trip to Iceland!"

There were a few cheers across the way, and then silence as the door to Tahira's room closed. For a long moment, no one said a word, and Ariana's very fingertips started to itch. Should she follow Tahira or stick with her first instinct? She had to have the right friends here at APH. Needed to align herself with the group that would introduce her to the right clubs, the right people, the right future. Which of these two factions would do that for her?

"So obnoxious," Maria said finally, shaking her head as she walked over to the mirror, which hung on the wall near the door. She took her hair and twisted it, piling it atop her head. She held it there, checking herself out from every angle. "I'm surprised you didn't get into it with her," she said to Brigit.

"Get into what with who?" Ariana asked, playing catch-up.

"It's a *long* story," Brigit said as she dropped down on Allison's bed, leaning back on her elbows. Clearly she wasn't going to elaborate further, which made Ariana feel even more left out. "Guess Tahira decided to room with Zuri this year."

"Well, who wants to live with Allison?" Soomie put in. She was texting again, her fingers flying deftly over the mini keyboard. "A) The girl snores like a freight train; B) she's totally OCD about her teeth; and C) she's always getting those smelly care packages from home and letting them fester under her bed for weeks at a time."

Ariana swallowed hard as her cluelessness started to eat away at her. Everyone here already knew everyone else—and she knew no one. She had to start from scratch, figure out which girls were worth befriending and then get them to trust her. But how would she even begin deciding that when she was sure that each group would feed her lies and jaded opinions about the other? She wished she had been here to witness whatever history there was between these two groups. Wished she could have seen it unfold for herself so she could make an informed decision. It was awful, feeling like the outsider, the girl not-in-the-know. A hot flush of anger started to creep up the back of her neck. She shouldn't have to do this. Shouldn't have to be starting over from square one like this. If it hadn't been for that bitch Reed Brennan . . . if Thomas Pearson hadn't been so taken in by her . . . if it hadn't been for all that unpleasantness . . . she would be at Princeton right now instead of standing here trying to ingratiate herself to a bunch of girls two and three years younger than her. Why did all of this have to happen to her?

Just breathe, Ariana, she told herself.

In, one . . . two . . . three . . .

Out, one . . . two . . . three . . .

She had to contain herself. Cut herself some slack. Give herself some time to catch up.

"You don't want to go over there. Trust me," Soomie said, eyeing Ariana in a discerning way. Obviously she could tell that Ariana was at war with herself. "Tahira and her friends . . . they're fun, but frivolous . . . tacky. And you, I can tell, are a serious person. Serious and all class."

Ariana smiled wanly at the girl. Suddenly Soomie was full of compliments. Could it be more obvious that she was just trying to keep Ariana from defecting to the other side? That she simply wanted to win? Ariana felt the power shift slightly in her favor. Now *she* was the one who would be doing the evaluating. Deciding which group was most worth her time. Perhaps this was a good development.

"Thanks. So what did Allison mean when she said she wouldn't be my roommate for long?" Ariana asked, placing the unopened envelope down on her desk and feeling slightly more in control. She unzipped her small cosmetics bag and started to unpack.

Brigit glanced at the others and they all exchanged a look. "Shall I?" Brigit asked.

"Just don't leave anything out." Soomie sat down at Allison's desk and continued to text.

"Okay, anal. I know you won't let me," Brigit said to Soomie. Then she turned to Ariana. "It has to do with that envelope," she explained, her plethora of jewelry clinking and jangling as she shifted on the bed to face Ariana better. "Every year during Welcome Week, the entire campus is split up into three teams, and there's this whole weeklong competition."

"Right. I read about that," Ariana said. "There are three events: academic, athletic, and philanthropic."

"Exactly," Soomie said.

"But what you probably didn't read is that whichever team wins the competition gets to live in Privilege House for the year," Brigit added.

"That's what Allison meant by 'not for long,'" Maria put in. "She figures she'll get into Privilege House and leave good old Cornwall behind. Once you get in, you can choose to live with whomever you want."

All the little hairs on the back of Ariana's neck stood on end, her skin prickling with a mixture of excitement and what could only be called fear. In all her reading she had never heard of Privilege House. Was this some sort of secret thing only known to the students of APH? The secrecy intrigued her almost as much as the name "Privilege House." How could it not? It was clearly something sought after, and right away she wanted in. Needed in. And feared that somehow she would be left out.

"So what's Privilege House, exactly?" Ariana asked, placing her bottles of moisturizer atop her dresser.

"Its true name is Wolcott Hall," Soomie explained, finally lowering the BlackBerry. "It's that large dorm up on the hill overlooking the river. The one with the two towers."

Ariana nodded. "Right. The only coed dorm on campus."

"That's the one," Maria said with a grin. She fished a pot of lip gloss from her bag and touched up her lips in the mirror. "Plus it's completely cush. New furniture, satellite TV, private bathrooms . . ."

"Wow. So what's in here?" Ariana asked, picking up the envelope again. Suddenly she felt as if she had to open it. Would die if she didn't get to see its contents soon.

Patience, Ariana. Just breathe.

"That would be your team assignment," Soomie said. She glanced at her BlackBerry and stood, smoothing her plaid skirt. "Speaking of which, we should go. The rally's going to start soon."

"Yay!" Brigit said, as they all quickly started to gather their things. She grabbed Ariana's free hand and squeezed. "You are *so* going to love this! I hope we're all on the same team!"

"Brigit," Soomie scolded, rolling her eyes. Brigit blushed and dropped Ariana's hand. Obviously her friends sometimes grew weary of her overly enthusiastic attitude.

As Soomie slipped out, followed by Maria, who averted her eyes, Ariana's face burned. She wished at least one of them had echoed Brigit's sentiment, even if it was just to be polite. She felt a niggling uncertainty again and wondered if she shouldn't be hanging out with Tahira and her crowd right then. Would they make her feel more accepted, more wanted? Brigit seemed to be all over her, but Maria and Soomie were so hot-and-cold it was making her feel a bit nauseated.

"It's too bad Lexa's not here," Brigit said, gripping the strap on her messenger bag as Ariana closed the door behind them. "Do you guys think they'll let her compete even though she's coming late?"

"Of course they will. She's Lexa Greene," Maria said matter-of-factly.

"Who's Lexa Greene?" Ariana asked.

"Oh, Lexa is the *best,*" Brigit said. "You're going to *love* her!"

Suddenly the three girls were all walking ahead, gabbing about this Lexa girl. They wondered if she was going to bring back presents from her tour of Europe, debated over whether she'd kept her hair short this summer or grown it out and whether she'd hooked up with any hot Italians behind her boyfriend's back. Another conversation in which Ariana could not participate. These girls clearly didn't need her. They even had a fourth whom she hadn't known about. A person who, from the sound of it, was the leader of their little group. Feeling stung by rejection, Ariana sighed quietly, looking over her shoulder at Tahira's closed door, listening to the muted laughter coming from inside. For a moment, she hesitated. Should she just walk away? Knock on Tahira's door and try that group on for size? But Allison had been so rude. And there was something about Tahira that had rubbed her the wrong way. She was too imperious, too loud. And the immodest way in which she wore her uniform was too . . . What was the word Soomie had used? Tacky. And then Brigit called up the steps to her.

"Ana! Are you coming?"

Ariana took a deep breath. She didn't want to be rude. "Yeah! I'm right here!" she replied, hurrying down the stairs.

All she could do was hope that she *was* choosing wisely.

FREE FALL

The quad at the center of campus was a sea of blue and gray, all the students clad in their Atherton-Pryce Hall uniforms. Plaid skirts with gold accents or plain gray pleats for the girls. Blue or gray pants for the boys. Some of the guys sported well-worn, old-school cabbie hats with the APH crest on them, undoubtedly hand-me-downs from generations of their fathers and grandfathers who had attended the school before them. Everyone was shouting hellos, throwing their hands up, grabbing each other into hugs. Ariana felt like the new, unknown in-law in the middle of a family reunion. The very inappropriately dressed in-law. The only other people who were not in uniform were freshmen—easily identifiable by their bad skin and thinly veiled terror—and other transfers, all of whom looked so lame and lonely Ariana had to avert her eyes.

I don't look that sorry, she told herself. *I already have friends here.*

"You *must* go to the school store after this," Soomie said, her eyes flicking over Ariana's dress in a disapproving way. "You need school colors."

Ariana's face burned. "My thoughts exactly."

Suddenly, a murmur of excitement tore through the crowd and the noise dulled to a hum. Everyone seemed to be looking toward the chapel at the north end of the quad, which had a set of tall, stone steps leading up to its huge, whitewashed doors. Ariana hid a smirk as she took in the redbrick building and its bright white trim. It was such a happier-looking chapel than the damp, cold, gothic one at Easton. A happier chapel for a happy new her.

A tall African-American woman in a perfectly cut black suit strode out to the center of the stage, wielding a microphone. She smiled out at the crowd and tapped the mic a few times. The crowd grew silent.

"Welcome, students, to a new school year at Atherton-Pryce Hall," she began.

The crowd cheered and applauded. Some of the guys threw their hats into the air and a ripple of laughter raced through the crowd. Brigit smiled at Ariana. Everyone was excited to be back on campus. Fresh-faced and relaxed and ready for first term. Giddy anticipation rushed through Ariana. She was back. She was back where she was supposed to be. With people who wanted to learn. People who valued tradition. People who weren't psycho, drooling bed wetters with substandard vocabularies and violent tendencies.

"For those of you who do not know me, I am Headmaster Jansen," the woman continued. There were more cheers, which she politely allowed to die down. Ariana looked around at her peers. They seemed to genuinely like their headmaster. "And I am here to welcome you all to this year's Welcome Week competition!"

This got the loudest response yet. Ariana laughed and clapped her hands along with the rest of the students. She saw a few people pulling their envelopes from their pockets and drew hers from her bag. Her fingers trembled and she grasped it tightly to keep from dropping it. Her heart pounded with excitement. Easton had a lot of traditions—the opening rite at the beginning of each term; the Firsts competition every semester; the Billings initiation, the thought of which brought a particularly nostalgic pang to Ariana's heart—but nothing this exciting and uplifting. Nothing this light.

"The Welcome Week competition dates back to the very earliest days of our academy," Headmaster Jansen continued. "There are three events. First a debate—this year's topic will be nuclear weapons and whether or not the United States should disarm."

A murmur went through the crowd as everyone reacted to the topic. Clearly the students had been mulling over the possible topics for the debate and were intrigued by the announcement. Ariana smiled to herself. Somehow she couldn't imagine Gage Coolidge and his posse of party-minded brethren spending their summer discussing what hot-button issues the headmaster might throw at them during the first week of school.

"Next, philanthropy—the funds raised by this year's events will go to the Red Cross for hurricane and wildfire relief."

There was a smattering of applause at this news.

"And third, athletic . . . a crew race on the Potomac."

At this, a small but very loud group of guys toward the front of the crowd let out a cheer, their voices low and rumbling. Ariana's heart caught. Something about boys being boys always made her tingle.

"Oh my God. Palmer and Landon are so happy right now," Maria said with a fond eye roll.

"What do you mean? Do you see them?" Soomie asked, standing on her toes.

"Down, girl," Brigit said, patting Soomie on the back.

Ariana filed away the boys' names. Clearly Palmer and Landon were of some consequence. She would have inquired about them, but she wanted to refrain from asking too many questions. It would only serve to remind the girls that she was new and ignorant of their lives.

"But you don't all want to stand out here and listen to me talk. You'll get enough of that during the semester," the headmaster continued with a wry smile. "So now I'll leave the rest of the explanations to one of your own. Please welcome your student body president, Palmer Liriano."

Ariana nearly jumped out of her skin at the explosion of applause. She stood on her toes as everyone clapped their hands together above their heads to welcome their president. She got the faintest glimpse of a blue blazer bounding onto the stage, but it took a few minutes before the mania died down and she was able to get her first good look at the school president. His latte-colored skin, his jet-black hair, the broad shoulders that perfectly filled his blue blazer. And the smile. The smile that told everyone there that he knew they were looking at him. Admiring him.

Ariana stopped breathing. She experienced a moment of pure weightlessness, like the exhilarating split second at the top of a free-fall ride, knowing what's about to come and being blissfully unable to stop it. And then she was falling. Falling right toward Palmer Liriano. He was so beautiful, so powerfully perfect, he was like human gravity.

Ariana had always believed in love at first sight. She'd just never experienced it until now.

Calm yourself, Ariana, she thought, taking a deep breath. *You don't know anything about this guy.* But still her heart pitter-pattered away like a bunny rabbit on speed.

"I trust you all had a productive summer," Palmer said with a teasing lilt to his voice, a mischievous glint in his dark eyes. "And by productive I mean full of parties, exotic destinations, and . . . other things."

As the crowd cheered, he cast a glance at Headmaster Jansen, who had stepped aside. She gave him a warning look and a smile that was a "Watch it, pal," and "You know you can do whatever you want" all rolled into one. The vibe between the headmaster and the students was vastly different from any Ariana had ever experienced at Easton. Always one for order and respect—where it was warranted, of course—she wasn't yet sure if she liked it.

"But now we're back and it's time to get down to business." He whipped a white envelope from the back of the waistband of his gray pants and held it up. Hundreds of envelopes were thrust in the air in response. "These envelopes hold your team color. Each student has been selected by one of three teams. *I* am the captain of the gold team."

Here he paused for more cheers.

"Elizabeth Darrow is the captain of the gray team."

Here he stepped aside and held out his arm to welcome a beautiful, preppy blond girl to the stage, her hair pulled back in a French braid and her argyle socks stuffed into a pair of traditional penny loafers.

"And Martin Tsang is the captain of the blue team."

A tall, handsome Asian boy with shaggy dark hair joined them at the top of the stairs.

"Now, whichever team wins the Welcome Week competition will win the right to exert the five privileges," Palmer continued, pacing slowly back and forth in front of Martin and Elizabeth. "Privilege one."

"One!" the crowd shouted in unison as Palmer raised one finger in the air.

"Extended curfew," he said, his gaze sliding across the crowd. "That means lights out an hour later than the rest of campus, people."

"Privilege two."

"Two!" the crowd called out.

"The freedom to leave campus without a pass!"

Cheers greeted this announcement. Ariana's heart fluttered with excitement and joy.

"Privilege three."

"Three!"

"The right to take one class pass/fail. Privilege four."

"Four!"

"Prime tables in the dining hall and library," Palmer said. "And finally, privilege five."

His voice grew low and sexy as he said "privilege five." Ariana's pulse quickened and she felt nearly ill with attraction. Everyone around her hooted and hollered.

"This one was established when the school went coed in 1974 and Wolcott Hall with it . . . the right to have a member of the opposite sex *in your room!*"

The crowd went wild with cheers.

"With the door open of course," Palmer added in a flat tone.

Boos rang out, and Headmaster Jansen glared sternly at her students.

"So now that we all understand the Welcome Week competition and what's at stake, we will open our envelopes together on the count of three," Palmer instructed.

Ariana squeezed her eyes shut, holding fast to a mental image of Palmer and that incredible smile. *Please let it be gold, please let it be gold, please let it be gold.*

"One . . . two . . . three!"

She tore into her envelope and opened her eyes. In her hand was her golden ticket. Literally.

"Yes!" she cried as everyone around her squealed and hugged and checked each other's cards. On the top step, Palmer held his own gold card above his head, laughing as he took in the chaos from above.

"You got gold too!" Brigit cried, grabbing Ariana's hand and jumping up and down. "We're all on the same team!"

Ariana looked around at Maria, Soomie, and Brigit. She'd been so entranced by Palmer, she'd practically forgotten they were there. But they were, in fact, each clutching a gold card. On the same Welcome Week team as Palmer Liriano and her three new friends. Or, at least, the girls she planned to win over as soon as she found a way. The universe, clearly, was smiling on her. And suddenly she knew with absolute certainty: This new life of hers was going to be perfect.

BOYS OF CONSEQUENCE

"I can't believe we're all on gold," Ariana said as she squeezed between a rack of white blouses and a wall display of striped APH ties, monogrammed scarves, preppy ribbon belts, and argyle socks in the school store. She picked up a few shirts in her size, adding them to the two plaid skirts and two gray skirts on her arm, and turned around to select some accessories. "What are the chances?"

"Sometimes things just work out," Maria said, sliding a gray and blue tie through her fingers. She exchanged a brief look with Soomie. They quickly dropped their eyes when they saw Ariana watching. Ariana's heart contracted as she realized that, once again, there was something unspoken going on between them. Something she wasn't supposed to know. "You should definitely get the gold accessories. They'll make your hair pop."

Ariana almost contradicted her. She had always found that darker colors like black or navy blue really accentuated her blond hair. But then she remembered she no longer had blond hair. She was an auburn girl now. Feeling the burn of her near mistake, she gripped her arm with her fingers under the bundle of clothes and stepped over to the gold and blue ties.

"So true," she said, pretending to be distracted by the ties while she let her pulse slow. The store was jam-packed with students stocking up on supplies and new uniform pieces. Everyone around Ariana was comparing Welcome Week team colors and trash-talking over which team was going to kick which other team's ass. She tried to let the merry conversation soothe her.

It was just one near mistake. It won't happen again. Get a grip. You're home. This is home now.

"So, Ana. Where're you from? Your accent is so exotic," Brigit said, flipping through a rack of skirts.

"Yeah, but you're from Norway. You think nachos with cheese are exotic," Soomie pointed out, flicking her straight hair over her shoulder with a manicured fingernail.

"Okay. Now I'm hungry," Brigit said with a pout, glancing toward the counter at the front of the sunlit store. "Who wants a candy bar?"

"Not you. Remember? Chocolate is not your friend," Maria said, dropping the tie and moving on to a blue baseball cap with APH embroidered on the front. She tried it on and checked every angle of her face in a nearby mirror, sucking in her perfectly defined cheeks.

"Right." Brigit looked down at her slightly doughy stomach. "The diet."

"We're just trying to help," Soomie told her, checking her Black-Berry. "You told us you wanted us to help."

"I know, I know. And I do!" Brigit suddenly brightened again. "I'm going to lose ten pounds," she told Ariana. "Have you ever been on a diet?"

"No. Not really," Ariana replied.

Unless one were to count those few days after breaking out of prison when she'd been on a lack-of-money-induced fast. But she wasn't thinking about that now. Never again.

"Dammit. This thing keeps freezing up and I have to restart it every time," Soomie said, pressing down hard on the off key on her PDA.

"Maybe that's because you're asking it to do way too much," Maria suggested.

"Please. I'm barely using seventy percent of its memory," Soomie replied as she checked out a gray sweater.

"It scares me that you even know that," Ariana joked.

She turned the corner and nearly walked right into Tahira, who was flanked by Allison and another girl.

"Hey there, Transfer," Tahira said with a smile. She glanced at the other girls in a knowing way. "So, bored yet?"

Ariana could feel Maria, Brigit, and Soomie watching her and knew this was an important moment. It was time to show them how she handled herself. Display her loyalty. Even if she hadn't completely decided to stick with them just yet.

"No. But thanks for your concern," Ariana said coolly.

Tahira's eyes narrowed. "This is Zuri," she said, indicating the pretty black girl hovering just behind her left shoulder. A hot pink scarf held her long dreadlocks back from her face, and her shimmery eye makeup was expertly applied. It was too much for day, in Ariana's opinion.

"We're going to host a party in our room tonight," Zuri said in a quiet, but somehow commanding voice. "You should come."

"Definitely," Tahira said with a bright smile. She looked at the other girls derisively. "You're going to need a break from all the excitement," she added sarcastically. "What do you girls have planned, a chess tournament?"

"Oh, shut up, Tahira," Brigit said, rolling her eyes. She stepped from the skirts and stood between Tahira and Ariana. "If you want to know what's boring, it's you constantly telling everyone how lame we are."

"Just calling it like I see it. So, Brigit, tell me . . . how are your parents?" Tahira's voice dripped with disdain.

"Here we go," Maria said under her breath, looking at the ceiling.

Brigit crossed her arms over her chest and lifted her chin, shaking her blond hair back in an imperious way. "They're well. And yours?"

"Fine. Fabulous, actually," Tahira replied, glancing at her fingernails. "And your summer, I trust, was adequate."

"Better than adequate," Brigit sniffed. "I spent eight weeks in Greece as the personal guest of Princess Christine of Denmark."

Tahira looked impressed for a moment before slamming her lips back into a frown. "I toured India with the emir."

"That must have been a test of your patience, what with his lazy eye and wandering hands," Brigit shot back. Behind her, Maria and Soomie slid their palms together triumphantly. Ariana feigned interest in a pair of charcoal gray kneesocks, always keeping her ear on the conversation. Emirs? Princesses? What was the deal with these two?

"Will you be attending Prince William's Christmas party this year?" Tahira asked. "My invitation arrived last week."

"Sadly, no. Queen Noor is having an intimate gathering that same week and I have been granted the extreme honor of an invitation," Brigit returned. Tahira visibly paled at this news. Another point for Brigit, Ariana assumed. "You know what they say. No one ever declines an invitation from Noorie."

For a long moment Tahira simply glared at Brigit. Ariana could tell the girl was grasping for something with which to one-up Brigit, but was coming up blank.

"No," she said finally. "I suppose not."

Finally, Ariana couldn't take it anymore. She looked at Maria, her brow knit and her voice low. "What's all this about?"

"Brigit is princess of Norway. First in line to the throne. Tahira—"

"Can speak for herself," Tahira interrupted. She tilted her head and looked at Ariana, with a staid smile. "Tahira is daughter of Dubai's emir."

"They kind of get on each other's nerves," Soomie added.

"And the Princess War continues!" Suddenly Palmer Liriano appeared behind Tahira and placed a hand on one of her shoulders, the other on Brigit's back. Behind him were three other boys, all of whom were caught in the maze of clothing racks with nowhere to go. "Now come on, ladies, kiss and make up. I will not have Civil War among my team."

Ariana's pulse sped up so fast she almost felt faint. Palmer up close was even more magnetic than Palmer on stage. She could see the crinkles in his cheeks when he smiled. The tiny birthmark just to the left of his perfectly straight nose. The insanely long lashes fringing his dark brown eyes. As he greeted Tahira, Allison, Zuri, Maria, Brigit, and Soomie with cheek kisses, warm smiles, and interested questions, Ariana paid close attention. Palmer definitely spent more time chatting with the "vanilla brigade," as Tahira called them, than he did with Tahira, Allison, and Zuri. It wasn't a huge discrepancy, but it was there. Ariana felt reassured that she had made the right decision. Palmer was obviously the center of the APH universe, so clearly Maria and her friends knew the right people. If they could get her closer to Palmer, then vanilla she would be.

She waited as Palmer finished catching up with his friends and prayed that her mind would come up with something witty to say when he finally noticed her standing there. She also couldn't help noticing that he was surrounded by guys. No girlfriend trailing adoringly after him. This was a very good sign.

At long last his eyes fell on her and he broke into a wide smile. Ariana's skin sizzled as he took her in. He clearly liked what he saw. The force of her relief, mixed with the insane weightlessness of anticipation, made her feel light-headed.

Control yourself, Ariana. Control.

"Who do we have here?" Palmer asked, sliding out into the aisle to stand in front of her.

He smelled incredible. A clean, crisp aftershave scent. Expensive, definitely.

"Ana Covington," she said with a hint of a smile. She lifted her hand toward him. "It's an honor to meet you, Mr. President," she added slyly, looking directly into his eyes.

Palmer's smile turned satisfied. He liked the acknowledgment of his position, however teasing it might be. He shook her hand with a firm, warm grip, and Ariana's heart all but stopped.

"And you, Miss Covington," he said, picking up on her jokingly formal tone. "But wait . . . I thought it was Briana Leigh."

Ariana started. Why did everyone here seem to already know her name? "It . . . it is," she said. "But I prefer Ana."

"All right, Ana," he replied. "So, what classes are you taking?"

Ariana hesitated. The last thing she wanted to do was reveal her embarrassingly simple schedule—the result of Briana Leigh's substandard entrance exam scores—especially since she planned on having it altered as soon as possible.

"Palmer's in all advanced and honors courses," Soomie explained with an affectionate smile. "He measures everyone's worth by the level of their intellect."

Intriguing. A guy who actually cared about school and preferred to surround himself with like-minded people. Ariana was both surprised and pleased. She'd never known a popular, handsome, privileged guy to also be a serious student. But now she definitely couldn't tell the truth about her schedule. Her only choice was distraction.

"I'm impressed," she said, looking up at him. "No guy has ever shown interest in the size of my *intellect* before," she added with a flirtatious smile.

His friends all reacted exactly as Ariana predicted, laughing and making suggestive noises. Palmer simply grinned and Ariana felt an instant connection. He appreciated her joke but didn't feel the need to be lewd about it. Palmer was definitely a rare breed. Mature, serious, and insanely gorgeous.

"Guess I'm different than other guys," he said.

"And I'm different than other girls," she said, glancing at Tahira in a derisive way. "So I guess we have a lot in common."

Palmer laughed, his eyes sparkling.

"You know what? You're no longer invited to our party tonight," Tahira said with a sniff.

Ariana smiled stiffly. "I wasn't coming anyway."

Brigit laughed as Maria and Soomie slid their palms together once more.

Tahira's eyes narrowed in a threatening way. "You are *so* going to regret that."

Ariana felt the slightest twinge of fear. After all, who knew what the princess of Dubai was capable of? But then Tahira walked over to one of Palmer's friends—a tall, muscular guy with thick, wavy, dark hair—to whisper something in his ear, and the fear passed. Retreating to her guy? Maybe Tahira wasn't as formidable as she made herself out to be. Palmer, meanwhile, simply smirked and looked back at the guys.

"This girl is going to be a definite asset on gold." The guys laughed again and Palmer looked around at the group. "We're gonna meet up with some of the other guys in the Hill. If you get done shopping you should head over."

"Cool. We'll stop by," Maria said.

Ariana, meanwhile, tried to pick apart his words. *In* the hill? What did that mean?

"See you later, Ana," Palmer said, slipping by.

"Wait. How did you know I was on gold?" Ariana asked.

Palmer lifted his palms. "I'm the team captain. I know all."

Then he sauntered away, greeting almost everyone he saw with a wave or a hug or a peck on the cheek, just like a real politician.

"Palmer. Such a flirt," Maria said in a fond way.

Ariana felt a hint of irritation at the implication that Palmer treated all girls this way, but she let it slide. She was too busy basking in her new crush. Then Soomie nudged her arm and woke her up from her Palmer-related stupor.

"Ana, meet our friends," she said, her voice almost breathless. For the first time Ariana noticed that the three boys were still loitering nearby. The guy Tahira had retreated to now had his arms around Tahira as they whispered directly into each other's faces. "That's Robert," Soomie said, pointing at Tahira's boyfriend. "And *this* is Landon Jacobs."

Landon pushed his hands into the pockets of his well-worn gray chinos, which he wore with a studded leather belt and battered black boots. His tie was slung around his neck and then over his shoulder like a scarf, and his white shirt was open to reveal a faded T-shirt depicting the British flag. His jacket was rolled up at the sleeves, with the cuffs of his shirt just peeking out at the ends, and his blond hair was long on top and pushed forward over his blue eyes, as if he was trying to hide behind it.

"Hey," he said with a slow, practiced smile, which Ariana could tell was supposed to make her swoon.

"Hi," she said. He was definitely not as tingle-inducing as Palmer.

Landon blinked, as if confused. So did everyone else around them.

"Oh, and this is Adam." Landon stepped aside and gestured over his shoulder at the curly-haired boy hanging behind him. "He's new too."

"Nice to meet you," Ariana said.

"You too. Is this place overwhelming or is it just me?" he asked in an endearingly vulnerable way.

"It's not you," Ariana lied, taking pity on the poor guy. He looked kind of lost-puppy-doggish with his light brown curls and big brown eyes. Like someone who needed looking after. "Speaking of which, what's 'the hill'?" Ariana asked the group.

"The Hillary Rush Junior/Senior Lounge," Soomie replied. "It's off the dining hall. We call it 'the Hill' for short."

"Yeah, and the freshman/sophomore lounge is called 'the cave,'" Brigit added. "Because it's so much lamer than the Hill."

"I definitely miss the cave," Landon said with a shudder. "Well, see you girls around." Then, with one more confused glance at Ariana, he sauntered away, trailing Allison, Zuri, Tahira, and Robert.

"Later, Norway," Tahira said over her shoulder.

"Hopefully *much*," Brigit replied.

Ariana almost cringed. So immature. She was going to have to help Brigit with her comebacks. Or possibly just teach her the art of aloofness.

As soon as they were out of earshot, Soomie gripped Maria's sleeve. "Oh my God. Landon is *so* hot!"

Ariana blinked. If someone had asked her ten minutes ago, she would have sworn that Soomie was the type of girl who didn't do giddy. But here she was, practically trembling in the wake of Mr. Floppy Hair.

"Eh. He's all right," Maria said, looking away. Ariana caught a hint of a blush at the top of Maria's high cheekbones. "It's just the fame thing. It makes objects in the rearview mirror appear hotter than they are."

"He's famous?" Ariana asked, looking after the boys, who were just sidling out the door into the sun.

All three girls gaped at Ariana. "Uh, yeah? Youngest artist ever to have two albums premiere at number one on the Billboard chart?" Soomie said, ticking a list off on her fingers. "First under-thirty ever to win *People*'s Sexiest Man Alive? Winner of dozens of AMAs, Grammys, and MTV Video Music Awards, and star of the upcoming feature film *First Son*?"

An embarrassed blush crept up Ariana's face from her neck. Clearly this was a person whom every red-blooded American teenager was supposed to know about. She dimly recalled a conversation back in her dorm room—something about a worldwide tour and an inflated ego. They must have been talking about Landon. If she hadn't been so distracted by her new room, her fresh start, she would have tuned in and would never have made such a slip.

"You're not from the South. You're from Mars," Brigit said with a laugh.

"Sorry," Ariana said quickly. "I'm just not the biggest pop culture junkie."

This excuse seemed adequate. Adequate enough for the topic to be dropped, but with some dubious looks.

"I am so going to make him my boyfriend this year," Soomie said, biting her bottom lip.

"Really?" Brigit asked as Maria looked, ever so briefly, alarmed. Then Maria saw Ariana noticing her expression and quickly glanced away.

Soomie whipped out her BlackBerry, turned it on again, hit a button, and showed them the screen. "It's on my top ten goals for the year."

And there it was. Right underneath "Earn straight A's" and "Perfect SAT scores." Number three read, "Make Landon mine."

"Well, then you should go talk to him!" Brigit said, grabbing Soomie's hand in excitement. "Come on! They're probably out on the quad!"

"Now?" Soomie looked suddenly terrified. She reached back to smooth her hair.

"Sure. Why not?" Maria said, picking at her fingernails as if wholly uninterested. "I'm dying to see your technique for 'making Landon mine,'" she said, throwing in some air quotes.

"Okay." Soomie rolled her shoulders back. "'Don't put off until tomorrow what you can do today,' right? Let's do it."

"I just have to pay for these things," Ariana told them. "I'll catch up with you."

But the girls were already halfway out the door when they waved to her. Ariana felt a scalding rush of irritation. What was she, invisible? She forced herself to breathe in, then clenched and unclenched a fist—letting it go. She was still new. The three of them—and this elusive Lexa girl, apparently—had been best friends for a while. It would take some time for her to rise to integral status in the group.

She was going to have to be patient. Even though she was older than them, even though she should have been at Princeton by now and would have been if not for the betrayal of certain people . . . even though she should have been well beyond these girls and any need of their approval . . . she wasn't. That was just how it was. And the sooner she accepted that, the better.

With a deep breath, Ariana returned to the task at hand. She gathered a few more pairs of socks, then browsed through the blazers and selected an array of accessories. By the time she was done her arms were laden with clothing, hangers, and various little touches that would add some personality to her uniform. She had just joined the long line snaking toward the center of the store when her phone beeped.

Startled, she flinched, sending the silky ties and scarves sliding to the floor. Quickly, Ariana stooped to gather them before flipping open her purse to find her phone. She had a feeling she knew who was trying to contact her, and her chest filled with dread.

The text, as predicted, was from Ashley Hudson. Of course it was. He was the only living person with this number.

Am @ Easton Acad. No one here ever heard of Emma Walsh. Where R U? Whats going on??? WB. PLZ.

The phone nearly slid from Ariana's now-sweaty palm, but she gripped it before it could fall and hit the ground. Hands shaking, she deleted the text and turned off her phone, glancing around to see if anyone had noticed her panic. No one was watching her, however. They were all too busy browsing and buying and catching up with friends. Living their lives.

Which was exactly what Ariana was going to do. Live this life and put the old one behind her. As soon as she got herself a new phone number.

RARE

"I must say, it's the rare student who comes in here and asks for *more* work."

Ariana smiled slightly. She rather enjoyed being deemed "rare."

If only you knew my real story, she thought. *"Rare" would take on a whole new meaning.*

Seated in a leather chair across the desk from her new guidance counselor, Mr. Pitt, Ariana folded her hands in her lap and took a deep breath of the musty air. There were piles and piles of books all over the tiny room, on the floor, on the desk, on top of the printer, all along the windowsill. When Ariana had first walked in, she had almost recoiled in horror at the mess. But after sitting for a few minutes and letting her eyes slide around the area as Mr. Pitt yammered away about her adjustment period and his open-door policy, she realized there was a method to the madness. Biographies and nonfiction to her right, each stack organized alphabetically by author. Mysteries behind her. Russian classics to her left. Early American lit next to that. African-American poetry on the windowsill. Everything had its place.

Organized chaos. She had a feeling she was going to like this man.

"Ah. Here it is." He turned his computer screen slightly so that they could both see it, and placed his glasses on his bulbous nose. His thick forearms stuck out of the rolled-up sleeves of his light blue oxford shirt, which was topped by a green sweater vest and a yellow bow tie. All the color made him seem jolly. Like an overweight elf. "I'm sorry to say that your entrance exam scores were simply not high enough to place you in honors courses. I believe the schedule you have will be challenging enough, Briana Leigh. Don't try to overextend yourself. You're at a new school, making new friends. . . . The last thing you need is *more* stress."

Ariana's smile tightened. She was not leaving here without a new schedule. Her entire future depended on it. Not to mention the small matter of impressing Palmer.

"No offense, Mr. Pitt, but you don't know me," she said. "The more challenged I am, the better I do. And as for the entrance exams, I'd like to retake them, please."

The man blinked behind his thick glasses. "Retake the entrance exams."

"Yes. I was going through a horrible breakup when I took them the first time," Ariana lied smoothly, wrapping her hands around her knees. She inadvertently kicked the plastic bags full of Atherton-Pryce

Hall uniform pieces and bit the inside of her cheek. All she wanted to do was get this done with so she could go back to the dorm and try on her new wardrobe. Start fitting in around here. "Needless to say, I was a bit distracted."

Mr. Pitt sat back in his chair and exhaled loudly, blowing out his chubby cheeks. "Well, this is a first. You would have to take them all this week so I could have a new schedule for you before classes start a week from Tuesday."

"Done," Ariana said.

"Not so fast, Miss Covington. There are five exams. And the Welcome Week competition takes up a lot of time," he said. "Are you absolutely sure you're up for this?"

"I'll figure it out. I have to," Ariana said firmly. "These courses are not going to get me into Princeton."

Mr. Pitt smiled and sat forward again, resting his elbows on his cluttered desk, atop Briana Leigh's open file. "Ah, so Princeton is the goal, is it?"

"That's the goal," Ariana said, her heart fluttering. She had been sidetracked for a time, but that was over now. All she had to do was ace five exams this week and she'd be back on track. And maybe she'd even be placed in a few of Palmer's advanced courses, which would just be an added bonus.

He sat back, opened the top drawer of his desk, and pulled out a well-worn black baseball cap with an orange, block-letter *P* just above the bill. With a flourish, he placed it proudly on his head.

"I'm a Princeton man myself," he said with a grin.

Ariana leaned forward as well, as if she and Mr. Pitt were old chums. "Then you understand."

There was an excited gleam in Mr. Pitt's eyes. Ariana could tell that he was going to take her under his wing. That she had just made it *his* goal to get her into Princeton as well. She officially had someone on her team. Someone who, as a Princeton alum *and* guidance counselor watching her progress keenly, could be *very* helpful.

"We'll start tomorrow at eight a.m. with your history exam," Mr. Pitt said. "There's an examination room, down the hall from here. Room one-ten. I'll be proctoring, so if you don't show up, it's me you'll have to answer to."

"I'll be there," Ariana replied happily. She stood up and grabbed her bags, smoothing her dress down as she turned toward the door.

"Oh, Miss Covington. One more thing," Mr. Pitt said, removing the hat. "There was a problem with your enrollment form."

Ariana paused. "A problem?"

"Yes. Every student at Atherton-Pryce Hall is required to participate in a team sport," Mr. Pitt said, looking down at the papers inside the open folder before him. "You didn't specify a sport."

He looked up at her and smiled expectantly. Ariana placed her hand on the doorknob and squeezed. When she was at Easton Academy, she had been excused from the team sport requirement thanks to a doctor's note, written by a close friend of her mother's. Sports had never been Ariana's thing, and the woman had been more than happy to help her avoid the requirement. But she no longer had that option. She was just going to have to suffer through and deal with

all the athletic spirit and competitive trash-talking and . . . sweat.
Disgusting.

"Your entrance essay about your equestrian experience was quite
inspiring," Mr. Pitt said, pulling out a few stapled pages. Ariana stared
at them, imagining Briana Leigh at her computer, typing away about
horses and jumper competitions, getting the essay over with so she
could get back to the country club pool and her all-important tan. For
a moment, a smile twitched at Ariana's lips at the thought, but then
the happy picture of Briana Leigh was suddenly replaced by a mental
image of the girl's face as Ariana shoved her underwater. Her wide, terrified eyes as she was held down. As she flailed and struggled for life.
Ariana closed her eyes and gripped the doorknob tighter.

Breathe. Just breathe.

In, one . . . two . . . three . . .

Out, one . . . two . . . three . . .

"Are you all right? You look pale," Mr. Pitt said.

Ariana's eyes wrenched open. She was back in the counselor's
office. Back in the now. Everything was fine. Briana Leigh was in the
past. The horrible, awful past. There was nothing Ariana could do for
her now.

"Fine. I'm fine," she said.

"Good. So shall I put you down for the equestrian team?" he asked,
his fingers hovering over his keyboard. "They're quite accomplished,
actually. I—"

"No!" Ariana blurted, as the Briana Leigh images threatened to
resurface. "No. I'm over horses."

Mr. Pitt blinked. "Over horses?"

"Tennis," Ariana said and forced a smile. "I'd like to be on the tennis team."

Mr. Pitt shrugged and typed it in. "All right then. Tennis it is." He hit a button and locked it in.

As Ariana thanked her counselor and strolled out the door, she felt a twinge of uncertainty. If Briana Leigh had been so into riding that she had written about it in her essay, it must look kind of odd that now, just a few months later, she was so avidly *dis*interested. Would it make Mr. Pitt suspect something? But when she looked back at Mr. Pitt, he had already busied himself with something on the computer. He had no reason to suspect her. She was just a kid to him, and kids changed their minds all the time.

I am Briana Leigh Covington now, Ariana reminded herself. *The world is just going to have to get used to the new me.*

And anyone who didn't like the new her . . . well, she had ways of dealing with them.

OF COURSE

It wasn't until Ariana was back out on the quad that the panic set in. She had been in prison for almost two years. Two years since she had studied history or French or science or anything other than the novels housed in the Brenda T.'s library. If she was going to pass these exams, she was going to have to study.

A pair of guys rushed by, trying to tackle each other for a Frisbee, and came close enough to nearly crush Ariana's feet.

"Sorry!" one of them called out, lifting his hand as he was slammed into the ground.

Ariana took a deep breath, told herself not to strangle them, and turned around. At the back of the school store was a whole section filled with laptops and desktops and printers. She noticed a sign for textbooks behind it, with a big arrow pointing down a set of stairs. She was about to rack up one hell of a credit card bill for Grandma Covington. But it was the start of the school year.

She needed a uniform and supplies. The old woman would have to understand.

"So, did you get my text?"

Ariana's heart jumped into her throat as she almost strode full force into Palmer Liriano. He had appeared out of nowhere and was now walking backward in front of her so he could look at her while he talked. Somehow, as distracted as she was by his sudden appearance, Ariana managed not to miss a step.

"What text?" she asked, the handles on the heavy plastic bags cutting into her suddenly sweaty palms. She took a deep breath and tried to stay cool, calm. Why did sweat exist? It was so unattractive.

"I texted everyone on gold to let them know about the first team meeting," he said, still ever-so-confidently walking in reverse. "Three o'clock. Gymnasium. You didn't get it?"

"My phone's turned off," Ariana said, recalling Hudson's earlier text. "How do you have the numbers of everyone on your team? Wouldn't that be more than a hundred people?"

"One hundred and eight, actually . . . if you count the freshmen, which I rarely do," he joked, finally turning to walk beside her. He produced a worn baseball from his pocket and rolled it between his palms. She noticed his hands were large and powerful, with long fingers. "I got the numbers from admissions. Rosie loves me, so she gives me pretty much anything I want."

"Rosie the receptionist, I presume," Ariana said with a smile.

"Yep. Actually, I'm pretty sure all the receptionists on campus love me," he said, tilting his head. "Maybe I have a receptionist-targeted pheromone."

He had pheromones all right, but they affected more than just receptionists. Ariana was about to shoot back a flirtatious remark when a cold wave of dread hit her in the face and snaked right down her spine. She was so startled she stopped walking and it took Palmer a few steps to realize she was no longer with him.

Palmer had texted the number he'd gotten from admissions. That would be Briana Leigh's old phone, not Ariana's current one. The phone which had been stolen along with all Briana Leigh's things on the night Briana Leigh had been murdered.

Stolen by Kaitlynn Nottingham. Kaitlynn, Ariana's completely psychotic former roommate from the Brenda T. The girl who had no idea of Ariana's plans to assume Briana Leigh's identity and attend Atherton-Pryce.

Ariana's vision started to prickle over with gray spots as panic seized her heart.

But wait, you canceled the phone, you moron, a little voice in her mind reminded her. *Calm down. It's all good. You took care of it.*

"Are you all right?" Palmer asked.

Breathe, Ariana. Just breathe. . . .

In, one . . . two . . . three . . .

Out, one . . . two . . . three . . .

"Ana?"

"I'm fine," Ariana said.

Her vision cleared and there was Palmer. Handsome, concerned

Palmer, looking down at her with those earnest brown eyes, probably ready to whip her over his shoulder and fireman-carry her to the infirmary if she needed it.

"Fine. I'm fine," Ariana said shakily. "I just . . . thought I forgot to do something. But it's okay."

"Okay, good. For a second there I thought you were going to pass out on me," Palmer said with a grin that made her heart tap-dance. "Not that girls haven't had that reaction in the past."

Ariana smiled. "You're kind of full of yourself. Anyone ever tell you that?"

Palmer blinked, tossed his baseball up, and caught it. "Not in those words, no. You're the first."

The first. It was always nice to be the first something in someone's life.

"So, you never told me which classes you were taking," Palmer said, strolling along.

Right. That old question. Ariana thought back to her conversation with Mr. Pitt and how impressed he'd been by her dedication to her future. Was it possible that Palmer, with the importance he placed on school, would find it impressive as well?

"Actually, that's not quite clear at the moment," she said, eliciting a confused glance. She tilted her head and said with chagrin, "I'm retaking my entrance exams."

"Really?" Palmer said, pausing again.

"I had kind of a bad day the first time I took them," she said. "Let's just say my scores were not up to my usual standard."

"Which is?" Palmer asked.

"Straight A's," Ariana replied firmly. "No exceptions."

"Wow. You sound like me," Palmer replied. "That's cool that they're letting you retake them. I doubt they do that for everyone."

"I guess I'm not everyone," Ariana replied, loving how mysterious it sounded. It wasn't lost on her that Palmer had decided not to pry into the reason behind her bad day. He was a gentleman. Another point in his favor.

"I guess not," Palmer said, popping the baseball up with the back of one hand and catching it with the other.

"So, if we win this competition, we move into Privilege House?" Ariana asked.

"Not *if . . . when,*" Palmer replied, raising his eyebrows. "And only the juniors and seniors get to move in."

"Okay, *when.* So how does it work, exactly?" she asked, looking up at the two towers, which could be seen from almost anywhere on campus. "Guys and girls living together, I mean."

Palmer chuckled. He paused in his tracks and crossed his arms over his chest, tucking the baseball under one bicep. "Well, the north tower is for guys, the south for girls. We only really mix in the common areas, but it's cool. You don't have to walk all the way across campus to meet up with your friends, and it's easier to get study groups together. It's definitely a privilege. I'm glad my uncle came up with it."

"Your uncle?" Ariana asked.

"Yeah, on my mom's side. The whole thing was his brainchild," Palmer said. "He was kind of a big deal around here. When he graduated he gave the school this huge endowment, but said he wanted to leave his mark on Welcome Week, so they let him create the fifth privilege—which was turning Wolcott Hall into a coed dorm for the upperclassmen winners. I guess he didn't appreciate the fact that he had so little access to females while he was here, and wanted to make it easier for future generations," he added with a laugh.

"Wow. That's so cool. Your family's part of the history of Atherton-Pryce," Ariana said, feeling a thrill of excitement. Palmer was more than the president of the student body, more than Mr. Popular—he was Atherton-Pryce Hall royalty. And apparently, his family had an insane amount of money, if his uncle could make that large of an endowment upon graduating from prep school.

"Yeah. It *is* kind of cool," Palmer said with a nod. "But it puts a lot of pressure on me to win and get in, you know? Keep it in the family."

Family pressure. Ariana knew a little something about that. "Sure."

"So three o'clock. Gym. Be there."

He tossed his baseball into the air and turned to walk away.

"Actually, I have a new number," Ariana said, hoping she sounded casual and composed when, in fact, she was almost panicked by the idea of him walking away right then. This was their first one-on-one conversation and she wanted it to last as long as possible. Long enough, at least, for her to make a lasting impression.

Palmer whipped his cell out of his jacket pocket without hesitation. "I'll be needing that."

Ariana blushed, flattered, and Palmer smiled, noticing.

"For team business, of course," he clarified teasingly.

"Of course."

She gave him the number, adjusted her shopping bags in her hands, and kept walking, hoping he would fall into step with her. He did. Ariana smiled to herself. Clearly there were ten million other places a guy of his stature and popularity could be right now, but he was choosing to stick with her.

"So, Ana, before I let you go, do you have any special talents I should know about?" he asked, looking her up and down in a suggestive way.

Ariana's blush deepened.

"For the competition, of course," he added, grinning. He realized the effect he had on her and was obviously loving it. Ariana didn't mind, however. She was loving it too.

"Of course," she said again. "Well, Mr. President, I'm not sure exactly what you're looking for."

They had come to the crossing of the pathways in front of the school store. Ariana paused and looked up at him, the sun lighting his handsome face perfectly. He took a step closer to her. So close she could feel the warmth radiating from his body.

"Don't worry. When I need you, you'll know." Then he tossed his baseball up in the air, caught it, and strode away.

Ariana breathed in the fresh, late-summer air, enjoying the excited rush of her pulse, and looked down at her purse. There would be no getting rid of her phone now. Palmer had the number. And if there was one thing she wanted in this life, it was Palmer being able to get hold of her whenever he damn well pleased.

She was just going to have to find a way to deal with Hudson.

ROOMMATES

Ariana had never missed Noelle Lange more than she did at that moment. As she tried on her new uniform pieces, each stiffer and itchier than the last, Allison sat on her bed with her earbuds cranked up and a magazine open on her lap, watching Ariana's every move. She watched as Ariana shimmied in and out of skirts, as she buttoned and unbuttoned blouses, as she tried on a cardigan sweater, then a blazer. When Ariana turned to the side to check out her profile, Allison snorted. Ariana shot her an irritated look and the girl trained her eyes on her magazine, as if she hadn't been observing Ariana for the last fifteen minutes.

You have no idea who you're dealing with, Ariana thought, her nostrils flaring slightly as she glared at the unsuspecting girl. *I can think of five different ways to end you right now.*

When Allison looked up again, Ariana made sure to hold her gaze until the girl blushed and glanced away first. Then Ariana sighed, bored now, and went back to her private fashion show.

Allison was not a person Ariana could live with for very long. Unfortunately the girl was also on gold, just like her pal Tahira. Ariana could only hope that once they got into Privilege House, the two of them would decide to room together and there would be someone cool who needed a new roommate. In the meantime, being sequestered with the girl for the last hour just brought home how amazing it was to be paired with a real friend. She missed the sound of Noelle's voice, which filled every room she entered. Missed her bald-faced honesty. Her humor. Her advice. Missed living with someone she loved.

Or had loved. Until the girl turned her back on Ariana and chose Reed Brennan over her.

Maybe Allison as a roommate wasn't half bad. If they never became friends, there was far less of a chance that Allison would end up betraying her.

"Allison? Can I ask a question?"

The girl rolled her eyes and made a big, exaggerated show of removing her earbuds from her ears, as if Ariana were making a huge imposition.

"What?"

"How does laundry work around here? I didn't see a laundry room," Ariana said, holding tightly to her patience.

Allison heaved a sigh and sat up straight. "See that bag?"

She pointed at a light blue bag that was folded and placed atop the shelf above Ariana's desk.

"You put your dirty clothes in that bag and leave it in the hallway before eight p.m. In the morning it comes back to you all clean and neatly folded. It's like a miracle," Allison said facetiously, her eyes wide. Then she flopped back down on her pillows and put her earbuds in again before noisily flipping the pages of her magazine.

"Thank you!" Ariana shouted. No need to let this girl stop her from being polite.

She slipped her arms into the navy blue cardigan again and ran her fingers over the gold APH crest on the breast pocket. Ariana had always wished that Easton Academy had required uniforms. She liked how neat and cohesive they made the student body look. She cherished the tradition of wearing the school colors and proudly displaying the crest. Uniforms instilled pride. Integrity. Loyalty. Qualities that many of the people at Easton had lacked.

Even though the short-sleeved shirt was making her itch and the pleated plaid skirt needed to be hemmed, Ariana decided she would wear them to the three o'clock team meeting, along with a blue and gold tie. Her comfort was far less important than her inconspicuousness. She didn't want to stand out like the newbie she was. She wanted to blend. To fool everyone into thinking she had been here all along.

Allison laid her magazine aside and picked up a copy of the *Washington Post*. As she lazily turned the pages, Ariana reached back to French braid her hair. Then, suddenly, Allison paused and looked up from the paper. She stared at Ariana, her eyes slightly narrowed, her lips slightly taut. Ariana's heart started to race. Every day since Briana Leigh's exhumation from the lake, Ariana had checked the newspaper for any stories on herself or Kaitlynn, just to make sure no one had started to ask questions. But today she had been so busy, she hadn't thought to look. What if there was something in there about her funeral? A picture of Ariana or a story about Kaitlynn that mentioned her old friend Briana Leigh Covington?

Instantly she began mentally cataloging everything in the room, trying to find something that could be of use to her. There were plenty of neckties in the closet, a pair of large scissors on Allison's desk, and pillows. Pillows could be helpful. But there were people everywhere, chatting in the halls, hanging in the lounge. A struggle would definitely be heard. What was she going to do?

"I'm out of here," Allison said, suddenly rising from the bed. She curled the newspaper up, tossed it in the trash can, and brushed by Ariana, slamming the door behind her. The second she was gone, Ariana dove for the paper and ripped through it, making sure to take in every line of every last page. There was nothing. Nothing but stock quotes and football scores and stories of human suffering.

Ariana was just being paranoid.

With a sigh, she returned the newspaper to the trash and turned toward the mirror. So Allison hadn't seen anything to make her suspect Ariana. She was simply prone to staring. Which was just one of her many drawbacks. Taking a deep breath, Ariana wiped the newsprint from her hands with a tissue from Allison's desk and tossed that in the trash as well. She couldn't help looking forward to the gold team's imminent win and to getting out of Cornwall and into Privilege House. Because her perfect new life could not include an imperfect roommate.

STATEMENT OF TRUTH

Ariana stepped out into the sun, feeling giddy even as the super-starched pleats of her skirt scratched her bare thighs. She wondered if her new friends had thought to wait for her, and her smile widened when she saw Maria, Brigit, and Soomie loitering on the quad a few feet from the dorm's back door.

But the smile died a moment later. Not one of them was in uniform. In fact, no one on campus was in uniform.

Maria took a sip from the paper coffee cup in her hand and snorted a laugh. She looked comfortable as could be in a cream linen dress and strappy leather wedges. Brigit had changed into jeans and colorful, layered tanks, and Soomie wore a black skirt, a crisp white tee, and a pair of Chanel flats.

"What are you wearing?" Brigit asked breathlessly as Ariana stepped toward them, her face burning.

"Everyone was in uniform at the rally," Ariana whispered back as Brigit took her arm in a solidarity kind of way. "I thought—"

Suddenly it dawned on her. The reason Allison had been staring at her. Hiding laughs. Making that odd face. She hadn't recognized Ariana. She'd been trying not to crack up. The girl knew that Ariana was going to walk out here in her uniform and look like a moron, and she had simply let her do it.

Bitch. Bitch, bitch, bitch.

"We all wear our unis for the rally, but not again until classes start," Soomie informed her matter-of-factly.

"Guess we should have told you," Maria added, sounding like she didn't much care one way or the other.

"I have to go change," Ariana said.

"There's no time," Soomie told her. "You don't want to be late."

Ariana's face stung over being told what to do, but Soomie's tone left no room for negotiation. Clearly punctuality was a must for Miss Organized. Ariana had just been starting to win her and Maria over with her dissing of Tahira back at the school store. She didn't want to make waves now.

"Okay," Ariana said. "Let's just go."

On the way across campus to the gymnasium, which had its own parking lot and sat at the north end of campus, Ariana noticed more than a few amused glances being shot in her direction. She did her best to ignore them, but her body heat had risen to a dangerous level by the time they stepped through the blue doors to the gym's lobby. It only made the itchy fabric itchier. She tried to distract herself by taking in her surroundings. Hung from the ceiling were dozens of championship banners for all kinds of sports, and glass trophy cases lined the cinder-block walls, crammed with hundreds of years' worth of gold and silver trophies. Ariana would have loved to stop and peruse the history, but the rest of Team Gold was streaming through the inner doors to the basketball court. Including Tahira, Robert, and Allison. Ariana caught Allison's eye, and she and Tahira both cracked up laughing. Rob snorted and doubled over, an over-the-top reaction that was obviously for his girlfriend's benefit.

"Thanks a lot," Ariana snapped as she strode past Allison into the gym, the heady scent of the freshly waxed floor filling her senses. "It's so nice of you to make me feel welcome."

"Anytime!" Allison sang back, her eyes wet with laughter.

Maria, Brigit, and Soomie trailed after Ariana.

"Hey, Norway. Or should I say, Muffintop!" Tahira commented, rather loudly. Her words echoed throughout the lofty gym, and everyone around them turned to stare. Brigit froze in place, her mouth open in horror. Tahira strolled up to her from behind and looked her up and down as she passed by. "I *thought* you looked hefty in your uniform, but those jeans really show off your new curves," she added in an obnoxious tone.

A strangled squeak escaped Brigit's throat. Maria and Soomie exchanged an anxious look, but Ariana could tell they were at a loss as to how to help. She stepped up to Brigit's side and took her arm.

"Don't listen to her, Brigit," Ariana said, staring at Tahira's purple kitten heels. The girl really was all about bold color choices. "At least you're not carrying all your weight in your cankles."

Brigit laughed as Tahira's jaw dropped. Ariana tugged her new friend along toward the bleachers, which were rapidly filling with dressed-down students. They found a spot in the bleachers, front and center, where girls of consequence should be sitting. Maria and Soomie gathered around her and Brigit, settling in.

"Thanks, Ana," Brigit said under her breath. "I don't know what happened to me back there."

"It's not a problem," Ariana replied, feeling proud over making herself so useful to Brigit.

"You should be careful, though," Maria said. "You don't want to overdo it when it comes to Tahira."

Ariana's heart panged. She had thought she was doing something right. Something that would endear her to these girls.

"But I thought you didn't like her," Ariana said.

Soomie and Maria exchanged a look. "It's a fine line," Maria said.

Ariana stared straight ahead. She had no idea what that meant. She was supposed to be mean to Tahira, but not *too* mean? Were they kidding? Clearly there was yet another nuance here she didn't understand. How was she ever going to catch up, especially if they didn't fill her in? She curled her fingers into fists and bit back her frustration.

All in time, Ariana. Just give it time.

"Hi, girls!" A pretty redhead paused on her way up the bleachers with a couple of friends trailing behind her. "We brought iced coffee." Her friends handed cups to Maria, Brigit, and Soomie, who took the frosty drinks as if they'd been expecting them. The redhead, meanwhile, looked around in confusion. "Where's Lexa?"

"Not getting in till tomorrow," Maria said, taking a sip. "You can give hers to Ana," she added, waving a hand in Ariana's direction.

"Ana, this is Quinn," Brigit said. "She's a sophomore."

"I'm on coffee, if you ever need one," Quinn said with a smile. "Hope you like skim latte. It's Lexa's drink of choice." She seemed disappointed to be handing the drink to someone other than Lexa.

"Sure. Thanks," Ariana said, nonplussed.

"We'll be up top if you need anything," Quinn said, the smile returning. "Later!"

"'Bye," the girls said vaguely.

"What does she mean, she's on coffee?" Ariana whispered to Brigit.

"The underclassmen were always asking us if we wanted anything, so last year Lexa decided it would just be less of a bother to assign people certain chores," Maria said with a shrug. "Quinn brings coffee to any interclass event, but we also have girls on snack duty, clothing patrol, library runs—"

"Clothing duty?" Ariana asked.

"Like if you spill coffee on your sweater and you need a new one, they'll get it for you," Brigit explained, sipping at her straw.

Ariana's jaw dropped. "Wait a minute, you have errand girls?"

"It's not as bad as it sounds," Soomie said. "They want to do it."

"Of course. Lexa would never make anyone do something they didn't want to," Maria added.

"I like to think of them as ladies-in-waiting," Brigit said, staring up toward the ceiling. "It's much more civilized. You'll have to give Quinn your drink order the next time you see her."

Ariana tried not to look as shocked as she felt. But this was way better than having a few grousing Billings newbies at her beck and call. It was a whole troop of *willing* lackeys. She sipped Lexa's latte and glanced back at Tahira. Quinn and the other girls had passed her by, so clearly the Dubai princess was not in on this particular perk. Ariana had *definitely* chosen wisely.

Just then Palmer strode into the room with Landon and Adam in tow, and excited chatter raced through the assembled crowd. Landon and Adam walked over to Ariana's clique. Ariana kept her eye on Landon as he made his way up the bleachers and dropped down next to Soomie, who turned purple at his closeness.

"*Chicas*," he said by way of greeting.

"*Buenas tardes*," Soomie replied.

Ariana glanced at Maria, who stared pointedly straight ahead. This triangle was very intriguing. And potentially something Ariana could use to her advantage once she figured out a way to play it.

"Hey," Adam said, sitting down next to Ariana. "I almost wore my uniform too, but my roommate told me to change."

Ariana smiled politely. "If only we were all so lucky."

Adam smiled back, showing some adorable dimples. "So, are you new to the prep school thing, too?"

"Me? No. I've been to a ton of schools like this," Ariana replied, recalling Briana Leigh's history of bootings from various illustrious academies.

"You're lucky. Public school is *way* different," Adam said, wiping his palms on his jeans.

Obviously, Ariana thought, but didn't say. Instead she gave him a bolstering look. "Well, you've obviously fallen in with the right crowd. Being friends with these guys, you should have no problem."

"That's exactly what Palmer told me over the summer," Adam said, brightening considerably. "My mother works for his mother. That's how I got my scholarship."

Ariana considered telling him that this was the kind of information he might be better off keeping to himself, but at that moment, Palmer decided to start the meeting. He stepped up to the center of the bleachers and smiled.

"Welcome, Team Gold!"

Everyone cheered. Ariana crossed her legs at the knee and clapped her hands. She wasn't sure whether to hope he would look for her. Why had she changed into this stupid, itchy uniform? She glanced over her shoulder to find Allison sitting a few rows behind her, smiling haughtily. She tossed her short blond curls back from her face and Ariana's fingers twitched, thinking of those silver scissors on her roommate's desk. Girl didn't know who she was messing with. She'd be lucky if she woke up with all her hair tomorrow.

"Let's get right down to business," Palmer continued, rolling his baseball between his palms. His eyes scanned the crowd, making solid eye contact with all assembled like a good public speaker, and fell on Ariana. His lips twitched and she fought the urge to sink back, instead sitting up straight and holding her head high. "Uh . . . we have three events at which to dominate."

Ariana smiled. She had thrown him off for a moment. Mr. Composed was not impenetrable. Too bad it had been because he was trying not to laugh at her.

"First will be the debate. I've put APH's resident debate king, Sumit Medha, in charge of that. Sumit, please stand and wave," Palmer said, gesturing toward the right side of the bleachers. A scrawny South Asian guy with short black hair stood up and raised his hand, earning some applause from the crowd. "If you're interested in participating in debate, please see Sumit after the meeting. That includes anyone who wants to do research, run for coffee, make support signs, and all that."

"I'm on research if any of you want to join," Soomie whispered.

"Please," Maria scoffed, sipping her coffee. "I'd rather do the coffee runs, thanks."

"I'm totally in," Brigit replied. "It's not like I'm going to be helping *her*."

Ariana kept her mouth shut. She could guess whom Brigit was referring to, but she had to hear all the options first.

"Our resident heiress, Tahira Al Mahmood, has generously offered to take the helm for the fund-raising event," Palmer continued.

Brigit sank lower in her seat as Tahira stood up and waved like a beauty pageant contestant.

"So please see Tahira for the details on that. And I will be captaining the crew team," Palmer said, tugging at the front of his T-shirt as though at jacket lapels. The guys in the crowd whooped while the girls shrilly cheered. Ariana raised an eyebrow. Palmer certainly was a rock star around here.

"We need a girl to act as coxswain for the boat, so anyone interested, please see me," Palmer said. "Practice starts Tuesday morning at the boathouse at five a.m. sharp."

"Yeah. So not happening," Maria said. "Coffee runs it is."

"All right. That takes care of the events," Palmer said, glancing to his left. "Ladies, if you please?"

He took a step back and four girls—sophomores or freshmen, Ariana guessed—jumped up from the bottom row, each wearing a gold armband around her bicep. They started to make their way up the bleachers, distributing armbands to the group.

"From this moment on, you will wear these bands wherever you go," Palmer instructed, pacing in front of the bleachers. "To meetings, to bed, to the bathroom, to the welcome dinner tonight—especially to the welcome dinner tonight. We want the alumni to know who's representing gold. Team pride, people. It's more important than fashion."

Here he glanced at Ariana again and smirked. Ariana felt the color rising in her cheeks.

"Okay, once you have your armband, you can go. But if you're in for debate, stay back and see Sumit!"

Palmer slapped Sumit on the back as he strode from the room, tossing his ball up and down as he went, as if perfectly confident that he was leaving everything in good hands.

"So, you staying?" Soomie asked Ariana as the room filled with chatter and everyone rose from their seats. "You seem like a research person."

"Actually, I just want to get back and change," Ariana said as she cinched her armband around her bicep.

"You're required to participate in the competition in some way," Maria told her. "As a transfer you should really be aware of that. People pay attention to this."

Ariana glanced at Maria. Why did she seem hostile all of a sudden? And who, exactly, would be paying attention to her level of involvement?

"I'll be involved. Don't worry," Ariana said. "I'll see you all later."

As she strode from the room, trying to ignore the torturous scratching of her skirt and shirt, Ariana had the awful feeling she'd just made some kind of social faux pas, only she had no idea what it was. But being seen for another five minutes dressed like this had to be worse than whatever infraction she'd committed.

Tomorrow she would get involved somehow. After she aced her history exam. She heaved a sigh and shoved her way through the gym doors. Turned out that creating a new life from scratch was a lot of work.

SNAGGING THE BOY

"This room is stunning," Ariana said, gazing up at the domed ceiling looming over the gilded Atherton-Pryce Hall ballroom. The vast chamber was at the center of the Pryce Building, which was a huge, colonial-style structure situated on a crest overlooking the Potomac. The building housed several art collections, an exclusive library, a catering kitchen, and several smaller gathering rooms. Ariana had seen photos of this room in the school's glossy catalog, but not one had done it justice.

"That's why it's booked five years in advance for weddings during the high seasons," Maria informed her, hugging her slim arms as she looked around. "Only alumni can get married on campus and have their receptions here." She fixed her eyes on Ariana. "And only *important* alumni, at that," she added, as if giving Ariana one of many reasons to become important.

"Duly noted," Ariana replied.

"There are currently six APH alumni in the Senate and twenty-three in the House of Representatives," Maria said, looking around the room. "Not to mention White House staffers and Wall Street millionaires and international business gurus. There are more power players circulating in this room than there are at most state dinners."

"I had no idea," Ariana lied. She had, of course, seen the numbers in the APH brochure, but she was starting to get the feeling that Maria was the type of person who enjoyed knowing more than the people around her. She could let her feel that way, for now.

"You should mingle. Meet as many of them as you can," Maria instructed, fiddling with the cowl neck of her sleeveless black dress. Her face was practically makeup free, and her hair tumbled in natural waves down her back. She was one of those rare, lucky girls who could get away with such simplicity at a formal event. Just standing next to her, Ariana felt envious. Many people had called her beautiful, but that was before. Back when she had blond hair and an ivory complexion and was comfortable in her own skin. Tonight she had taken almost an hour to get ready, trying out different makeup schemes and shedding dress after dress before finally settling on the short-sleeved, belted, blue Donna Karan because it didn't clash with her gold armband. She was still learning to be a tan, auburn-haired girl from Texas. Still finding her way as Briana Leigh Covington.

"I will," Ariana told her.

A petite girl with cocoa skin and curly black hair appeared at Maria's elbow and handed over a light blue pashmina. "I couldn't find the black, but I thought this would go well with your dress," she said.

Maria sniffed. "Fine. Thank you, Jessica."

"Anytime." Jessica quickly disappeared into the crowd.

"See? Clothing duty," Maria said to Ariana as shrugged her arms into the sleeves.

Ariana smiled. She really was going to have to find a way to put these ladies-in-waiting to use.

"Maria! Landon's parents are here," Soomie announced breathlessly, lifting herself onto her toes as she joined them. "You must introduce me."

Maria blushed and sipped her water. "I doubt they'd even remember me. We've only met once."

"Like anyone could forget you," Soomie said, rolling her eyes. "Please? You know impressing the parents is one of the five keys to snagging the boy," she begged. "Even if the boy thinks he hates his parents. Which Landon does not," she added as an aside to Ariana. "He totally loves them, which just makes him all the more perfect, don't you think?"

"Definitely," Ariana acknowledged. "What are the other four keys?'

"One, be in his space, but not in his face—"

"Which you are utterly failing at," Maria pointed out.

Soomie hesitated, but chose to ignore this comment. "Two, have your own life and interests. Three, never leave the house without mascara. Four, flirt with other boys, and five . . . make sure his friends and family love you," she finished, looking pointedly at Maria.

Ariana laughed. "That's some list."

"It better be, after two years of interviewing and cataloging the responses of girls aged thirteen to twenty-one who were in successful relationships of more than six months."

"Wow."

"Yeah. She can be a little scary." Maria let out an impatient sigh and Ariana shot her a knowing look. She understood why Maria didn't want Soomie to meet Landon's parents. Right now she had a leg up, knowing the family. She was slightly more important in Landon's life than Soomie was. An introduction would make them equal. Why had Maria never told Soomie about her feelings for Landon? They were supposed to be best friends. Best friends told each other everything.

Except, of course, when the boy in question was supposedly unworthy. Which was why, years ago, Ariana had kept her relationship with Thomas Pearson a secret from Noelle, as much as it was possible to keep a secret from Noelle. But Landon, obviously, was not unworthy.

"Fine," Maria said, rolling her eyes and placing her glass on the tray of a passing waiter. "We'll be back," she said to Ariana. "Mingle," she added again over her shoulder. "Don't forget, this is a big event."

"I've got it," Ariana told her. This was the third time that day she felt directed by Maria. She wasn't sure whether to feel grateful because the girl was looking out for her, or offended because Maria obviously thought she couldn't fend for herself.

Soomie paused before scurrying off, glancing at Ariana as if she'd just realized she was standing there. "You look amazing, by the way," she said matter-of-factly. "Very event-appropriate. That won't go unnoticed."

"Thanks," Ariana said, looking down at her dress and touching her pearl necklace with her fingertips. The two girls hurried off and

Ariana watched them go, her brow furrowed. Again, she felt as if she was missing something.

With a confused sigh, Ariana looked around the room at all the well-dressed smiling people chatting and downing drinks all around her. Suddenly she realized that this was the first cocktail party she had attended in ages, and she decided to forget about Maria and Soomie and their odd behavior and just let herself sink into the light and airy atmosphere. Nothing much had changed about these events during her two years in prison. There were still trays of hors d'oeuvres and flutes of champagne, overdressed women eyeing one another's choice of frock, and underdressed men checking their watches. And as always, the vibe was festive. Bubbly. Full of froth. Not a care in the room. Which suited Ariana just fine. She was due for a carefree evening.

A familiar laugh caught her ear and she turned. Palmer stood in the center of the ballroom's marble dance floor, wearing a perfectly cut suit, an APH tie, and an American flag lapel pin, chatting with a couple who could only be his parents. He was the spitting image of his father, who had a few wrinkles around the eyes, but not many other signs of age. His mother had light brown hair, blue eyes, and the straightest posture in the room, but Ariana could tell by her broad gestures and unabashed laughter that she wasn't the least bit uptight.

Impressing the parents is key to snagging the boy, Ariana thought.

She smiled, matched her posture to Mrs. Liriano's, and, feeling confident in her event-appropriate choice of dress, strode over to join Palmer and his family. Palmer did a double take as she approached, and his smile widened.

"Good evening," Ariana said, completing the circle by standing across from Palmer.

"Hello," Mrs. Liriano said.

"Mother, Father, meet Ana Covington," Palmer said in his low, sexy voice. "She just transferred to APH."

"Very nice to meet you, Ana." Palmer's mother offered her hand.

"Likewise," Ariana said, making sure her Texan accent was intact.

"You made a wise choice, transferring here," his father added. "Mrs. Liriano has nothing but fond memories."

"You graduated APH?" Ariana asked Mrs. Liriano.

"Ages ago," she replied, taking a sip of her champagne.

"Not that long ago, Mother," Palmer said, causing his mother to laugh. He looked at Ariana and leaned in, lowering his voice. "The congresswoman likes to pretend she's older than she is. She thinks it will help her gain more respect on the Hill."

"Not that she needs any help in that arena," Mr. Liriano added.

"I've trained my men well, as you can see," Palmer's mother said to Ariana in a conspiratorial tone. "Nothing but compliment after compliment."

"Believe me, I'm taking mental notes," Ariana replied with a laugh. "You're a congresswoman?"

"Fifth district, Arizona," she replied with a nod.

"That's incredible," Ariana said. "I don't believe I've ever met a congresswoman before," she lied. Her father had been fast friends with many a politician in Georgia. They used to gather out on the porch on warm summer evenings, smoke cigars, and talk about how to improve the state. Ariana used to love to listen to their throaty laughter and rumbling voices from the settee inside the parlor, letting the sounds of the creaking rocking chairs lull her off to sleep.

She found her throat welling at the memory but swallowed it down. She was Briana Leigh Covington now. Briana Leigh had no such fond memories.

"Well, I'm happy to be the first," Mrs. Liriano said.

"And what do you do, Mr. Liriano?" Ariana asked, glancing at Palmer from the corner of her eye. She could tell he was watching her closely, and that he appreciated her good manners and her ability to chat with the adults. Points were definitely being scored.

"Nothing much, I'm afraid. Retired ballplayer. All I do these days is sign baseballs, make appearances, and head up my charitable foundation," he said.

"Really? I'd love to hear about the foundation," Ariana told him.

"No, you wouldn't," Palmer joked.

They all laughed.

"Dad was also instrumental in shaping the anti-performance-enhancing-drug bill that was signed into law last year," Palmer said, clearly proud of both parents. "He's the one who taught me everything I know about sportsmanship and fairness."

Ariana smiled. So sportsmanship and fairness were important to Palmer as well. She was glad she'd come over to chat with his family. Already she was learning more about him. Ariana was just about to ask a follow-up question when a photographer stepped up and touched Mr. Liriano's shoulder.

"Mr. Liriano, Congresswoman . . . would you and your son mind posing for a few photos for the alumni magazine?" he asked.

"Of course not," Mrs. Liriano said.

Ariana's heart skipped a beat and she slunk back a few steps. The last thing she wanted was her photo appearing in a magazine. Even in her disguise, someone out there might recognize her.

"No, Ana, stay," Mrs. Liriano said, touching her arm. "The magazine loves to get as many students and alums in each photo as they can."

Ariana's pulse raced as the Lirianos all looked at her expectantly and the photographer looked on. She didn't want to be rude, but she could not have her photo published. Her life might depend on it.

"It's okay. Actually, I'm not very photogenic," Ariana said, still backing away.

"I find that hard to believe," Mr. Liriano said matter-of-factly.

"Thanks, but . . . you should just make it a family picture," Ariana said. She glanced around and spotted Tahira out of the corner of her eye, wearing a bright green dress that couldn't be missed. "Besides, I promised Tahira I would meet some of her friends and she's waiting for me, so . . . it was nice to meet you both!"

Then, not wanting to look at their baffled faces any longer, Ariana turned and strode toward Tahira, who was talking to a group of elderly alumni. Not because she in any way wanted to, but because she had to in case the Lirianos were watching.

As she marched toward what was sure to be a lethally boring conversation, she wondered what the five keys were for keeping her new identity safe.

LEXA GREENE

Ariana decided to take the long, scenic route back to her dorm after the alumni welcome party. It was a clear, balmy, late-summer night, and the Atherton-Pryce Hall campus glowed in the light emanating from dozens of old-fashioned iron lampposts set along the walkways. Alcove lamps at the entrances to the class buildings and dorms illuminated the APH crest, which was etched above each door, along with each building's date of construction. Ariana could hear the Potomac River burbling along as she strolled the outer paths of the school, and she sighed contentedly. Even though Atherton-Pryce had fewer students than Easton Academy, the campus was twice the size. The facilities were state-of-the-art, the setting gorgeous and bucolic and serene. She looked up at the dual towers of Privilege House and imagined herself gazing out one of the huge plate glass windows, watching the sun rise over the river. Imagined how perfectly happy she would be there. Then she thought of her former friends, who had long since finished their days at Easton, and felt a sense of satisfaction.

This place was a vast improvement over Easton Academy. Who cared if she was a few years behind where she should have been? Her experiences here were going to be unparalleled. She could feel it. Easton Academy and everyone associated with it could kiss her ass.

With a private grin at her crassness, Ariana walked back toward the center of campus. She heard laughter and conversation coming from the direction of the boys' dorms—guys saying their good-byes to their parents, seeing them to their cars—and turned her steps in that direction. Hanging back near the corner of one of the brick buildings, she watched as Adam shook hands with his father and hugged his mother before the woefully underdressed couple walked over to their blue Ford Taurus. Surrounded by the other families in their expensive suits and dresses, loitering around their Mercedes and Audis and Cadillacs, Adam's family looked completely out of place. Ariana could only imagine that they were relieved to be going. Relieved at the thought of returning to their own world.

Ariana scanned the area for Palmer, and saw him lifting a hand in a wave as his parents pulled away in their black Lexus. Her heart skipped a beat in anticipation. He hadn't seen her yet, but he was about to turn to head back to the dorm. Any second now, he would spy her standing there. Watching. What would his reaction be?

He turned. Saw her. Smiled.

Pure elation.

Ariana struggled to compose herself as he strolled over to her, his hands in the pockets of his blue suit trousers.

"You sure know how to work a room," he said, stepping closer to her than was absolutely necessary. "And my parents specifically."

Ariana glowed with pleasure. Apparently they hadn't lingered on her uncomfortable exit after she was gone. "I'll take that as a compliment."

"Walk you back to your dorm?" he offered.

"Definitely."

They walked together, side by side, straight across campus. Palmer was silent, but Ariana didn't mind, because she could feel him looking at her. Studying her. Admiring her. When she hazarded a glance in his direction, he was smiling down at her with an almost giddy expression. Like he wanted something. Like he knew he was about to get something. As long as she was willing to give it.

The tingling of her skin intensified the closer they got to Cornwall. Ariana could actually feel the attraction between her and Palmer. So thick it was almost tangible. She couldn't help feeling that she had been sent here somehow. That she had been meant to meet him. That all the awful, ridiculous, heartbreaking moments of her life had led her to this place at this time for this reason. She and Palmer were soul mates. So what if she had only known him for a day? A girl knew these things. She just knew.

"Here we are," Palmer said as they arrived at the imposing front door of the dorm.

The arched alcove just outside the entry provided a bit of shelter, a bit of privacy, shielding them from the parking lot and arced drive-way in front of the dorm. A few small klatches of people were still saying good-bye at the curb, but they were far enough off that Ariana couldn't make out specific voices.

"Yes. Here we are," Ariana said.

She leaned back against the cool brick wall and looked up at him through her lashes. Palmer smiled and placed his hands in the pockets of his trousers.

"So, what made you come over to meet my parents tonight?" he asked. "Got a yen for aging ballplayers?"

"Not exactly," Ariana said coyly.

She had never been one to make the first move, except on the odd occasion when she lost control of herself. But that was before. Here at APH, she hoped to keep her emotions from consuming her the way she had in the past. The results of that behavior had often been messy.

"Then what was it, exactly?" Palmer's grin widened and he took a step toward her. Ariana was light-headed with glee. He was going to kiss her. She was sure of it. Here it was, her first day at APH, and already she had landed the most eligible bachelor on campus. President of the student body.

"You're a smart guy. You can figure it out."

Just then, a car door slammed and a girl's voice called out, thank-ing the driver. Palmer leaned back to see out the entryway of the alcove. Ariana wanted to grab him and pull him into her, but no. Control. She had to be in control. Then the yawning chasm between them grew even wider as Palmer took a full step back and turned away from her.

"Lexa!" he shouted cheerily.

Lexa? Lexa Greene? Even as Ariana hankered for a glimpse of the infamous group leader, her brain was processing that something wasn't right here. Palmer was way too happy to see this girl.

"Hey! What are you doing here?" Lexa's voice replied merrily. "Did Maria tell you I was coming back early? She was supposed to keep it a secret!"

In a blur of red dress, the girl raced into the alcove and threw herself into Palmer's arms. She was slight but tall, her long dark hair shaped into a perfect, long blunt cut with bangs straight across her forehead. Ariana's gaze automatically flicked to her shoes. Tasteful black peep toes, Charles David, Ariana guessed. When Palmer released her, Ariana got a good view of the girl's gorgeous, pixieish features. Tiny nose, big blue eyes, pretty smile, glossy lips . . .

Lips that were now pressing against Palmer's.

Ariana's face stung as she watched the embrace. What the hell was going on here? That was *her* kiss. That was *her* soon-to-be boyfriend.

"I missed you," Lexa breathed, keeping her arms locked around Palmer's neck as she leaned back.

Palmer smiled. A relaxed, happy, intimate smile. As if the girl he'd been *about* to make out with wasn't standing mere inches away watching him maul some other girl. "I missed you too."

Finally, Ariana couldn't take it anymore. She pushed herself away from the wall and cleared her throat.

Palmer looked over at Ariana but kept one arm around Lexa's tiny shoulders. Ariana couldn't help noticing that the girl had a perfectly taut, athletic body, obvious under the clingy material of her red wrap dress.

"Oh, hey. Lexa Greene, meet Briana Leigh Covington. Ana for short," Palmer said in a formal way. "She's a transfer."

She's a transfer. The dismissive, detached nature of the comment made her skin crawl.

Yeah. The transfer you were about to hook up with.

"Hi," Ariana managed to say. "I've heard a lot about you."

Lexa looked at Ariana and her eyes narrowed. She took a step toward Ariana and for a split second Ariana was sure the girl was going to slap her across the face. Why not? She could tell with one glance that Lexa was not stupid. She had to see what was going on here.

Then, suddenly, Lexa's pretty face lit up like the Fourth of July. "Briana Leigh! I heard you were transferring in!"

Lexa threw her slim arms around Ariana and hugged her so hard Ariana could hardly breathe. Then, just as suddenly, Lexa leaned back, clamping her hands onto Ariana's shoulders.

"You look so different! I never would have recognized you!"

Ariana's pulse raced and her mind reeled, thinking back to every inane conversation she'd had with Briana Leigh. She had never mentioned anyone named Lexa Greene. Never. Ariana was sure of it. So why was this girl acting as if she and Briana Leigh were long-lost friends? What had Ariana missed? And what was it going to cost her?

"It's me! Lexa Greene!" Lexa said, her brow knitting in disappointment as she finally released Ariana. "You don't remember me, do you."

"I . . . sorry," Ariana said.

"I was your main competition in jumper at Camp Triple Star. The summer before fourth," Lexa continued, growing more animated. "Oh my God. I was so jealous when you took home that trophy, I cried for, like, twenty-four hours straight. Not that I'm proud of that fact." She studied Ariana's face for a long few moments and Ariana's stomach lurched. Any second the words were going to fall from Lexa's mouth:

"Wait a minute. . . . You're not Briana Leigh Covington. . . ."

Ariana tried to mentally prepare herself for the moment. Tried to decide what she would say or do with Palmer looking on and all those people out in the parking lot gabbing away.

In, one . . . two . . . three . . .

Out, one . . . two . . . three . . .

"How can you not remember? It was such a huge deal," Lexa said finally.

Suddenly Ariana's whirling mind hit upon a dim memory. Something about equestrian camp. Briana Leigh had gone there during her grade school summers before transferring to Camp Potowamac when she was twelve.

"Right! Lexa Greene," she faked. "Of course I remember you. You were good."

Lexa smiled again. "Not as good as you! We called you 'Blue Ribbon Bitch' behind your back," she said, her cheeks turning pink. "I always felt bad about that because we were such good friends, but I guess that's how girls are when someone has what you want."

Ariana glanced at Palmer, who was standing a bit behind Lexa now. He quickly looked away toward the parking lot, but she could see the hint of an embarrassed blush on his cheek.

"I guess so," Ariana said.

"But I've improved a bit since then," Lexa said. "You inspired me to practice nonstop."

"She's the most accomplished rider on the APH equestrian team," Palmer announced proudly, squeezing Lexa's shoulder.

"That's great," Ariana said, forcing herself to smile at Lexa. All she could think about was finding a way out of this conversation and this awkward little threesome, but Lexa seemed hell-bent on keeping her there.

"Whatever. We had so much fun that summer! I can't believe you're here!" Lexa said, reaching out to brush Ariana's arm with her fingertips. "We are going to have so much fun!"

"Definitely," Ariana said. *As soon as this violent nausea subsides.*

"You look so different somehow," Lexa said suddenly, narrowing her eyes again. "Did you change your—"

"And you look exactly the same!" Ariana replied with a frantic laugh.

Lexa rolled her eyes. "God, I hope not. Otherwise the braces were for nothing."

Palmer slipped his arms around Lexa from behind and nuzzled her neck. "You have a perfect smile."

Lexa blushed and Ariana almost hurled. "My boyfriend. So sweet," Lexa said, cuddling back into his arms. She slid her hand up his arm until it found his gold team armband. Then she turned and looked from his band to Ariana's. "Hey! You're both on gold!"

"Yeah," Ariana said. "Lucky us."

"You are too, Lex," Palmer said. "I worked it with the headmaster."

Of course you did, Ariana thought.

"Yay! This is going to be so much fun!" Lexa trilled. Then she grasped Ariana's hand and squeezed. "Come on. Let's go inside. Palmer, can you help with my bags?"

"Sure," he said. He glanced over at Ariana and smiled as Lexa turned to flash her key card at the electric eye next to the door. Ariana leveled him with a stare that should have stopped his blood cold. But instead, he merely appeared confused.

As Palmer and Lexa jostled all her things through the door, Ariana hesitated. Had she completely misread Palmer over the last twelve hours? Had he not been flirting with her in the school store, on the quad, at the party? Their mutual attraction had seemed completely obvious. But then, Maria *had* said that he was a flirt by nature.

It doesn't matter, Ariana told herself, fighting off a crushing wave of disappointment. *Whether or not he was flirting with you, he's obviously with Lexa. And you need to be friends with Lexa and her friends.*

She had made her choice and she'd already pissed off Tahira. If she wanted to have any chance at a social life here at APH, there was no going back now. Suddenly months of hanging with Lexa and Palmer, watching them kiss and flirt and be adorable together, stretched out before her like an extended death row sentence.

So much for her perfect new life.

GULLIBILITY

Ariana lay perfectly still in her bed, listening to Allison snore, trying to remind herself of all the reasons it would be unwise to murder her roommate in her sleep. First, she would instantly be sent back to jail, which would mean that all the work she had done for the past two years both inside the Brenda T. and out would be for nothing. And secondly, it wasn't Allison she wanted to get rid of, however annoying her snoring was. If she killed the girl, Ariana would just be taking out her ire on an innocent bystander. Bitchy, but innocent.

No, it wasn't Allison she wanted to kill. It was Palmer. Or maybe Lexa. Or maybe both.

Ever so slowly, Ariana's fingers gripped and released her blanket. Gripped and released. Gripped and released. She repeated the motion over and over as she breathed deliberately and tried to calm her racing thoughts.

Lexa would be tricky to deal with. After studying all evening for her history exam, Ariana had e-mailed Briana Leigh's personal maid back in Texas and asked her to dig up any mementos she could find from Briana Leigh's days at Camp Triple Star. Ariana was hoping for diaries and photo albums, but even ribbons and trophies or plane tickets would do. If she could just know which events Briana Leigh had won or the dates she'd attended the camp, she would be in much better shape. After that, all she had to do was keep the conversations vague and hope that Lexa didn't ask as many questions as Brigit did. Because *that* could eventually pose a problem.

Why did there have to be someone at this school who actually knew Briana Leigh? How could Ariana possibly be that unlucky?

But she wasn't going to think that way. She was going to think positively.

She could deal with Palmer. She just had to stop thinking about him. Ariana squeezed her fists hard. No. She didn't need him. The last thing Ariana needed was a guy who cheated like Daniel Ryan had. A guy who thought it was perfectly fine to toy with a girl's emotions like Thomas Pearson. To lead girls on. To dally with several people at once. The first two loves of her life had been total players. Schemers. Cheaters with charm. And look how those relationships had turned out.

Ariana sighed as she thought of Hudson. Beautiful, kind, uncomplicated Hudson. If only she had met him in this life instead of her interim one. He would never mess with her the way Palmer had.

But he hadn't seemed in the least bit guilty. Did he have no conscience, or had Ariana actually misread his signals? She had posed this question several times over the past few hours and every time she came back to the same conclusion. It wasn't possible. She couldn't have misunderstood him. He was interested in her. She knew he was. But clearly he was more interested in Lexa.

Suddenly, Ariana's cell phone trilled. She had turned it back on that afternoon hoping Palmer might call her. She darted up in bed and grabbed for it, wondering if Hudson had psychically realized she was thinking about him. Or if, perhaps, Palmer was calling to explain himself.

Allison groaned and rolled over in her bed as Ariana finally glimpsed the caller ID screen. Her blood ran cold. The caller ID read *Briana Leigh*.

"Oh my God," Ariana said under her breath. Her fingers shook, and for a moment the specter of Briana Leigh hung over her, as if the girl were phoning her from the grave, but then the call clicked over to voice mail and the reality of the situation settled in. It was Kaitlynn. Kaitlynn was calling her from Briana Leigh's phone.

But how? She had canceled the service. This was just not possible.

The phone rang again, obliterating the silence. Allison sat up in bed. "Will you please take that outside!?"

Ariana flung her covers aside, shoved her feet into her slippers, and grabbed a cashmere hoodie on her way out the door. In the hallway, her bare toes dug into the soft carpet as she stared down at the still-ringing phone, considering what to do. She could simply ignore the call. Let it go to voice mail again and shut it off. But if it *was* Kaitlynn, she knew the girl would not give up. What if she came to campus? She could blow Ariana's cover with one word. Maybe it was better to deal with her now. Find out what she wanted and get it over with.

She hit the talk button and walked toward the floor's common lounge. "Hello?" she said, whispering tersely.

"Hey *Briana Leigh*!" Kaitlynn's voice sang. "Didja miss me?"

Ariana clenched her teeth. She shoved one arm into her sweater, then the other, holding the phone away from her to keep from gnawing on it in anger. Slowly she sank down on one of the room's cushy leather chairs, remaining perched on the very edge of the seat. The big-screen television in the corner was dark, but the green numbers on the cable box beneath it were flashing, begging to be set, casting an eerie dim glow over Ariana's face at two-second intervals.

"What do you want?" she demanded.

"I just want to see you, B.L.," Kaitlynn teased. "I showed up at that fancy school of yours, but when I refused to show them my ID, they wouldn't even call up to your dorm. May as well be the Pentagon. Very impressive."

"What do you *want*?" Ariana repeated, gripping the phone so hard she was surprised it had yet to shatter.

"I want you to meet me tomorrow afternoon, two p.m., at the Belle Haven diner," Kaitlynn said, her voice syrupy sweet. "We need to have a little chat, Briana Leigh."

"Stop calling me that," Ariana said through her teeth, standing up. She paced around the wooden coffee table, strewn with fashion magazines left behind by her floor mates, and walked over to the large, single-pane window.

"Why? Isn't that your name? Isn't that why you drowned poor Briana Leigh in the lake that night?" Kaitlynn replied.

Ariana closed her eyes against the onslaught of images. Briana Leigh struggling for life, her lifeless form sinking to the bottom of Lake Page. Suddenly a rush of anger crashed in on her from all sides and she wanted to scream at Kaitlynn. Tell her it was her fault that Briana Leigh had died. She was the one who had fooled Ariana into thinking Briana Leigh was a murderer. She was the one who had manipulated Ariana into going to Texas and wheedling her way into the girl's life. If not for Kaitlynn, Briana Leigh would be alive and well right now.

Except that you did need the authorities to find a body, a little voice reminded her. But she chose to ignore that little detail. This was Kaitlynn's fault. All Kaitlynn's fault. Still, she couldn't get into a screaming match about culpability right now, not with all her new friends and classmates slumbering within hearing range. She gripped her arm with her free hand to rein in her anger, held her breath, and stared out the window at the glowing lights of the APH campus. "What if I don't come?"

"Well, then, I'll just have to send this little e-mail I've composed to your Headmaster Jansen, telling her all about the violent tendencies of the imposter they have living on campus," Kaitlynn said. Ariana could hear the sound of a computer keyboard tapping away in the background. "I'm sure that with all the dignitaries' sons and daughters they have strolling around campus, they'll be sure to investigate right away."

Hot tears seared at Ariana's eyes. She wanted to throw something.

Hit someone. Break something. She imagined her fist going through the glass in front of her, the satisfying crash, the blood pouring down her arm.

"You'll be there," Kaitlynn said confidently. "See you at two."

The line went dead.

Ariana turned and hurtled her phone against the wall, shattering it into a zillion pieces. She let out a quiet groan and sank to the floor, pulling her knees up and holding her head in both hands, struggling for breath.

Why had she trusted Kaitlynn? Why had she let her out of prison? Why couldn't she have just seen the girl for what she really was— a lying, manipulative, murderous psychopath?

She took a deep breath and pushed her fingers up into her hair. This was her own fault. Her own gullibility had brought her here. Kaitlynn had played her, used her as her unsuspecting puppet.

I hate her, Ariana thought, pulling at her hair as the depth of her own stupidity slapped her in the face again and again and again. *I hate her, I hate her, I hate her.*

The pain was what brought her back from the edge. She pulled her hands away from her scalp and with them came an alarming amount of hair. Ariana's jaw dropped, appalled by her own lack of control. She stood up, her hands shaking, and breathed.

In, one . . . two . . . three . . .

Out, one . . . two . . . three . . .

In, one . . . two . . . three . . .

Out, one . . . two . . . three . . .

Slowly, her blood pressure began to return to normal. Yes, Kaitlynn had played her. It was the most frustrating fact of all to accept, but there it was. And she had to deal with it. She had been naïve enough to believe in Kaitlynn, and now she had to figure out a way to correct the mistake. Somehow. Some way. She had to get Kaitlynn Nottingham out of her life.

Ariana breathed in, her mind completely clear now, and gazed across the room at the shards of plastic and metal that had once been her cell.

And now she definitely needed a new phone.

FOCUS

Ariana stood in front of the mirror and smoothed the front of her white Calvin Klein top. Her hand trembled and she stared at it for a moment defiantly. It would not tremble again. She would not let Kaitlynn see her sweat.

"Everything's fine," she told herself. "You aced that history exam this morning and you're well on your way to getting your schedule changed. Now all you have to do is deal with the bitch from hell and you'll be back on track."

She gave herself a tight smile, grabbed her suede hobo bag, and strode into the hallway. A burst of laughter greeted her, and she looked up to find Maria, Brigit, and Soomie strolling down the hall, led, of course, by Lexa, who was looking very Audrey Hepburn in a perfectly chic black sundress and flats. Ariana's first instinct was to clench her fist, but she forced herself to smile.

"Hey, guys," Ariana said brightly.

"Briana Leigh!" Lexa's eyes lit up as she stepped forward, but then she stopped abruptly. "I'm sorry. I mean, Ana. The girls reminded me you want to be called Ana now."

Ariana registered the fact that they had been talking about her. But that, she supposed, was to be expected. She shrugged casually. "Well, Briana Leigh is kind of a mouthful."

Lexa appeared confused by this, but let it go.

"Where're you going?" Brigit asked, eyeing Ariana's purse. "Got a hot date?"

"No. I just—"

"Good! Because we're off to Georgetown to burn up the credit cards," Brigit said, looping her arm through Ariana's. "Want to come?"

"Yes! Come with us!" Lexa put in, leading the way to the stairs, her hair swinging behind her shoulders, not one strand out of place.

Ariana glanced at her watch. "I wish I could, but I can't."

"Why not? There are no events or meetings scheduled until this afternoon," Soomie pointed out unhelpfully. She pulled out her BlackBerry as if to double-check, and clucked her tongue. "Damn. Frozen again."

"Why don't you just get a new one already?" Maria groused, looking bored as she toyed with her hair.

"Who has the time to deal with that?" Soomie asked.

"So order one online," Lexa suggested. "You can do it when we get back." Then, as if that ended that conversation, she looked at Ariana again. "So, you in?"

Ariana hesitated. Part of her was dying to go with them. She needed to solidify herself as part of this group if she wanted to have the social life she craved here at Atherton-Pryce. But staying at APH wouldn't be in the slightest bit possible if Kaitlynn made good on her threats. There would be time to bond with the girls later. If she bailed on Kaitlynn now, who knew if the psycho would give her another chance?

"Actually, I have a meeting scheduled with my guidance counselor," Ariana lied as she descended the stairs behind the rest of the girls. "There was a mix-up with my schedule."

"You have all week to do that," Maria said over her shoulder, donning a pair of aviator sunglasses as she shoved through the outer door of the dorm. "Blow it off."

"I can't. I just want to get it over with," Ariana said, keeping her voice in check. Maria seemed intent to tell her what to do at every turn. "But thanks for the offer."

"Your loss," Maria said with a shrug. "Let's go, ladies."

"Wait. Let me give you my number," Lexa said, holding out her dainty hand. "Then you can call and meet up with us after your meeting."

A lump of embarrassment formed in Ariana's throat. She envisioned her phone in a hundred pieces on the lounge floor. Pieces it had taken almost half an hour to gather up last night.

"My phone died." *Because I killed it,* she added silently. She flipped open her purse and pulled out a pen and the small pad she always kept with her, flipping quickly past the pages full of Briana Leigh's practiced signature. *Mental note: Burn the evidence of all those hours she spent perfecting her new autograph.* "Here. Write it down."

Lexa giggled as she took the pen. "I feel so old-school."

Ariana laughed as well, but felt the sting of unworthiness.

"There you go," Lexa said, handing the notebook and pen back. Ariana couldn't help noticing that the girl's penmanship was big and bubbly. Like a little girl's. It totally worked with her personality. Lexa was so unapologetically sweet. And kind. And giving. She was trying to reach out to the new girl, include her. Something she definitely didn't have to do. Something Maria and Soomie had been reluctant to do all day yesterday. And yet she also had an air of authority, power.

Ariana could see why Palmer, Brigit, Soomie, and Maria liked her so much. Why she would be a valuable friend.

"The car's here," Maria announced.

She was just about to shove through the door when Tahira walked into the dorm, trailing Allison and Zuri. Tahira paused for a split second before a wide grin lit her face.

"Lexa! So good to see you!" she said.

"You too, T!" Lexa replied, with what sounded like genuine enthusiasm.

As the two girls double air-kissed, the rest of their friends stood back a respectable distance and shot each other impatient but resigned glances. Ariana swallowed her surprise. Lexa and Tahira were friends?

"Where are you girls off to?" Tahira asked, her contempt for the other girls simmering just below the surface of her wide-eyed smile. She was faking it for Lexa's sake, clearly.

"Shopping, of course. Want to come with?" Lexa asked.

Brigit, Maria, and Soomie visibly stiffened, but Tahira was quick to answer.

"I have ten zillion things to do for the fund-raiser, but thanks," she said, stepping past Lexa. "But you should stop by later. I'd love to hear your thoughts. And I want to hear all about your tour of Italy."

"I'm in!" Lexa replied. "I'll come by when we get back. Oh, and Tahira, did you get those sheets for me?"

Tahira's smile suddenly appeared stiff. "Of course. I had my maid fly to Pakistan especially."

"She had these insanely soft eight-hundred-thread-count sheets last year and I just *had* to have them," Lexa explained to Ariana. "But it turned out they're made by this tiny company in Pakistan, so Tahira was nice enough to offer to pick them up for me over the summer."

"I'll put them in your room for you," Tahira said.

"Thank you *so* much, T," Lexa said brightly.

"Anytime," Tahira said. There was a tiny bit of strain behind her polite demeanor, but it was so slight Ariana wasn't sure anyone had picked up on it but her. "Later!"

Zuri followed Tahira up the stairs, but Allison hung back. "I'd appreciate it if you wouldn't use my stuff," she said to Ariana, without so much as a greeting.

Ariana blinked. "What?"

"My tissues. I saw one in the garbage and I know I didn't use it," Allison said, crossing her arms over her chest. "You make a habit of taking things without asking?"

A tissue? She was going to make a big stink about one tissue? Ariana could feel the other girls watching her and felt unsure of what to say. Was she supposed to back down and apologize, or tell the girl she was insane, like she wanted to? After their comment about the fine line with Tahira the day before, and this new development of a friendship between Tahira and Lexa, she felt completely thrown.

"No. Of course not," Ariana said. Then, adopting a slightly sarcastic tone, she added, "I owe you one tissue. I'll make a note of it."

Maria and Soomie laughed and Allison narrowed her eyes. "And who are you getting calls from in the middle of the night, anyway?"

Ariana's heart nosedived into her toes.

"You got a call in the middle of the night?" Brigit asked excitedly. "Was it your secret lover?"

"Ooh! You have a secret lover?" Lexa asked with a grin.

"No," Ariana said quickly.

"Whoever it was pissed her off," Allison said with a derisive chuckle. "I saw the pieces of your phone in the trash this morning next to the tissue."

Ariana saw the lie she had told to Lexa registering on the girl's face and her cheeks burned. "What do you do, go through the garbage as soon as you wake up every day?" she snapped at Allison.

"I thought your phone died," Lexa said, her pretty brow creasing.

"It did," Ariana replied, fighting for control. "It died on me in the middle of the call and while I was trying to figure out what was wrong with it, it slipped out of my hand."

"So who called you? Because the next time they call I'm picking up and telling them off," Allison said.

"It was my grandmother," Ariana said flatly, leveling Allison with a stare. "She's old and she gets disoriented sometimes. She had no clue what time it was, but if you want to pick up the phone and scare the life out of a frail old woman next time, be my guest."

Lexa slipped a protective arm around Ariana. "I think you should go now, Allison," she said.

Ariana was surprised by the gesture, but then she realized that her barely contained ire must have been coming off as grief over her grandmother's "illness." She gave herself a mental pat on the back for a job well done. Allison, meanwhile, simply turned and walked away without another word. Between this exit and Lexa's exchange with Tahira, it was clear that Lexa had some real power around here, even with the enemies of her friends.

"Are you okay?" Lexa asked Ariana.

Ariana sniffled for good measure. "I'm fine, thanks," she said. "You guys go."

"Are you sure?" Brigit asked. "If you want to talk about your grandmother, I'd love to hear all about her."

I'm sure you would, Ariana thought. "Thanks, but I have to get to that meeting."

"We should go. The driver's waiting," Maria said, pushing the door open.

Idling at the curb in front of the dorm was a black Town Car. Maria walked over and waited for the driver to open the back door for her. Brigit and Soomie both waved before they joined her. Lexa, however, hung back.

"So, we'll see you later?" she said.

"I'll call you," Ariana said, even though she knew she wouldn't. She would be too busy meeting with her archnemesis over diner coffee.

"Cool," Lexa said. "I'd really love it if you guys could all bond, Bri—Ana, I mean," Lexa said. "I think it's so great that you're here."

Ariana's heart twinged at the unabashed honesty. "Thanks."

Then the car horn honked and Lexa turned and jogged off to join her friends, giving Ariana a wave as she got into the car. Ariana smiled back, but the moment the car was gone, she cursed under her breath.

Whatever Kaitlynn had to say to her, it had better be good.

OUT OF CONTROL

By the time Ariana filled out the three separate forms it took to get a pass off campus, figured out the bus line into Belle Haven, and finally arrived at the appointed diner, she was more than ready to wring Kaitlynn's neck. Even more so when she strode into the glass-walled diner and ascertained that the girl hadn't arrived yet. There were two elderly couples in back-to-back booths, a loud group of girls in garish cheerleading uniforms, a few single men at the counter, and a completely punked-out girl at a free-standing table, slumped over her coffee and pancakes. Ariana approached the hostess's stand.

"Hey, hon. Table for one?" the rotund hostess asked, picking up a menu.

"Actually, I'll be meeting a . . . someone," Ariana said, unable to get out the word *friend*. "Hopefully she'll be here soon, so—"

Ariana's words died on her tongue as the punk chick lifted her hand, looked Ariana right in the eye from across the room, and waved.

It took a full five seconds for Ariana to reconcile the image of the girl before her and the Kaitlynn Nottingham she knew so well. Her thick brown curls had been shorn to a buzz cut with long bangs which were dyed half black, half blond. Blue contacts covered her light brown eyes. A silver ring marred her perfect lips, which were painted a deep purple. Ten piercings lined one ear, with three in the other. Not to mention the clothes. Torn denim vest over a babydoll dress. Black fishnets and black combat boots.

Ridiculous was the word that came to mind.

"Never mind," Ariana said.

The hostess glanced at Kaitlynn and made a disapproving face as Ariana squared her shoulders and walked over. She placed her purse on an empty chair and sat down. "Interesting look for you."

"I could say the same," Kaitlynn replied, her eyes running over Ariana's auburn extensions. "When I saw you by the lake I should have guessed what your plan was. Like you'd ever have chosen that color unless it was for a purpose."

"What can I get you?" the waitress asked, appearing at Ariana's side.

"Nothing, thank you. I'm not staying," she said, never taking her eyes off Kaitlynn.

The waitress sighed and walked off. Ariana folded her arms on the cracked Formica table.

"What do you want, Kaitlynn?" she asked.

"Call me Teresa," Kaitlynn replied, leaning back in her chair, her legs spread wide just like the anarchist she was supposed to be playing.

"What's with the attitude, B.L.? Aren't you happy to see me? Don't you want to catch up? Ask how I've been?"

"What do you want, *Kaitlynn*?" Ariana repeated, her blood starting to curdle.

"What do I want . . . ?" Kaitlynn said. She picked up a straw from the table, tore the wrapper off with her teeth, and started gnawing on the end. "I can't believe you haven't figured it out yet. Weren't you and that BFF of yours, Noelle, always up for firsts in your class every semester? You were always going on and on about how you two loved to compete with each other. Remember all those nights in our room when you told me all your little secrets and dreams?"

Ariana's eyes burned at the memories, not just of the idiotic amount of trust she'd placed in Kaitlynn, but of Noelle and their friendship. How dare Kaitlynn trot out those memories for her own amusement, using them to remind Ariana of how gullible she'd been.

"You want money," Ariana said through her teeth. "How predictable of you."

"Yes. I want money." Kaitlynn sat forward again, dropping the punk persona and mimicking Ariana's ramrod posture exactly. "I've been staying at the Palomar on Dupont Circle and I want enough money to keep me in the manner to which I've become accustomed for the next two weeks. Until my flight to Australia."

Ariana's heart leapt with hope. "You're going to Australia?"

"Just like we always planned," she said, her voice bitter. "I'd say you can come, but I'm still a bit pissed that you screwed up with Briana Leigh's money."

"*You're* pissed at *me*? You must be joking," Ariana hissed under her breath. Kaitlynn smirked. Indignation ate away at Ariana's stomach like acid through tin, but she tried to squelch it. Sure, Kaitlynn was playing her, but in two weeks she'd be gone. Wouldn't it be worth it to swallow a little pride if it meant getting rid of her forever?

"Fine. Tell the front desk that Briana Leigh Covington is taking over payment for the room. I'll call them with my credit card number," Ariana said flatly.

"Why not just give me the number? Make it easier on both of us?" Kaitlynn asked, her eyes twinkling.

Because you'll go on a shopping spree and max the thing out, Ariana thought. "No."

Kaitlynn sat back in her chair and smirked. "Have it your way."

"As if any of this is *my* way," Ariana shot back.

"Attitude!" Kaitlynn scolded, taking a sip of her coffee.

"Are we done here?" Ariana asked, reaching for her bag.

"Not quite." Kaitlynn placed her cup down carefully in its saucer. "I also want you to get me a million dollars to help me start my life down under."

Ariana felt the walls of the diner shrinking toward her. The edges of her vision went blurry as the table full of cheerleaders cracked up laughing—awful, cackling laughs. Under the table, her fingers gripped her arm until the nails cut into her skin.

"Where do you think I'm going to get a million dollars?" she gasped.

"You'll figure it out. You always do," Kaitlynn said, taking a syrup-soaked bite of her pancakes. "Or, well, you usually do."

Ariana's cheeks stung at this thinly veiled reference to her failures of the past. "There's no way I can get a million dollars," she said. "Briana Leigh never had access to that kind of money."

"I'm sure that if she really wanted it, she could have gotten it," Kaitlynn said, staring into Ariana's eyes. "And you *really* want it, B.L., because if you don't get it, I'm going to blow this little charade of yours out of the water."

The lump in Ariana's throat was large enough to choke on, but she managed to swallow it down. She couldn't let Kaitlynn see the effect her threats were having on her. Could not let the girl walk out of here feeling she'd won. Ariana extracted her wallet from her hobo bag and removed five one-hundred-dollar bills, the only cash she had on her.

"Here," she said, swallowing her pride as she slid the bills across the table. "It's all I have."

Kaitlynn barely glanced at the money as she picked it up, folded it, and stuffed it into an inside pocket in her vest. She popped a strawberry into her mouth from her plate and looked at Ariana sympathetically.

"Come on, Ariana," she said, using her real name for the first time. "I hate to see you like this. Don't underestimate yourself. I know you can do it."

Ariana stared Kaitlynn down. What she wouldn't give to be able to pick up that fork and just jab it through the girl's eye. Just have it over and done with right now. She glanced around, wondering if anyone in this place had really noticed her. Had noted her appearance. Wondered if those guys at the counter would try to tackle her when she made a run for it.

"You may not have gotten Briana Leigh's inheritance money, but you got something much more valuable," Kaitlynn continued in a coddling tone. She looked Ariana up and down and smiled. "You got her life."

Under the table, Ariana's fingernails drew blood. She could feel it creep down her arm, but she didn't flinch. Didn't move. The waitress strolled by and slapped Kaitlynn's bill down on the table. Kaitlynn sighed as she plucked it up and looked it over.

"Of course, you couldn't have done it without the information I fed you those two years, so that means you owe me. I think one million dollars is a small fee to pay for your new life, don't you?"

"What's to stop me from just calling the police with an anonymous tip?" Ariana said through her teeth. "Telling them exactly where the Brenda T.'s most recent escapee is holed up?"

Kaitlynn let out a condescending laugh. "Are you not paying attention? If you do that, the first thing I'm going to tell them is how to find *you*. All I've done is broken out. You've committed a murder since skipping jail," she whispered, leaning in low over the table. "They find you and you'll *fry*. No questions asked."

Tears of anger and desperation stung Ariana's eyes. It wasn't her fault, the Briana Leigh thing. It was all Kaitlynn's fault. Kaitlynn's misdirection. Her mind games. Kaitlynn had tricked her into thinking Briana Leigh was a hateful, backstabbing murderer who didn't deserve to live. And now she was holding it over Ariana's head and there was nothing Ariana could do about it. How could her perfect new life already be crumbling around her?

Kaitlynn rose from the table, placed the bill in front of Ariana, and patted her shoulder. "You'll take care of that, right? I'm sure Briana Leigh's credit card will cover it."

Ariana's whole body trembled from the effort of holding back her fury.

Just grab the fork. Grab the fork and pin her down. It would be so easy. . . .

But of course it wouldn't be. It would be public and messy and basically end her. But it was still satisfying to imagine.

"Oh, and nice try on canceling my phone," Kaitlynn said, pausing on her way out. "Good thing I had Briana Leigh's social security number memorized so I could have it turned back on. Thank that Palmer guy for me, would you? He sounds hot. And if it wasn't for his text, I never would have known where to find you."

Then she slipped a pair of dark sunglasses over her eyes, turned, and shoved the door open with the heel of her hand. Ariana sat, alone and silent, for ten full minutes, waiting for the anger to pass. Waiting for her pulse to return to normal. Waiting for her mind to return to her. Finally, she reached for the bill with a quaking hand, her palm marked with blood. She was a mess. A sweaty, bloody, trembling mess. How had this happened? Yesterday she had been so happy, so full of hope, and now she was sitting in some crappy diner in the middle of nowhere looking like a pathetic waif who'd rolled in off the street in search of charity.

You are *a pathetic waif,* a little voice in her mind taunted her. *Look at you. Kaitlynn just took control of your life. There's nothing you can do to stop her.*

Staring at the blood, Ariana felt her meager breakfast making its way up her already sore throat. She jumped up from the table and ran for the bathroom, about to put the capper on what had to be the worst morning of her life. And just like that, she had no control over anything anymore. Not even her own stomach.

PERSONAL SHOPPER

The moment Ariana stepped inside the airy, sunlit shop, she knew she'd made the right decision calling Lexa. The boutique was called Vintage and the space was two stories tall, with floor-to-ceiling windows for walls. Hundreds of glittering rainbow-colored orb lamps hung from the ceiling like lollipops suspended from sticks. The clothing racks along the walls were stuffed with colorful clothing—everything from pencil skirts to bell-bottom jeans. If it came from another decade, it was represented here, either in true vintage fashion or by current designers *doing* vintage. As Ariana strolled through, looking for her friends, she heard carefree laughter over the driving disco music and spotted Lexa and Soomie near the back of the store. She felt more relaxed already. She was going to get her bonding time after all.

Ariana swung the small, colorful shopping bag that held the box for her new phone as well as a gift for Soomie she had picked up at the wireless store. The new cell phone—or *phones*, really—definitely qualified as an emergency purchase, which was what she would say to Grandma Covington if the old bat happened to call to discuss the charge. What Grandma C. would never know was that the emergency was a near nervous breakdown on Ariana's part and that this shopping trip was the only possible remedy.

Of course she had no idea how she was going to explain Kaitlynn's hotel charge. Maybe she'd say the card had been stolen. Briana Leigh *had* been on the careless side. Her grandmother had probably been forced to cancel a number of lost cards over the years. It wouldn't be totally out of the ordinary.

But these explanations were going to wear thin fast. She could only get away with so many strikes before Grandma C. started to get annoyed and cut her off, or at least put more restrictions on her spending. Or even worse, until she got suspicious and dropped in for a visit. Did Kaitlynn really not see the jeopardy involved in all of this? If Ariana got caught, they were both screwed.

But we're not thinking about that now, Ariana told herself, running her hand along a gleaming glass counter filled with countless colorful beaded necklaces, sparkling rings, and boho bracelets. If she kept dwelling on Kaitlynn, she was going to drive herself crazy. She needed distraction. And there was nothing more distracting than a little retail therapy. Even if she had to refrain from buying anything for the moment. Another luxury that Kaitlynn had stolen from her along with her pocket money.

She grabbed a light blue cashmere cardigan with felt appliqué flowers on the left breast and slipped into it, all the better to hide the nasty crescent moon–shaped indents in her arm. Then she plastered on a smile and joined the girls over by the dressing rooms. Reflecting the colorful, retro vibe of the shop, each room had a candy-colored lacquer door, and there were five brightly hued leather benches situated in an arc around them, perfect for impromptu fashion shows. Soomie sat on a hot pink bench, scrolling through her BlackBerry. Lexa hovered behind another, checking out a rack of designer purses.

"Hey, girls!" Ariana greeted them, hoping she sounded at least somewhat cheery.

"Ana! There you are!" Lexa cried, dropping a Michael Kors bag on the floor so that she could hug Ariana.

"You got a new phone," Soomie said instantly, staring at Ariana's shopping bag.

"Yes, I did," Ariana said. She reached into the bag and pulled out the heavier of the two boxes inside. "And so did you."

Soomie's eyes widened and Lexa's jaw dropped. "The one with the new touch screen! This is for me?" Soomie asked, jumping up and grabbing the box out of Ariana's hands.

Ariana shrugged blithely while her heart swelled with glee at a job well done. "This way you don't have to wait for it to be shipped. I know how important it is for you to be organized."

"She bought you a new BlackBerry?" Maria asked from inside one of the dressing rooms.

"That's so sweet!" Brigit added, her voice coming from behind another door.

"Ana, you really didn't have to do this," Soomie said.

"But it was so thoughtful of you," Lexa added, placing her hand on Ariana's back. They both watched as Soomie tore into the box and pulled the phone from its plastic wrapper.

"I think I'm in love," she said happily, hugging it to her shoulder.

"So much for Landon!" Brigit joked.

Soomie beamed at Ariana, her expression completely open for the first time since they'd met. "Thank you so much, Ana. Really. I'm going to call right now and activate it. This is going to make my year!"

"You're welcome," Ariana replied. Apparently she had played her cards right with this one. Soomie had officially been won over.

"You're just in time," Lexa said, grabbing Ariana's hand as Soomie walked off to call her wireless company. "We're trying to decide which dress Brigit should wear when she goes to Princess Tori's birthday-slash-slumber party next month."

"I still think the red," Maria said, stepping out of one of the dressing rooms in a shapeless, mustard-colored dress straight out of the seventies that did nothing for her skin tone and made her skinny frame look absolutely scrawny. Her hipbones jutted out at unpleasant angles and her collarbones and shoulder bones looked like chicken wings. Ariana revised her stance on Maria's effortless beauty—this was plain unhealthy.

"I do too. You haven't taken it off yet, have you?" Lexa asked the ceiling.

"No! I'm coming out," Brigit replied from behind a grape-colored door.

"Wow," Ariana said as Brigit emerged.

The dress was full-skirted and apple red, with a gold belt and wide neckline, all of which helped to balance out Brigit's slight pear shape. It made her blond hair pop and brought out her rosy cheeks and blue eyes.

"You look positively ScarJo in that," Ariana said, bringing a pleased smile to Brigit's face.

"See? We told you," Soomie said, holding the phone away from her ear.

"There's just one thing," Ariana added, settling herself onto a turquoise leather bench. "Isn't Princess Tori the one from Spain? The one who's known for being . . . slightly less attractive than the rest of the royal family?"

Maria snorted a laugh as Brigit's face fell. "I guess. Kind of," Brigit said.

"Well, then, since it *is* her birthday, maybe you want to avoid looking *that* good," Ariana said. "It's like wearing white to a wedding. You don't want to outshine the girl who's supposed to be sucking up the spotlight."

Maria glanced at Lexa. "She's good."

Ariana tried not to beam. It was the first outright nice thing Maria had said about her or to her since she'd arrived.

"Yes. She is," Lexa replied with an almost proud tone.

Okay, what that was about? Was Lexa taking some sort of responsibility for her because she used to know Briana Leigh? But she didn't dwell on it. Instead she focused on the positive. They appreciated her input.

"What do you think of this?" Maria asked, striking a pose in her ugly dress.

"That? Just no," Ariana said bluntly.

Lexa, Soomie, and Brigit glanced at one another nervously, as if they were afraid of what Maria's reaction to this comment might be. Maria, however, nodded.

"Exactly what I was thinking." She smiled at Ariana. "I'm glad you came along. All these bitches do is 'yes' me to death when we go shopping." Then she walked back into her dressing room and slammed the door.

Ariana smiled to herself. It was just like old times. Back at Easton she was always helping her friends when it came to etiquette and taste quandaries.

Soomie ended her call and tossed her old BlackBerry into her bag. "Well, we *have* a reason," she whispered. "If she wasn't so freaking paranoid about her body, we—"

"I can hear you!" Maria shouted. "If you're going to talk about me, kindly do it when I'm not around."

Lexa swallowed hard, looking green. "Anyway!" she said brightly. "Brigit, maybe you should get the black dress instead. Thank you, Ana." Brigit slipped back into her dressing room to change, and Lexa sat down next to a pile of shopping bags that clearly belonged to her. "So, Ana, how did your meeting go this morning?"

Ariana instantly thought of Kaitlynn, even though that wasn't the meeting to which Lexa referred, and felt her stomach turn. She forced a smile. "It went well. I think that by Monday I'll have the schedule I want. And I also joined the tennis team."

"What? No! I was so looking forward to riding with you again!" Lexa lamented, looking positively devastated. This was definitely a girl who not only wore all her emotions on her sleeve, she wore them in big, bright colors. "We were going to kick ass all over the eastern seaboard with you on the team!"

"Lexa told us you were some big jumper champion," Soomie added. "Why would you just give it up?"

"I didn't *just* give it up," Ariana replied. "I haven't ridden since the seventh grade. I just lost interest in it."

Briana Leigh had, of course, still ridden all the way up until the summer before she died, but they had no way of knowing that.

"I can't believe you could just lose interest in something when you were that good," Lexa replied.

"Well, I did," Ariana said with a shrug. "I'll leave the riding to you, Lexa. From what I understand, you don't need me anyway."

"Yeah, but Tahira doesn't exactly need you either," Soomie said matter-of-factly.

"Soomie!" Lexa scolded, swiping at the girl's knee.

"What? I'm just warning her." Soomie laid her new BlackBerry aside.

Ariana felt her stomach twist. "Tahira's on the tennis team?"

Soomie nodded. "Ana, there are three things you need to know about the tennis team. A) It's Tahira's baby. APH didn't even have a team until she showed up at school and basically whined them into creating one. B) She takes it very seriously. Like, if you lose a match, she berates you for days on end. And C) even if you do win your matches, you'd better not be better than her, because then she will be *truly* insufferable."

Brigit bounded out of her dressing room, back in street clothes, a black crepe frock slung over her arm. "Are you better than her?" she asked, salivating. "Please, please, *please* say you're better than her!"

Ariana laughed. "I don't know. I haven't played her yet. How good *is* she?"

"Who knows? We've never bothered to go see her play," Maria said, emerging from her dressing room as well. She had left the clothes she'd tried on behind in a heap on the floor.

"But we'll go now that you're on the team," Lexa assured Ariana. "Right, ladies?"

"Can't wait," Maria said sarcastically.

"Tahira claims she's good enough to be on the tour," Soomie said, rolling her eyes. "Which is highly unlikely." She looked Ariana up and down and tilted her head. "But I bet you can take her," she said with a smile.

Ariana smiled back. She had a feeling that Soomie would have said something a lot less friendly and supportive if they'd had this conversation an hour ago. Now she knew she had Brigit, Soomie, and Lexa's good opinion. All she had to do was work on Maria. Which she resolved to focus on from here on out. Her social standing was just as important as her academic placement.

"We'll see," Ariana said.

"Can we bounce? I'm so over this conversation," Maria said, curling a lock of hair around her finger and tilting her head. "And I need an espresso, like, yesterday."

"That'll make three this morning," Soomie said.

"And no food to speak of," Lexa put in.

"God! Fine! I'll have a scone. Let's just go," Maria said. She turned and stormed out of the store, shoving her sunglasses on as she walked outside.

"Ballerinas," Lexa said under her breath. "Can't live with 'em . . ."

"Can't feed 'em," Brigit joked.

Ariana gave them a slight smile as she followed Brigit to the cash register, watching Maria through the glass doors. She was starting to understand a little better why Maria always seemed so tense and mood-shifty. Not eating and downing espressos could do that to a girl. "Were you going to buy that sweater, miss?" the salesclerk asked, eyeing Ariana suspiciously.

"Oh, I'm sorry," Ariana said, her face flushed as she snapped back to the present and realized she was going to have to expose her arm. How was she going to explain away the fresh cuts on her skin? "I forgot I was wearing it," she stalled.

"It looks really nice on you," Brigit said. "Here."

She reached up and yanked the tag off at the back of Ariana's neck, then handed it to the cashier. "Add it to mine."

Ariana's blush deepened. "Brigit, no. You don't have to do that."

"You just kept me from making a huge fashion faux pas," Brigit said. "Consider it your personal shopper's fee."

Ariana smiled. "Thanks."

"Anytime. I'm so glad you're here, Ana. It was getting a little boring, just the four of us."

It took all of Ariana's inner will to control her giddiness. She had already made herself indispensable. This was where she belonged. This was her future. Kaitlynn was in her past. Now she just needed to figure out how to keep her there.

A DECISION

The late-summer sun beat down on Ariana's back, searing the skin on her neck. She shifted uncomfortably in the heat, cursing herself for scratching her arm so badly yesterday at the diner. Everyone else on the quad was wearing tanks and tees, keeping as cool as possible. But not Ariana. No. She had been forced to wear a long-sleeved boatneck tee in order to cover up the ugly wounds. Not only did she feel ridiculous and overdressed, but she was basically melting in the sun.

"Why don't they hold the debate in the auditorium?" Ariana asked Lexa as they took their seats in the front row of folding chairs, facing the fountain. Two podiums were set up in front of the burbling fountain. Gold would be debating blue first, and the winner of that debate would be facing gray. Each team had to prepare both pro and con arguments, and the side they would argue would be determined by luck of the draw.

"I guess they like to have as many outdoor events as possible before the weather turns on us," Lexa replied. Lexa was, of course, wearing a perfectly weather-appropriate sundress in a stunning shade of blue. It made her eyes look like round sapphires.

"Hi, Ana. Hi, Lexa." Quinn, the sophomore on coffee duty, appeared at the end of their aisle. She and her friend were toting trays of iced coffees, and Quinn handed one to Lexa. "How was Italy?"

"*Fantástico*," Lexa said with a bright smile. "Did you guys have fun in Ireland?"

Quinn's grin widened as she handed Ariana her iced cappuccino, the drink order she'd passed along to the sophomore during dinner the night before. "I can't believe you remembered! It was incredible. We hiked *everywhere* and stayed in these amazing little inns."

"I'd love to see the pictures," Lexa said kindly. She looked at Quinn's friend. "You can leave the other drinks here. They're running late."

"Okay," Quinn said, taking this as her cue to leave. She grabbed the tray from the other girl and placed it on the empty seat next to Ariana. "Let us know if you need anything else!"

"Thanks!" Ariana called after them.

She glanced at Lexa, who was sipping her drink as she watched Quinn and her friend scurry off, her expression completely normal. She wasn't feeling self-satisfied or cocky over having errand girls at her beck and call. It was as if nothing out of the ordinary had just happened. As if this was her birthright rather than some kind of power trip. Ariana thought of Noelle and her imperious stares, how she got off on ordering people around. Lexa seemed like her complete opposite. While Noelle was a ruthless dictator, Lexa was a benevolent ruler. It was odd, intriguing, and almost refreshing.

"Do you want to go back and change?" Lexa asked. "I'll hold your seat for you."

"No, thanks. I'm fine," Ariana replied, trying her best to look cool and poised.

It took all her willpower not to hold her cold drink cup against the back of her neck. The scrapes on her skin stung from the sweat. She should have just told Kaitlynn to piss off. She should have walked out. Better yet, she should have never shown up there. Kaitlynn wouldn't really make good on her threat to expose Ariana, would she? What could she possibly have to gain from seeing Ariana get hauled back to jail? Kaitlynn wouldn't have even been free right now if it wasn't for Ariana. Didn't that gain her any leeway here?

Ariana gripped her coffee cup. She knew the answer was "no." Kaitlynn would turn her in just for the sheer pleasure of watching the newsfeeds and seeing Ariana, as she so eloquently put it, "fry." The girl was going to ruin Ariana if she didn't get what she wanted. The problem was, Ariana had absolutely no chance of getting her hands on a million dollars. Kaitlynn might as well have asked for a billion. She might as well have asked for her own personal space shuttle with a five-star chef, a water bed, and a flight plan to Jupiter.

I should have killed her. I should have just ended her right there.

"We missed you at breakfast," Lexa said, ruffling her own bangs with her fingertips to make them fuller. "Soomie went over the entire debate from the con side. I thought Maria was going to spear her with her fork. I swear it was touch and go there for a while."

Ariana glanced at Lexa, alarmed at the mention of forks and spearing. "What?"

"I'm just kidding," Lexa said with a laugh. She sipped her coffee and glanced up as the debate teams made their way to their chairs behind the podiums. "So, where were you?"

"Oh, I . . ." What did people do in the mornings that would make sense? She didn't want to tell the girl she had been retaking her English entrance exam. It was a secret only Palmer knew about, and with him she had been able to use it to her advantage, but the fewer people who knew about it, the better. It would definitely raise too many questions. Especially from Brigit. Ariana saw a guy walk by in athletic shorts and the lightbulb went off. "I went for a run."

Lexa's face lit up. "You run? Me too! We should go together sometime. There's a great jogging path down by the river."

Ariana's fake smile was so stiff it actually hurt. "Great."

"Hey," Maria greeted them, grabbing her coffee from the tray before settling in next to Lexa. "Did we miss anything?"

"Nope," Lexa replied.

"Here, Ana!" Brigit handed Ariana a white waxed paper bag as she walked by. "It's a raspberry muffin. My favorite. Not that I can eat them anymore. I wasn't sure if you liked raspberries, but I figured you'd be hungry since you missed breakfast. *Do* you like raspberries? What's your favorite fruit?"

"Can we twenty-questions her later?" Soomie asked, slipping past

Ariana to sit at Lexa's other side. "A) I'm sure she's not in the mood, and B) the debate is about to start."

"Thanks, Brigit," Ariana said, touched by the gesture. "And I love raspberries."

Brigit grinned happily and sat back in her chair.

"Hey, ladies."

Palmer picked up the empty coffee tray and dropped into the seat next to Ariana's, wearing a dark teal Izod polo and light shorts and looking country club perfect. He stashed the tray under his chair and grinned at Lexa. Ariana instantly stiffened and turned her knees away from him.

"Hey! Just in time!" Lexa whispered back.

"The party never starts till I get there anyway," Palmer joked. "Hey, Ana."

Ariana turned further away from him and nudged Lexa. "Do you want to switch with me?"

"Oh, that's okay," Lexa replied.

"No. Go ahead. Sit next to your boyfriend," Ariana said, emphasizing the word *boyfriend* a bit so that Palmer would definitely hear.

Lexa tilted her head. "Okay. Thanks."

The two of them got up and slid past each other, exchanging seats. As soon as Ariana was seated between Lexa and Maria, Palmer shot her a bemused look. She completely ignored it, focusing instead on her raspberry muffin, which was way too delicious to have been made by a school cafeteria staff.

As Headmaster Jansen got up to call the crowd to attention, a cloud slid over the sun, giving Ariana a moment's relief from the torturous heat. She glanced up, looked around at all the bright, expectant faces, the green lawn, the happily burbling fountain. The buildings were stately, the skies blue, the trees flowering. To the left was the administration building where she had aced the crap out of that English exam that morning. She should be excited about these things—these friends, these surroundings, the new academic year. But she wasn't. She was pissed. And scared. And helpless. As Soomie would say, the facts were these: A) There was no way she could pay Kaitlynn off, and B) if she didn't pay Kaitlynn off, all of this was going to be taken away from her.

There was only one thing Ariana could do. She had to kill Kaitlynn. Not just fantasize about it, but actually do it. It was the only way to be free of her. It was the only way to protect her new life. It wasn't the best-case scenario, of course. It would be risky and messy and could land her right back in prison, but it was her only chance. The only chance she had of preserving what she had worked so hard to achieve. It was Kaitlynn's own fault, really. She was forcing Ariana's hand. And if anyone deserved to die, it was her.

"And now, let the debate begin!" Headmaster Jansen announced.

"Let's go, gold!" Brigit and Soomie shouted as Maria and Lexa applauded.

A slight breeze kicked up, cooling the back of Ariana's neck, and she took a deep, cleansing breath. Suddenly, her heart felt as light as air. Simply making the decision, coming up with a proactive solution to the problem, had completely shifted her mood.

"Go, gold!" Ariana put in.

"That feels *so* much better," Lexa said, commenting on the breeze.

"Doesn't it, though?" Ariana replied. She sipped her iced coffee, tore off a piece of muffin and popped it into her mouth, then sighed contentedly. Everything was going to be fine. She was back in control.

THE CHOSEN ONE

"Three cheers for Sumit Medha!" Palmer shouted, lifting his cup of lemonade.

"Hip hip, hooray!"

The celebratory crowd broke up, half of the people surging forward to slap Sumit on the back, the other half dispersing toward the food and drink tables. Gold had won the debate competition, which meant all the team had to do to secure Privilege House was win one of the next two competitions. And with Tahira in charge of the fund-raising event, everyone seemed about ready to start repacking their things for the move. Ariana sipped her lemonade and glanced back at the two towers of Wolcott Hall. Which room would be hers? She hoped it would have a view. And a much better roommate than Allison.

"I didn't think anyone hip-hip-hoorayed anymore," she said to Maria as they turned their steps toward the water. The celebratory pic-nic was being held at the edge of a quaint little pond on the outskirts of campus. A pond that was mercifully surrounded by huge maple trees offering lots of comforting shade.

"Oh, there are a lot of things done around here that you wouldn't think were done anywhere anymore," Maria replied. She paused and blinked. "Did that make any sense?"

"Strangely, yes," Ariana replied. Maria gave her a rare, tight smile. Progress. Maria tossed her empty iced-coffee cup—her fourth of the day—into a garbage can, and together they strolled toward the edge of the pond, where Tahira was calling a klatch of people to order.

"If you want to be involved in the fund-raiser, please, get your butts down here," Tahira called out at the top of her voice. "I've got a lot of info for you and not a lot of time!"

"So, Maria, what do you think of—"

"You should really be paying attention to this," Maria told her. "You have to sign up for something, and it's obviously not going to be crew."

Ariana's mouth snapped shut. So much for progress. Why was Maria so curt with her? Had she done something to offend the girl? She held her tongue and turned her attention to the Dubai princess, who was obviously enjoying the spotlight.

"I have the most fabulous fund-raising event planned. More fabulous than anything Welcome Week has ever seen," she began, sliding her eyes along the crowd to make sure everyone was properly rapt with attention. "Friday night, we will be holding a gala event at the American Museum of Pop Culture."

There were a few gasps, some impressed murmurs, and a spattering of applause. Ariana was duly impressed. This was one new development she *had* read about inside the Brenda T.—the opening of the fabulously hip museum, backed by some of the biggest directors, actors, and producers in film and television, plus a couple of magazine magnates and a few aging rock stars. It was jam-packed with memorabilia and exhibits from all forms of pop culture and was *the* place to hold parties in D.C. these days.

"Thanks to Kassie Sharpe, whose father is curator of the museum, we will have full access to all the galleries," Tahira continued. "And thanks to Micah Granger—our resident heir to the Jägermeister throne—"

Here she paused for the predictable hoots and hollers of the male population.

"We will have an open bar, stocked with all the finest spirits from around the world," Tahira continued. "But the *main* attraction will be our very own Landon Jacobs!" she announced, raising her arms over her head to applaud.

Landon bounded out of the crowd to stand at Tahira's side. He shoved his hands into the back pockets of his jeans and flipped his long bangs off his forehead with a twitch of his chin. Somehow, Ariana had the feeling that he adopted this pose often.

"I don't get it," Maria said, loud enough for only Ariana to hear.

"Landon has graciously agreed to be the centerpiece of the fundraiser," Tahira continued. "We will hold a silent auction where the sole prize will be a date with Landon to the New York premiere of his movie, *First Son*."

There was some happy, surprised, and approving chatter.

"Dude. We are so going to win," Tahira's boyfriend Rob said loudly.

"Not only that, but attendees will be able to pay ten dollars for an autograph or twenty-five dollars for a photograph with our little superstar," Tahira continued. "The night will be capped off by an acoustic performance by Landon himself."

Now the crowd really let out a cheer. Landon blushed under his shaggy hair and appeared to be struggling to hold back a smile. Apparently, smiling was uncool for a pop star.

"The museum is already promoting the event, and they have fielded thousands of calls from local schools, children's groups, and parents, asking how they can get their daughters in. Every tween within a two-hundred-mile radius is going to show up with their allowance money, not to mention their parents, who will probably be in serious need of an expensive drink once they've been exposed to all the swooning and screaming."

Everyone laughed. Everyone but Maria, who held her hand to her forehead and looked at the ground. "Oh my God. Why don't they just dip him in gold and mount him already?"

"What?" Ariana asked.

Maria sighed as the crowd cheered for Landon and he raised his arms and grinned, nodding in acknowledgment. "Nothing."

Ariana felt a surge of nervousness, the kind she always felt at the doorstep of an opportunity. She wasn't sure how Maria would respond, but she had to try. She had to get this girl to soften toward her at *some* point.

"Maria . . . is something going on with you and Landon?" Ariana whispered, turning her back to the crowd in an attempt to be discreet.

Maria's eyes flashed with surprise and what Ariana could have sworn was a twinge of fear. "What? No. Are you kidding me?"

Her reaction only solidified Ariana's suspicions. Her lie was written all over her face. "Sorry, it's just . . . you seem to get kind of emotional when the subject comes up."

Maria laughed, a short, uncomfortable laugh. "Well, clearly *perceptiveness* isn't your thing," she said blithely. She glanced over at Tahira and Landon, who were fielding questions from the masses. "I'm so over this party. Tell Lexa I went back."

Then she turned and slipped her sunglasses from her head over her eyes as she strolled elegantly away. Ariana eyed Landon, who was now waving his hands, trying to quiet the adoring crowd. She was more certain than ever that there was something going on between these two, but what was it? Unrequited love? A secret affair? Or perhaps just a shared secret. Whatever it was, she wanted to know.

"Hey," Palmer greeted her, stepping up from behind. "How's my favorite transfer?"

Annoyingly, Ariana's heart rate quickened. She took a sip of her lemonade and, much as it pained her, trained her attention on Tahira, who was now going on about e-mail blasts, flyers, and mailers.

"Okay. I get it. You're not talking to me," Palmer said.

Ariana sighed as she checked her watch. Her entire body throbbed, thanks to its proximity to Palmer, and she wanted to burn all her skin off in punishment. She was not going to be attracted to him anymore. She couldn't be. He was Lexa's. Lexa's, Lexa's, Lexa's.

"We'll also need plenty of people to work the tables at the event, so if you're interested, please see me!" Tahira shouted as the crowd started to descend into conversation.

"What I don't get is why," Palmer added.

Ariana looked at him, stunned. She couldn't help herself. "You *know* why," she said.

Palmer's forehead creased in concern. "No. I really don't. I'm sorry if you misunderstood something here, but . . ."

His expression was one of complete innocence, his eyes imploring. As if he truly wanted to make sure she wasn't upset over some fictional wrong. Ariana wondered again if Palmer really *was* innocent. If she really had misunderstood him. But the longer they stood there, color started to rise in his cheeks, and he pulled his baseball out of his pocket to fidget with it. He definitely felt guilty about *something*.

"Hey, guys. What's up?" Lexa asked, joining them.

"Nothing," Ariana answered automatically, looking away from Palmer. Her face was burning with frustration and unanswered questions, and she wanted to get out of there before either of them could notice. "I think I'm going to go talk to Tahira about working those tables."

"Wait. You don't have to do that," Palmer said. "Not if you're going to be the coxswain for the crew race."

"What?" Ariana and Lexa said in unison.

"What?" Palmer replied, sliding his hands into the pockets of his shorts. "You *are* going to do it, right? The team needs you."

Ariana blinked and looked at Lexa. This was the first time she had heard about this. What game was Palmer playing exactly?

"But . . . I thought I was going to be the cox," Lexa said, her sweet brow furrowing. "We talked about it over the summer. . . ."

Palmer reached for Lexa's hand and squeezed it. "I know, Lex, but Ana is just . . . smaller. And have you seen how the other teams are stacked? We need every advantage we can get."

Lexa's pretty face turned the color of marinara sauce. She extracted her hand from Palmer's and tucked it under her elbow. "Smaller? What are you trying to say? You think I'm fat?"

Ariana almost laughed at the total mortification on Palmer's face. "No! Of course not. No," he protested. "But you're supermodel tall. Ana is just a lot more . . . petite." He reached for Lexa, but she turned aside, avoiding his touch.

"Whatever," she said. "If I'm so huge, that's fine. I don't want to sink your boat."

"Real nice, Palmer," Ariana put in.

"Oh, come on. Don't be like that, Lex," Palmer said, stepping forward and wrapping his arms around Lexa. "It's really just that Ana here is freakishly short."

He looked past Lexa's shoulder at Ariana and smiled, telling her he was just kidding. Ariana rolled her eyes, but her lips twitched. She covered it with her hand, but it was too late. Palmer had seen, and now he was grinning as well. He leaned back, straightened his face, and looked at Lexa.

"Look, Ana has to contribute to the competition in some way, and are you really going to relegate her to the Dubai princess's slave squad?" he asked. "She'll transfer out before you even get a chance to give her one of your patented pedicures."

Lexa finally broke down and smiled. She glanced over at Ariana. "I do give excellent pedicures." She heaved a sigh and ran her hands down Palmer's chest, a gesture that made Ariana's own palms itch with longing. "Okay, fine. But you do realize that means *I* have to be Tahira's slave girl instead."

"Like Tahira would ever dare order you around," Palmer said with a smirk.

"True," Lexa said blithely. "But still. You both owe me."

Ariana filed this exchange away to dissect later. Why would Tahira order everyone around *except* Lexa?

"Fair enough," Palmer replied. He gave Lexa a kiss, then turned to look at Ariana. "So, you'll meet up with the team at the boathouse tomorrow at five. Don't be late."

Ariana groaned under her breath. Five o'clock. Fab. Not only did she have to be up at the crack of dawn, but she had a French exam at eight. She knew she should decline, more firmly this time, but one look into Palmer's eyes and she couldn't do it.

Palmer gave Lexa a last squeeze, then walked away, his arm grazing Ariana's as he passed by her, and she felt a rush of giddy triumph.

This time, at least, he had chosen her.

A CHALLENGE

Ariana couldn't have been happier when she saw the red slip in her mailbox that afternoon, indicating she had a package to be picked up at the window. Her toes tapped with impatience as the elderly gentleman behind the counter took his dear sweet time finding it, but she smiled when she was presented with a large FedEx box with some serious heft. Briana Leigh's maid had come through. There would definitely be something in here she could use to help her "reminisce" with Lexa about Camp Triple Star. As she emerged from the APH post office, a content smile played on her lips. Tonight she would study Briana Leigh's horsey past. Right after she ran a small errand.

She had an old friend to kill.

"What are you so smiley about?"

Ariana froze. Tahira strolled up behind her wearing a set of body-hugging tennis whites, a hot pink Adidas tennis bag over her shoulder.

"As if you care," Ariana said lightly, tilting her head.

Tahira laughed. "You're so right. I truly don't." She started to walk on by, but paused and looked Ariana up and down. "I heard you joined the tennis team. I was just about to go hit some balls off the machine, but I always prefer a living, breathing victim. Fancy a game or two?"

For a moment, Ariana hesitated, wondering if she could fit it all in—a tennis match, studying for her French exam, getting off campus again and up to Dupont Circle, doing away with Kaitlynn, and getting back in time to go through her box of B.L. memorabilia. But then she realized that the longer she hesitated, the more likely it was that Tahira would think she was intimidated. Which she definitely wasn't.

Besides, a little exercise might help clear her mind, get her focused for the task ahead of her at the Palomar Hotel.

"Why not?" she said finally.

"Good. Go get your racket and meet me over at the courts," Tahira instructed.

Ariana hesitated. When she'd gone shopping for her new life, she hadn't purchased a stitch of athletic equipment, something she was really going to have to remedy now that she had claimed to Lexa that she was a runner and had joined the tennis team. She glanced at Tahira, knowing the kind of reception her announcement was going to get, and dreading it.

"Actually, I . . . I'm still waiting for my grandmother to ship me a few things," she lied.

Tahira's jaw dropped. "You didn't bring your racket?"

Ariana's face burned. "I—"

"Whatever. You can borrow one of the school's." Tahira scoffed, utterly amused, and started down the sunlit pathway toward the gym and playing fields. "This should be a piece of cake."

"My point!" Ariana called over the net, turning to stride back to the baseline. She was wearing mesh APH shorts and a white T-shirt she'd bought spur-of-the-moment at the school store, along with a pair of cross-training sneakers she had borrowed from Maria. The shoes, unfortunately, were a size too big, which had caused her to trip and miss a point more than once.

"Oh, please! That was out!" Tahira shouted back.

Ariana turned on her heel and stared at Tahira, her jaw hanging open. The girl had to be joking. "That shot was on the line!"

"It *so* was not!" Tahira yelled, pointing her racket toward the sideline where Ariana's shot had hit. "It was like two inches out!" She turned to look at Rob, who, along with a few other classmates, including Maria, Brigit, Soomie, and Lexa, had shown up early in the second set to watch the proceedings. "Baby, wasn't that ball totally out?"

Rob, looking like a tool in his pink polo shirt with one side of the collar flipped up, swallowed hard and glanced at Ariana. His hesitation spoke volumes. Ariana laughed. "See? My point."

Tahira let out a frustrated screech.

"No, wait!" Rob said. "I didn't say that—"

"Forget it! Fine!" Tahira said, storming over to the baseline. "What-ever. Your point."

"It's nice that you're such a good sport about it," Ariana shot back, earning a few laughs from the small crowd in the stands. Brigit laughed the loudest.

Tahira's jaw clenched and she kept her gaze trained on Ariana, refusing to acknowledge the spectators. She got in her return stance, bent at the waist and swaying side to side.

"Just serve," she snapped.

Ariana smiled at Tahira's impatience, then decided to milk it. She bounced the ball a few times, jogging in place, pretending to be mull-ing her next move. Really she was marveling over the fact that this match had so far been a cakewalk. Tahira was a good player, but she wasn't *great*. She had taken the first set, but Ariana was well on her way to taking the second. And she hadn't played in a good three years. Well, except for that one match against Briana Leigh back in Hous-ton, but that had been even yummier, easier-to-swallow cake than this match.

Even though, in the end, she had let Briana Leigh win.

Which she had only done because, at the time, she had been cer-tain that Briana Leigh was a murderer—a murderer whose ire she did not wish to incite just because of a tennis match. Of course that had turned out not to be true. Kaitlynn was the murderer. Briana Leigh had been nothing but an innocent orphan.

And I killed her. I killed her because Kaitlynn turned me against her.

Suddenly, Ariana saw Briana Leigh's face again. Her happy smile that day as they volleyed. Her cliché fist pump whenever she won a point. The little dance she did when the match was over.

And then her bloated face the day they pulled her from the lake. Her hair matted with mud and muck and leaves. Her limp form as they lifted her onto the boat.

The ball bounced up. Ariana's fingers closed around it and squeezed.

"Oh my God, enough with the Djokovic act! Serve the damn ball!"

Ariana cleared her throat. The sun had dipped behind Tahira, throwing her into shadow and blinding Ariana. She felt hot. Hot and sick and light-headed.

Stop it. Stop thinking about it.

"You've got this, Ana!" Lexa cheered.

Ariana tossed the ball in the air and served. It hit in the center of the box and arced slowly toward her opponent. Tahira slammed it back over the net so fast Ariana never had a chance.

"Yes!" Tahira shouted. There was a smattering of applause from the crowd.

Ariana turned and walked over to the fence to grab another ball. Her vision was blurry as she stared down at her feet, the yellow and white sneakers against the green court. In her mind she could hear Briana Leigh cheering her own points. Laughing over her victory. Saying they'd play again. She'd give Ariana another chance.

"You can do it, Ana!" Brigit cheered.

Ariana bent down to grab a ball and had to brace her hand on the fence to keep from going over.

Dead. Dead. Dead because of me.

"What are you doing? Faking sick?" Tahira taunted her. "You're not going to get out of this that easily."

Ariana took in a breath.

In, one . . . two . . . three . . .

Out, one . . . two . . . three . . .

In, one . . . two . . . three . . .

She grabbed the ball and stood up, trying to let Tahira's teasing get under her skin. Trying to use it in some way. Trying to let it make her angry. She turned around and looked at her nemesis.

"Come on, transfer girl! Serve!" Tahira said.

Ariana strode over to the baseline. She could do this. Schooling this girl would be so much fun. It was the whole reason she'd accepted this challenge in the first place. To get relaxed. Get focused. Get her head clear for what she had to do tonight.

Tonight she would avenge Briana Leigh's death. Tonight she would ensure her own future.

She tossed the ball in the air and served. It went way wide. Tahira laughed and tossed the ball back to her.

"Please, *please* double-fault! If you do I win this game!" Tahira sang out.

I will not double-fault. I will not double-fault. I will not double-fault.

Ariana served. Double fault. Tahira's friends laughed and cheered as Tahira tossed her racket in the air, end-over-end, and caught it.

"My serve," she said. "This is where you go down."

Ariana felt the fight draining out of her. Her confidence was gone, fear and doubt creeping in to take its place. She wished she had never set yes to this match. Wished she could rewind her day to that moment on the quad and just say no. Because the last thing she needed on this particular day was to suffer the humiliating defeat she was about to endure.

ONE TASK

Ariana was still feeling the sting of her loss as she walked through the modern lobby of the Palomar Hotel that night. The trendy spot was buzzing with activity even though it was past midnight, with twenty-something partiers having just returned from some fete or other, all drunk and messy and loud. Ariana had dressed to blend in a pair of slim black pants and a gray ballet-neck top, her hair pulled back in a low bun, zero makeup on her face. As she approached the long line at the front desk, she told herself to remain calm. If she allowed herself to grow impatient, if she snapped in any way, all it would do was make her easier to remember later, when the police started asking questions. She couldn't have that. She couldn't let it all fall apart just because of some stupid tennis match.

She would take Tahira down sooner or later. That was certain. All she had to do was focus on that fact and she would be fine.

In, one . . . two . . . three . . .

Out, one . . . two . . . three . . .

This was not the perfect situation. Not by any means. Tomorrow morning some maid would find the dead body of fugitive Kaitlynn Nottingham in a hotel room reserved under Briana Leigh Covington's name. She would definitely be interviewed. Someone might even recall having seen her in the lobby on this night. The risks were huge. But they were risks she had to take. Kaitlynn had threatened her very existence, so Kaitlynn had to go.

Ariana bit her tongue as a drunken twentysomething with too much stubble almost slammed into her. She slipped by him without a word and kept walking, telling herself that the crowd was actually a good thing. It would make the security tapes more difficult to sift through. When she finally reached the front of the line, Ariana smiled in a perfunctory way at the man behind the counter.

"I'm Briana Leigh Covington. I misplaced the key to my room and I'd like another, please."

When the police came to Atherton-Pryce Hall, she would tell them she had never been to the Palomar. That of course Kaitlynn had used her name and stolen her credit card number—the girl was always obsessed with her. Everyone knew this. It was documented in every newspaper article that had been written about Briana Leigh's father's murder.

The front desk clerk hit a few keys on his computer without a word. Then he studied the screen for a moment, and smiled. "Of course, Miss Covington. Room five thirty-two." He produced a key card and handed it over, already on to the next task before Ariana had even slipped it from his fingers. She smiled to herself as she turned away from the desk. Forgettable. Exactly the way she wanted it.

Knowing there were always security cameras mounted in hotel elevators, Ariana opted for the stairs. She took them slowly, deliberately, to the fifth floor, making sure not to get winded. Not like she'd been on the tennis court. So gaspy and blotchy and sweaty. She got a sour taste in her mouth just thinking about those last few games in the second, and what turned out to be the final, set. The serves whizzing past her, the volley that ended with Ariana stretched out on the ground, diving for a ball she could never have hit. Tahira and her crew were going to be merciless tomorrow. Damn Briana Leigh. Damn Kaitlynn. Ariana knew she could have taken the girl. She was sure of it.

It wasn't until she arrived outside the door to room 532 that Ariana realized she hadn't thought once about what she was here to do. Not since she'd left the lobby, anyway. She paused and shook her head, banishing all thoughts of Tahira and her triumphant, smug face. It was time to focus. This wasn't just some tiny errand she was about to run. What happened on the other side of this door was going to determine the course of her entire future.

Ariana's breath caught and she curled her fingers into fists, her right hand closing around the edges of the flat key card.

You can do this. Just get it over with. Get it over with and you'll be free.

But don't screw it up, or you're dead.

Ariana closed her eyes and breathed.

In, one . . . two . . . three . . .

Out, one . . . two . . . three . . .

In, one . . . two . . . three . . .

Out, one . . . two . . . three . . .

She opened her eyes and was ready. The key slot made a low beeping sound as the door unlocked. Ariana winced. Luckily, Kaitlynn had always been a deep sleeper back at the Brenda T. Unless that, too, had been an act. Still, better safe than sorry. Ariana grasped the cold metal handle of the door and opened it as quietly as humanly possible.

The room was dark, save for a sliver of light coming through a crack in the blackout curtains across the way. Ariana felt a thrill of excitement at her luck. Kaitlynn hadn't decided to stay up to watch some pay-per-view movie or other. She was asleep. Ariana had been hoping for this. It would make the whole thing so much easier. Less struggle. Less mess. Less chance of being caught in the act.

As Ariana's eyes adjusted to the dim light, she saw that the closet door was open. Another stroke of luck. She grabbed one of the extra pillows off the top shelf and gripped it in both hands. Her heart started to pound and she felt sweat beads popping up along her hairline and above her upper lip.

Ariana savored her adrenaline. She would need it to help her overpower Kaitlynn, who was slightly bigger and probably stronger than she was. If she could just harness her anger, this could all be over in a matter of minutes. All she had to do was stay strong, stay focused, for that long. Then she would be free.

Tiptoeing ever so carefully, Ariana approached the bed. She could see the outline of Kaitlynn's slumbering form, turned on her side, away from the door. Suddenly, Ariana started to feel light-headed, and she realized she had no idea how long it had been since she'd last breathed.

In, one . . . two . . . three . . .
Out, one . . . two . . . three . . .
In, one . . . two . . . three . . .
Out, one . . . two . . . three . . .

Much better. She was at the very side of the bed now. Mere inches from Kaitlynn. Her fingers gripped the pillow even tighter.

Just think of the freedom. Do this and no one can touch you.

She took a deep breath, held it, and lunged. The pillow was about an inch from Kaitlynn's head when suddenly something wrapped around Ariana's neck from behind and jerked her back. Ariana tried to shout out in surprise, but her larynx was crushed and all that came out was a strangled choke. The pillow was wrested from her hands as her feet left the floor and she kicked out in a panic, taking down the bedside lamp with a crash. Still, the pressure on her throat only intensified. She couldn't breathe. Couldn't speak. Couldn't shout for help. Ariana grasped for her throat and realized there was an arm clamped around her neck like a vise. She tried to pry it loose, but all she could do was grasp in vain. Her vision began to blur over and she realized she was about to pass out. Then she was flung to the floor, the side of her head colliding with the corner of the dresser.

Pain radiated through her body as Ariana heaved for breath on all fours. The pillow she'd put so much faith in was tossed at her head and bounced off, coming to rest on the floor. The lights flicked on overhead, temporarily blinding her.

"Nice try, Ariana," Kaitlynn said. "But you're not going to get rid of me that easily."

Ariana's brain struggled for logic as she coughed painfully into the violet carpet. She pulled in a breath through her nose and sat back on her knees. Kaitlynn hovered over her, fully dressed in her punk-girl gear. Ariana looked at the bed, her neck muscles straining. Under the covers was a life-size stuffed doll. If there had been one more ounce of light in the room, Ariana would have realized it. Kaitlynn had tricked her. Again.

"You may be smarter than I *thought*, but you're not smarter than *me*," Kaitlynn said, sitting down on the corner of the mattress and patting Ariana on the back like a dog. "Nice touch getting me to put the room in your name so you could get the key, though. You do think ahead, I'll give you that."

Ariana sat back on her butt and finally got control of her breathing. She placed her hands on either side of her head, cupping her scalp. Every inch of her, save her burning throat, was numb. She had failed. Just like that. Two minutes ago her entire life was an open, endless book just waiting to be written. All she'd had to do was complete this one task. But she had been careless. Had thought herself lucky. Had gotten comfortable. And now, it was all over.

"So what are you going to do?" she asked, staring at Kaitlynn's horrid shoes. "Kill me?"

Kaitlynn let out a deep, throaty laugh. "I kill you and I get nothing," she said. "No, no, no. I'm going to keep you around, Ariana. We had a deal and you are going to make good on your part." She reached down, grabbed Ariana around her upper arm, and yanked her off the floor. Ariana had never felt so defeated. So humiliated. So stupid and lost and alone. Kaitlynn opened the door with her free hand, then shoved Ariana through it into the brightly lit hallway. If Ariana had a modicum of self-respect left, of hope, of pride, she might have resisted or struggled or fought back. But she just went limp. Kaitlynn stood in the doorway of her posh hotel room, looked Ariana up and down, and scoffed derisively. "Now let me spell it out for you in terms you'll understand. Get me. My effing. Money. You have until Friday."

Then she let the heavy door slam right in Ariana's face.

SHOUT IT OUT

By six o'clock the next morning, after a restless night of staring at the ceiling, Ariana's mood had miraculously improved. She felt much more positive. Much more herself. It was all the sanctioned yelling, she was sure. And the fresh air.

Plus, staring at a shirtless Palmer for the last half hour might have had something to do with it.

"Pull!" Ariana shouted, gripping the handles on either side of her flat seat with both hands. "Pull! Dig in and pull!"

Palmer let out a grunt of effort as he worked his oars. His dark hair had been blown forward by the wind, forming a sort of fauxhawk down the center of his head, and his face was ruddy from the effort of the workout. Ariana saw a tiny rivulet of sweat working its way down his perfectly smooth chest, between his very defined pecs. She continued to shout as she watched the droplet wend its way lower and lower. When it reached the waistband of his sweatpants she glanced away, her face searing. She looked past him to Adam—who was paler, skinnier, and less attractive—and shouted even louder.

"Pull! What kind of weaklings are you? Pull!"

The weaklings comment carried a few laughs from the guys. Palmer even broke concentration for a moment to look up at her and smile. But they dug in harder and the boat flew forward. Even Landon, who was almost as scrawny as Adam, grunted as he strained. Ariana was impressed. She would have thought that a pampered pop star like him would be averse to hard work. But then, as she had learned at the Brenda T., people were often surprising.

As the boat lurched forward, Ariana held on for dear life and smiled. Maybe she was good at this. Maybe Palmer had made the right decision when he'd picked her over Lexa. Somehow, Ariana couldn't see that sweet little thing finding the proper voice to motivate anyone. But Ariana had that voice inside of her. That pent-up adrenaline and rage. It was nice to put it all to good use.

As the boat sailed by the low-lying APH boathouse at the edge of the river, decorated with blue, gray, and gold flags and the APH crest, Ariana closed her eyes for a moment, just to feel. Just to absorb her surroundings. The warm breeze against her face, the salty, fresh scent of the river, the birds cawing overhead. Suddenly a voice in her mind spoke up out of nowhere.

It's going to be okay, she told herself. *Kaitlynn gave you till Friday. That means you have three days to figure it out, and you will. You always do.*

When she opened her eyes again, Palmer was looking right at her with obvious longing in his eyes. She felt the force of his gaze deep down inside her and, for a moment, allowed herself to relish it, and to relish the thrill of being right. He wanted her. A hot, desirable, unattainable boy was obviously attracted to her. It was the best feeling in the world.

But he had a girlfriend. Which made him scummier than the underside of this boat just for looking at her that way.

Control yourself, Ariana. Control.

But she really didn't want to.

STOLEN MOMENTS

The jubilant sound of guys' voices and laughter filled the boathouse as everyone celebrated a productive first practice. The cedar walls gleamed with a fresh coat of shellac, and the crew boats shelved along the walls were waxed to a shine. The guys had tossed their things— duffel bags, boxer shorts, T-shirts, sweatshirts, and sneakers—all along the benches that ran down the center of the room, creating a sense of carefree disarray. Ariana would have loved to loiter in the corner for a while and enjoy the camaraderie, the shirtlessness, and the testosterone-filled atmosphere, but she had an exam to get to in fifteen minutes. As the guys grabbed their clothes and towels off the hooks at the back of the room on their way to the showers, Ariana slipped her hobo bag over her head and tried to slink out.

Unfortunately, halfway through the doorway she slunk right into Palmer.

"Leaving so soon?" he asked, arching his eyebrows.

Somehow he had already showered, and his shoulders were dotted with little droplets of water. His arms were stuck through the armholes of his T-shirt, which he pulled over his head as he slipped by her. Ariana was breathless as she noted the various spots in which the soft gray cotton clung to his body.

Control, Ariana. Control.

"I have to go," she said.

"Second breakfast?" he asked as the guys emptied out toward the shower room. He tossed his towel into his APH crew duffel, which sat on a bench in front of a wall of lockers, and zipped it up. Then he slid his gold band up his arm, where it tightened over his bicep. "I'll come with."

"I'd rather you not," Ariana said tersely. No reason to tell him she was not headed back to the cafeteria. No reason to share anything more with him than she already had. She could not give him another inch. If she did, it could be dangerous.

Palmer blinked as he lifted the heavy bag onto his shoulder. "Okay, I have to ask . . . did I do something to offend you?"

Ariana simply stared at him. Off in the shower room, a few guys hooted and hollered. Laughter filled the air.

"You can drop the ignorant act. It's beneath you," she said, crossing her arms over her chest.

"What ignorant act?" Palmer said, gripping his bag strap with both hands.

Ariana scoffed. "You know you were about to kiss me the other night. You led me on."

Palmer laughed, tipping his head back slightly. "Led you on? I'd known you for one day."

Embarrassment heated Ariana's face, but she told herself not to let it get to her. She was right. She knew she was right. "Yes. And you led me on for *one* day." Palmer's smile waned slightly. Ariana walked toward him. "If Lexa hadn't shown up at that moment, you would have kissed me. Just admit it."

He took a deep breath and blew it out, studying her for a long moment. Ariana could have died from the strain of wanting to touch him. To just sink into his chest and wrap his arms around her. Then, finally, he spoke. "I can't."

She blinked, tearing her gaze away from his arms and looking into his eyes. "Can't because it's not true, or won't because you have a girlfriend?"

"A little bit of both?" he said with an annoyingly endearing smile.

"What the hell is that supposed to mean?" Ariana asked.

"Nothing," he said, averting his eyes. He adjusted the strap of his bag and started past her, avoiding her gaze. "Forget I said anything."

"No," Ariana said, her heart pounding. Palmer paused and placed his hands on either side of the doorway, leaning into them. He tipped his head forward and groaned, a noise that sent a skitter of nervousness through Ariana. "The other night you said . . . you *implied* that you're all about fairness, right?"

Palmer, his back still to her, snorted. "Right."

"So do you really think it's fair to say something like that to me and then not elaborate? To not tell me the truth?" Ariana asked, crossing her arms over her chest.

"No. I guess not." He stood up straight and turned around to face her. There was obvious conflict in his gorgeous eyes. Conflict that gave her hope. "So here's the truth. I love Lexa. I've been with her forever and I love her. I'm sorry if that hurts or whatever, but I do."

Ariana's heart shriveled like a raisin in the sun.

"But—"

And just like that it expanded again.

"But?" she repeated hopefully.

"But it's complicated. If I'm being totally honest, that night . . . maybe I forgot for a second that I was in love with her," Palmer said. "Just for a second."

Ariana stared at him. Did he have any idea how awful this made her feel? He kept dangling what she wanted just within her grasp, then snatching it away again.

"I do like you, Ana. You're . . . different than the other girls I know. But I just . . . I can't," he said. " I hope you understand."

Ariana swallowed hard. She was not going to play the victim here. Not going to let him see the hundreds of awful, warring emotions he had inspired in her. She was going to be the bigger person and put an end to this, right here, right now. For her own sake. For his. For Lexa's.

"I understand," she said in a clear, unaffected voice. "I completely understand."

"Good." The depth of his relief was obvious. "So . . . we're okay then. We're friends."

"Yes," Ariana said with a nod. "We're friends."

"Good. Then I'll see you at the faculty picnic later, cox," he said, backing away from her. "Good practice."

"Good practice," Ariana repeated.

Then he grinned at her one last time and walked out. Ariana's knees felt so shaky from the encounter she had to sit down. She backed up, dropped onto the wooden bench in front of the lockers, and placed her head in her hands.

This is a good thing, she told herself. *At least now everything is clear.*

Besides, she couldn't go around letting him look at her the way he had out on the water earlier. Couldn't be the girl who flirted with her best friend's boyfriend behind her back. She wanted to make it work here with Lexa and her friends. Undermining Lexa's relationship with Palmer was not the way to make that happen.

Ariana took a deep breath and glanced at her watch. Crap. She had ten minutes to get back up the hill and all the way across campus. She was about to get up and go for a sprint, when something caught her eye. One of the guys had left his watch on top of his gym bag. Ariana leaned over to check it out and her heart stopped. It was a platinum Rolex. Worth a quarter of a million at least.

Two hundred fifty thousand dollars, Ariana thought, her palms starting to itch. With that watch, she would be one quarter of the way to paying off Kaitlynn. Was it possible . . . ? Could she actually raise the money through petty theft? The idea had never occurred to her until now, but many of the wealthiest teenagers in the world attended APH. She didn't have much time, but if she could simply scrape a few things together . . .

Maybe she could get rid of Kaitlynn after all.

Ariana's pulse started to race, spurred by adrenaline and the slightest twinge of excitement.

Whose watch was it? And what kind of person left a two hundred fifty thousand–dollar watch just lying out in a public place? The kind of irresponsible person that practically deserved to have said watch stolen. No, not practically. He *did* deserve it.

Ariana heard a bang in the shower room, followed by more laughter, and grabbed the watch. It slipped right into the inside pocket of her bag as if it was made to fit there.

"Hey. What're you doing?"

Ariana whirled around, her heart in her throat, glancing at the wall for the nearest oar just in case she needed it. Landon was walking slowly across the room, a white T-shirt clinging to his chest as he toweled off his shaggy hair. What had he seen? And why did it have to be him? People were definitely going to notice if Mr. World-Famous Pop Star suddenly went missing.

"Nothing," Ariana said casually, lifting her shoulders. She started past him, focused on the door. "I'd better go."

Landon took a step back and to the side, blocking her path. "Wait."

Ariana's entire potential future passed before her eyes. He'd seen her pocket the watch. He was going to tell. Or threaten her. Or blackmail her. How could she have been so careless? She was going to be expelled from Atherton-Pryce before she even had a chance to take one class.

"I've known girls like you," he said, looking down at her with a smirk.

"What?" Ariana asked. His words didn't compute. When was he going to accuse her already?

"You think you're better than me, right? Better than my music? That's why you pretended you didn't know who I was in the school store," he said, tossing his towel on the nearest bench. "Just because it's pop doesn't mean it's crap, you know. Have you even listened to any of it?"

Oxygen flooded Ariana's lungs, filling her body with sweet relief. He hadn't seen her take the watch. His ego was so big he probably couldn't see *anything* past it.

"No. Can't say that I have," she replied coolly.

"I figured. I can spot a music snob from a mile off," he said, tugging his rope necklaces out from under his shirt. "I'll send you some mp3s. At least listen to my stuff before you judge me."

"Okay. I'll do that," Ariana said, sidestepping him. "You can get my e-mail from Soomie. Or Maria," she added pointedly, which caused him to blush. "Whoever you see first."

Then she walked out of the boathouse as slowly and deliberately as possible, even if it meant being a few minutes later for her test. She couldn't risk him or anyone else watching her as she ran up the stone steps cut into the hill.

Only the guilty ran.

MAKING THE CALL

That afternoon was the faculty picnic on the great lawn, which meant the professors were showing up on campus for the first time to mingle with the students. There were half a dozen buffet tables packed with food and drink, dozens of picnic tables dotting the grass, and colorful banners and sign-up tables for various clubs and organizations, each of which was mentored by a member of the faculty. Ariana signed up for the APH literary magazine. She'd always enjoyed working on Easton's literary magazine, but more important, her signature would prove that she had been there. After that, she quickly slipped away from the party. With hundreds of people milling around, it was the perfect opportunity to walk off unnoticed. She hurried back to her dorm, grabbed her leather gloves from her drawer, and commenced her life as a cat burglar.

Just like at Easton Academy, there were no locks on any of the dorm room doors, so it was beyond easy to slip in and out. Within minutes Ariana had gathered several pawnable baubles and trinkets, including a few diamond tennis bracelets, a ruby necklace, and several iPods. But when she returned to her room and laid it all out with the Rolex watch, she realized that the grand total of all the items would barely put a dent in the million dollars she supposedly "owed" Kaitlynn. If she could have gotten her hands on Tahira's pink diamond or some of Brigit's crown jewels, they definitely would have helped. But Ariana had a feeling that those things would definitely be missed—and that the royal guards would be sent out to find them. She stashed her stolen goods into the back of her desk drawer, covering them over with her notebooks, and sat down on her bed to think.

Two seconds later, her phone beeped. She grabbed it and checked the screen. It was a text from Kaitlynn:

3 days & counting! hope u have a good plan, BL!

Ariana's jaw clenched and she slapped the flip phone closed, then opened it again. Her one and only option had been hovering in the back of her mind ever since her encounter with Kaitlynn at the diner, and she scrolled to the phone book entry labeled "home."

Grandma Covington. The woman had access to serious money. And Briana Leigh was her one and only granddaughter, her one and only living relative. The least Ariana could do was ask. It couldn't hurt, right?

She glanced at her cell phone. The very idea of ringing up Grandma C. and putting on Briana Leigh's voice made her soul feel gray. But she needed the money in order to survive, and she needed it fast.

The sooner she bit the bullet and called, the sooner the ordeal would be over with.

Ariana hit the speed dial button. Grandma Covington's assistant picked up on the first ring. She didn't even hesitate when Ariana said it was Briana Leigh calling. One person fooled, one much shrewder person to go. Ariana held her breath as she waited for Grandma Covington to pick up the phone.

"Well, Briana Leigh, it's been over three weeks," she said by way of greeting. "I was beginning to think you were dead."

Ariana froze. The irony of the jibe, the morbid irony of it, was so overwhelming, her mind went completely blank. What was she doing? Who was she calling? Why, again?

In, one . . . two . . . three . . .

Out, one . . . two . . . three . . .

"Hello? Is anyone there?"

Ariana closed her eyes. Breathed. Opened her eyes. Spoke.

"Sorry, Grandma," she said in Briana Leigh's Texas drawl. "I've just been so busy getting settled in here and buying my books and all. And I'm retaking my placement exams. Trying to get into some tougher classes. So that's taken up a lot of my time."

Ariana's heart rate slowed closer to normal with each word. It was a stroke of genius mentioning this up front. Surely Grandma C. would notice the change in schedule when she started to receive Briana Leigh's progress reports. And surely retaking the exams to get into harder classes would win her brownie points.

"Well, I didn't know you had such initiative," Grandma Covington said cautiously.

"I'm turning over a new leaf here, Grandma," Ariana said, hearing the smoochy sounds of butt-kisses in her mind. "It's hard not to in a place like this. It just makes you *want* to learn."

"Interesting," Grandma Covington said. "As long as you stay out of trouble this time. That's all I care about."

Give me a million dollars and I will, Ariana thought. "Oh, definitely. You don't have to worry about that."

"Good." There was a pause. "Well, are you going to tell me the reason for this call or am I to believe you were just checking in? Because I find that highly unlikely."

Ariana laughed, mimicking Briana Leigh's giggle perfectly.

"Actually, I'm calling about this fund-raiser we're having," Ariana said, gripping her bedspread in her free hand. "There's this whole competition thing here during Welcome Week and, well, it's a long story, but whichever team wins gets all these perks for the rest of the year. Anyway, one of the competitions is a fund-raiser for the Red Cross, and whichever team makes the most money wins the event, so—"

"So you're calling for money," Grandma Covington said flatly.

"Yes." Ariana saw no reason to elaborate further just yet. Let it sink in first.

"How much money?"

Ariana closed her eyes, crossed her fingers, held her breath. "A million."

The laughter came as a surprise. Ariana didn't know that Grandma Covington was capable of laughter.

"And here I thought you'd changed," Grandma Covington said acerbically.

"What do you—"

"Did you not say this is a fund-raiser?" the woman asked. "I imagine they expect you to actually work a bit to raise the funds, not just call up your relatives and go begging."

Ariana's fingers dug into the bedspread and twisted. Begging? She was begging for her life here, not just for the money. And a million dollars was a drop in the bucket to this woman. Was she really going to turn her down?

"That's not what I'm doing, Grandma," Ariana said, trying to control the irate quiver in her voice. "I'm just trying to—"

"You're trying to take the easy way out, as usual," Grandma Covington said. "Why don't you just hand over your weekly allowance check when it comes? Give them your money instead of mine? Or is it because you've already thought of twenty-five frivolous ways to spend it?"

"I—"

"The answer, Briana Leigh, is no. Good-bye, dear."

And the line went dead.

It was all Ariana could do to keep from launching her phone across the room—again. But she couldn't afford to buy another one just now. Instead she placed the phone on her desk, dropped face-first onto the bed, and screamed as loud as she could into her pillow. Before she knew it, she was punching the bed over and over and over again with both hands, thrashing out her frustration and desperation.

Why did Briana Leigh have to be such a lazy, corner-cutting, money-grubbing loser in life? If she had been just a tad more responsible then, her grandmother wouldn't have been so quick to judge Ariana now. First the entrance exams and now this. Briana Leigh's laziness was screwing up Ariana's world.

After a few minutes, Ariana finally sat up, brushed her hair out of her face, and took a deep breath. She looked out the window at the party going on outside—the colorful tablecloths and banners, the heaping trays of sweets on the dessert table, the groups of students and teachers laughing and chatting and debating. She longed to join them. Longed to be part of all this for as long as she possibly could be. Ariana needed a plan B.

Unfortunately, she had no idea where to start.

OPTIONS

"Just so you know, I am not anorexic," Maria told Ariana as they sat down at the long wooden table at dinner that night. The places were already set and a menu stood inside a plastic holder at each plate, offering three choices of entrée. Table service at school. Ariana had never thought it possible until she'd experienced it on that first day. Easton could kiss Atherton-Pryce Hall's ass. "I mean, come on, an anorexic ballerina? How cliché. I just don't like food."

Ariana picked up her menu and perused the offerings. "Okay," she said. "But just so *you* know, even if you were anorexic, I wouldn't judge you. Everyone has issues."

Maria blinked, looking Ariana over as she placed her linen napkin in her lap. "I don't have issues."

Ariana glanced up at Landon, who was just slipping behind Maria's chair to join them. He squeezed Maria's shoulder under the blanket of her hair, then ran his fingers along the nape of her neck as he passed by. Maria's whole body tensed.

"Yes, you do," Ariana said. "You have a whole year's subscription."

Maria's face turned blotchy and she grabbed her own menu, pretending to be suddenly riveted. Ariana smiled as the rest of the usual crew started to filter in. Brigit, Soomie, and Adam were soon followed by Lexa and Palmer, who walked over hand in hand. Ariana wanted to look away, but instead she forced herself to stare at their entwined fingers. Forced herself to burn the image into her brain. All the better to remember it whenever Palmer's glances got her heart pounding.

"What's up, *Love*?" Tahira asked, pausing at the end of the table. Allison, Zuri, and Rob all stopped as well, as if none of them could make a move unless Tahira moved first.

Ariana glared up at her. "Oh, what is that? Some kind of witty tennis reference?"

"Yeah. Because you couldn't score a single point in that last game," Zuri said with a laugh. "Love, love, love."

"Is that really necessary?" Lexa scolded.

"Is it really necessary for you to always be telling everyone else what's necessary?" Allison shot back.

"Allison," Tahira said in a warning tone.

"Whatever. There *will* be a rematch and you *will* be going down," Brigit declared, rising out of her seat. "Right, Ana?"

Ariana didn't know how to respond. What if she claimed Brigit was right and then tanked even more swiftly next time? She wasn't sure she could handle that kind of humiliation without exploding. The silence seemed to drag on for an excruciatingly long time, until Maria finally spoke up.

"Move along, girls. We're bored with you now," she said to Tahira and her entourage.

Tahira scoffed. "Like anything could be more boring than vanilla." Then she and her friends moved off, obviously satisfied at having had the last word. Ariana's fists clenched under the table. Sooner or later, Tahira was going to get what was coming to her. She would see to that.

"Speaking of lame people," Landon said, glancing at Tahira over his shoulder. "Did you dudes hear that someone swiped Christian's Rolex this morning?"

Suddenly, Ariana was grateful to Tahira for her taunts. It meant her face was already red when this topic came up, so that when she grew even redder, no one at the table noticed. "What? Where?" Brigit asked. Her fingers touched the sparkling aquamarine and diamond pendant around her neck. Royal jewels worth hundreds of thousands, no doubt.

"He claims it was in the boathouse," Palmer replied, "but I think he must've left it back at the dorm. No one was down there but our teammates, and none of them would have taken it."

"Exactly," Lexa said, flicking her hair over her shoulder.

Ariana marveled at their certainty. Their absolute trust. Had nothing bad ever happened to these people?

"Hey, Texas, did you see anything?" Landon asked, lifting his chin.

There was a long pause, and Ariana suddenly realized that he, along with everyone else at the table, was looking at her.

"Texas. That'd be you," Maria said in a flat voice.

"Oh, right . . . um . . . no. I didn't see anything," Ariana said, looking at Palmer. "I left right after you did."

A girl at the next table backed her chair up so that it lined up with Landon's. "You know, one of my bracelets is missing too," she said, letting her long blond hair tumble down behind the back of her chair. "I thought I left it at home, but maybe someone took it."

"Interesting," Soomie said, raising her eyebrows. "It seems we have a thief on campus."

"What are they, admitting scholarship students now?" Maria joked.

Everyone at the table looked right at Adam, including Ariana. She couldn't help it. It was a knee-jerk response. The poor boy paled as his brown eyes flitted nervously around the table in a conspicuous way. Ariana was confused. *Was* Adam the first-ever scholarship student at Atherton-Pryce? Maybe he was simply the first one ever to hang out with this particular crowd.

"Oh, crap, Adam. Sorry," Maria said. Then she snorted an embarrassed laugh and looked up at the waiter, who had just arrived at the end of their table, a handsome if scruffy college-age guy in a white shirt and black pants who looked as if he'd rather be anywhere but there.

"She didn't mean anything," Lexa clarified to Adam, her tone kind. "The girl has a tongue-control problem."

Adam managed a laugh. "It's okay."

As Maria ordered her meal—making demands about oil and butter and salt—the rest of the table fell into an uncomfortable silence. Ariana tried to tell Adam with her eyes that she felt for him, but he had trained his gaze on his menu and refused to look up. Suddenly Ariana became aware that someone was repeatedly clearing his throat.

"Ana. Your turn to order," Maria said. "What's with you tonight?"

"Sorry." Ariana looked up at the hovering waiter and smiled her apology. He simply sighed in return. "I'll have the salmon," she said. "Thank you."

As the waiter made a note and moved on to Brigit, Ariana tried to relax her tense shoulders. She had, of course, known that people would notice when their things went missing, but what had she expected? That people *wouldn't* talk about it?

At least no one seemed all that angry or upset about the stolen jewelry. Probably because they could all easily afford to replace their things. But now people were talking about it, which meant it could become something big. A scandal. Would there be an investigation? How was she going to make sure she wasn't implicated? She could not get thrown out of APH for stealing. That would be way too pathetic an end to her grueling journey.

Tomorrow she would have to get a pass off campus and go into town to pawn those things. She couldn't have them lying around her dorm room for too long. Fab. Another pass, another trip into D.C., another wasted afternoon. And she still had no method for making up the rest of the cash.

Ariana clenched her arm under the table, avoiding the wounds that were still smarting from the other day. She wanted to kill Kaitlynn for doing this to her. But she had tried that, and she had failed. And now she was out of options.

THE BEST

"Why am I helping Tahira again?" Ariana asked, moving her fingertip around on the touch pad of her new laptop. She highlighted another list of e-mail addresses from a local high school's website and copied it into the ever-growing Excel chart on her desktop. It was Wednesday afternoon, and she had just finished her general science exam, the most difficult of the four she'd taken so far. When she'd returned to the dorm, she hadn't even had time to close the door behind her when Lexa popped in, asking if she wanted to hang out and help with the e-mail blasts for the fund-raiser. Maria was down at the dance studio working out, Brigit was on a video chat with the King and Queen, and Soomie was off meeting with her professors, trying to get some extra-credit assignments started early. Ana was Lexa's last chance for company. Although as Ariana sat back on Maria's bed, she was trying not to think of herself that way—as the final and least desirable option.

Lexa laughed. "Wow. The girls really turned you against her quickly, huh?" She looked up at Ariana from her twin-size bed, where she was seated with her own laptop, kicked back against a mound of plush light and dark gray pillows in cashmere, silk, and fur.

Ariana tilted her head. "It's not just that. I could tell from the beginning that she wasn't exactly my type of person. But you seem to like her."

"Well, Tahira and I have been friends for a long time. Since way before the Princess Wars broke out," Lexa said looking at her computer screen. There was something in her tone that told Ariana they didn't just go way back, but that they were somehow important to each other. "But I'm not going to try to change anyone's mind about her, especially not Brigit's." She took a deep breath and smiled. "So just don't think about it as helping Tahira. Think about it as helping the team. Team is a very big thing around here, in case you hadn't noticed."

"I did kind of get that," Ariana replied with a smile. She filed away her suspicions about Lexa and Tahira and vowed to observe the two more closely when they were together. There was nothing more intriguing than a dark secret between friends.

"So, how do you like it here? Is it better than . . . where were you last year again?" Lexa asked, a little line forming above her nose.

Prison? Ariana thought. "This rinky-dink day school in Houston," Ariana replied, waving a hand. "Believe me, you've never heard of it. This place is *way* better. I think I may stay," she said jokingly.

"Good. We'd love to have you," Lexa joked back, lifting her chin.

Ariana grinned. "So . . . what are the other two teams doing for their fund-raisers?"

"Blue is holding an art auction at the Smithsonian," Lexa said. "Martin's dad is this big collector, so he knows a lot of artists who are going to donate their work. And gray is doing a fashion show thing where you can bid on the gowns, but from what I hear, they had trouble getting any of the top designers, so they shouldn't be a problem."

"So all we have to do is win this or the crew race, and we win. We're in Privilege House?" Ariana asked.

"Yep. Winning debate was huge," Lexa said, typing away. Then she paused and looked over at Ariana. "You know, I'm glad the guys asked you to be the cox."

Her casual tone sounded forced. Ariana glanced at the girl from the corner of her eye and thought that her posture looked a bit more tense than it had a moment ago. She was lying.

"Really? I was a little worried about that," Ariana said.

"No. It's cool. It's a good thing for you," she said.

Ariana blinked. It seemed an odd thing to say. How, exactly, was it good for her? But she didn't want to harp on the subject. "Thanks."

"Anyway, back to Tahira. It can actually be a good thing to have her on your side," Lexa said, clicking her mouse before looking over at Ariana. "She does have the bitchy thing down, don't get me wrong, but she gets stuff done."

"Well, when you want to get stuff done, the bitchy thing is very helpful," Ariana replied, copying another list.

There was a brief pause and Ariana was aware that Lexa was watching her. Watching her closely. Her fingertips started to tremble ever so slightly over the keyboard. Had she noticed something? Some discrepancy between Ariana and the Briana Leigh whom Lexa once knew? Crap. She had let her accent slip for a second there. It had come out more Atlanta then Houston. Was that why Lexa was staring at her?

"You know, you can still join the equestrian team and drop tennis," Lexa said. "No one would blame you."

Already tense, Ariana saw red. "Why? Because I suck so bad at tennis and everyone knows it now?" she snapped.

Lexa blinked, her pretty face turning a stunned pink. It was obvious that she was unaccustomed to being snapped at. "No! No! That's not what I meant at all! I was there, okay? You had that girl on the ropes. You just . . . couldn't finish her off."

Thanks for the reminder, Ariana thought, keeping her eyes trained pointedly on the computer screen. Her jaw clenched as she vividly recalled her fabulous crash-and-burn, and the tension in the room enveloped her.

"No, I just meant no one would blame you if you wanted to avoid Tahira as much as possible," Lexa said, swinging her legs over the side of the bed to better face Ariana. She planted her hands at her side and clenched her knees together.

Ariana looked over at Lexa, feeling wary. Did Lexa really not mean to insult her? One look in the girl's earnest eyes and she knew—the insult was definitely unintended. Sometimes, after all Ariana had been through, it was difficult to remember that there were still some genuinely good and kind people in the world.

"Thanks," Ariana said, her shoulders relaxing. "But I can handle her."

Lexa smiled, and she stood up to shove the window open a bit wider, letting in the warm summer breeze. "Okay. I just wanted to make sure you knew there were options." She shoved her hands into the back pockets of her skinny-legged jeans and hovered there in the center of the room, looking down at Ariana. "Actually, to be perfectly honest, I was kind of relieved when you didn't want to join the equestrian team."

"Really?" Ariana placed her laptop aside, grateful for an excuse to take a break from all the lists. "You seemed so upset."

"It was an act," Lexa said matter-of-factly. She picked up one of many gold trophies from the shelf above her desk, which was also decorated with dozens of blue and red ribbons, and fingered the head of the rider atop the little gold horse. "I was actually terrified you'd be better than me. It's the only thing around here I'm best at."

Ariana was intrigued. She turned to face Lexa, sitting on the edge of Maria's bed now. "What do you mean?"

Lexa rolled her eyes and ducked her chin for a moment, shaking her head. "I've never told anyone this before. Not even Maria."

An excited skip of her heart left Ariana momentarily breathless. Not even Maria? She had assumed that Maria and Lexa were BFFs. If Lexa was about to share something top secret with her, then she was definitely in. And might even have a chance to usurp Maria on the friendship ladder. Her whole body tingled with possibility. She had to play this conversation exactly right.

"It's okay," Ariana said. "You can tell me. We go way back, remember?"

Lexa looked into Ariana's eyes. Ariana could tell she was dying to talk. As if she really didn't have anyone to talk to about anything deep. Ariana gazed back steadily, letting Lexa see that she was trustworthy.

"It's just . . . everyone has a thing, you know?" Lexa said finally, gesturing with the trophy. "Maria's the best dancer, Soomie's the best student, Brigit's the best party planner—"

"Really?" Ariana asked. "Better than Tahira?"

"Oh my God, with her money and connections?" Lexa said, widening her eyes. "You want Cirque du Soleil in the Riviera and Jude Law singing 'Happy Birthday,' she'll get it for you. But it's not just that—her events have this unique style. This, like, whimsy. She's totally going to be famous and successful for something creative. Forget the royalty thing."

"Interesting," Ariana said, filing this information away for later use.

"Anyway, horses are my thing. I'm good at riding. That's it," Lexa said, replacing the trophy on the shelf and adjusting it so that it was perfectly aligned with the others. Ariana smiled to herself. Lexa was a bit OCD, just like her.

"I don't think that's true," Ariana replied.

Lexa tilted her head, a quizzical wrinkle between her brows, and crossed her arms over her light blue T-shirt. "What do you mean?"

"You're obviously also good at taking care of your friends," Ariana said. "You're making sure Maria eats, helping Brigit with her diet, helping Soomie with Landon, trying to save me from Tahira torture. From what I've seen, you're the best at being a friend."

Lexa blushed, clearly flattered, and dropped back down on her bed. "You're cracked," she said modestly, looking at her computer screen. "Anyone would do those things for their friends."

"No, not anyone. Believe me, I know," Ariana replied. Lexa's expression grew serious, and Ariana felt a sizzle of apprehension. She had just opened the door to questions. Questions she did not want to invite in.

"Why? Did something happen with your friends at your old school?" Lexa asked, her voice tinged with concern. "Is that why you transferred?"

Oh, did something ever happen, Ariana thought, remembering in vivid detail that night on the roof of Billings. Reed on the ground near the edge, then Noelle with that stupid lacrosse stick. Did something happen? Yeah. Total backstabbing betrayal. Not to mention the ongoing torture that was the result of having been Kaitlynn's friend.

Lexa's eyes flicked to Ariana's hands, and she realized that Maria's white cashmere blanket was balled up at her side. She released it, breathed, and smiled.

"No. I just wanted the best, and APH is the best," she said lightly. Then she added, by way of distraction. "You know, all three of those girls were practically suffocating without you here. They could not *wait* to see you."

"Really?" Lexa said, pleased.

"Really."

"Thanks, Ana. That's so nice of you to say," Lexa told her.

"Just telling the truth," Ariana said, leaning back on the bed again and lifting her laptop onto her legs. "So, if Brigit is such the party planner, why did Palmer put Tahira in charge of the fund-raiser instead of her?"

She felt a twinge just saying Palmer's name to Lexa, but she was going to have to get used to it.

Lexa sighed, sitting back as well. "He had his reasons."

Ariana's skin prickled with interest. "What reasons?"

A blush lit Lexa's cheeks, as if she'd just been snagged saying something she hadn't meant to say. "It's hard to explain," she said quickly, tucking her hair behind her ears.

"What?" Ariana asked, trying not to sound as desperate for info as she felt.

"Nothing. It's just . . ." Lexa looked around the room, stalling for time. "They both . . . they both pitched him ideas, and I think he just liked the Landon thing better," she said finally, her words tumbling together so that Ariana knew she was lying. But why? What other reasons could Palmer possibly have for choosing Tahira over Brigit, especially when Brigit was so clearly one of his girlfriend's best friends? "And honestly, it *is* pretty brilliant when you think about it. We're going to take in so much cash, we're going to need to hire a staff to cart it all back here."

Ariana's breath caught in her throat. Her fingers froze over her keyboard. Suddenly, any thoughts of Palmer/Tahira/Brigit intrigue flew right out of her mind. "What do you mean?"

"Normally with these things we get all these credit card transactions and you have to pay a fee for each one, which eats into your bottom line," Lexa explained, leaning toward her screen as she continued to work. "But with this Landon thing we're going to get hundreds of girls with fists full of allowance money just salivating to throw it at their idol. We're talking bucket-loads of cash. And actual cash means no fees, which means more money for our tally. I mean, except for whoever wins the date with Landon. I figure that's going to be too expensive for any normal person to pay for out of pocket."

"Right," Ariana said. She stared at the door of the closet where Maria had taped up one of Degas's ballerina prints, but she didn't see it. All she saw was cash. Stacks and stacks of cash. All there for the taking.

"We are *so* going to win this challenge," Lexa said giddily, tapping away at her keyboard. "Two for two, baby! Blue and gray can kiss our butts!"

Ariana smiled, but she was barely listening. It looked like she was going to have to become a more integral member of the fund-raising committee. She had to figure out a way to steal some of the money without being caught. And the only way to do that was to be in on the plans.

Apparently she and Tahira were going to be spending more time together, a thought that made her cringe. But if it meant getting rid of Kaitlynn, it would all be worth it.

SURPRISE VISIT

Using a paint-spattered hammer she had borrowed from Cornwall's housemother, Ariana drove the final nail into the bottom corner on one of the two Jackson Pollock prints she had just bought at the school store. She stepped back to admire her work, then glanced over her shoulder at Soomie, who was supposed to be defragmenting Ariana's computer. Not that it needed it, being brand-new, but Soomie had offered and Ariana had seen it as an opportunity to bond. Instead, however, she caught Soomie remaking her bed.

"My hospital corners not tight enough for you?" Ariana asked, half annoyed, half amused.

"It's just something I do well," Soomie replied unapologetically, whipping her hands across the top blanket to smooth any wrinkles. She turned around and tilted her head as she regarded the painting. "That works."

"Thanks. I think so too," Ariana said.

Soomie pulled out Ariana's desk chair and opened her laptop. "So, are you totally sure about this whole tennis thing?" she asked. "Because the equestrian team is really—"

"Oh my gosh. Why is everyone so obsessed with me being on the equestrian team?" Ariana asked with a laugh, lifting another poster and holding it against the wall. She drove a nail into the top right corner and reached for another one. "Just because I beat Lexa a million years ago in one little dressage competition doesn't mean—"

"I thought it was jumper," Soomie said, whipping her head around.

The nail slipped from Ariana's fingers and bounced along the wooden floor with a faint tinkling sound. Her heart all but stopped. Was it jumper? She had gone over Briana Leigh's Triple Star mementos a thousand times and she had been sure it was dressage. Was Soomie just trying to make her slip up, or was she right? She glanced over her shoulder at the girl. Her eyes were sharp and discerning. Just one look at her and Ariana knew that Soomie was correct. Which meant that she, Ariana, had just screwed up.

Girl really *was* down with the details.

"It was. What did I say?" Ariana asked, hoping she wasn't visibly blushing.

"You said dressage," Soomie replied, one hand on the back of the chair. "Lexa said you didn't even compete in dressage."

Ariana's mouth was dry. Exactly how much had these people been discussing her behind her back?

"I didn't until later," Ariana clarified coolly. This was actually true. It was the reason for her mistake. If she hadn't looked at dozens of dressage ribbons last night the word wouldn't have even been in her head. She grabbed another nail and slammed it into the wall with slightly more vigor than necessary. "You're right, though. That year it was the jumper competition. I've been in so many I sometimes mix them up." Her skin grew warm under Soomie's gaze and she realized she was babbling, that she sounded like someone trying to cover up a lie. "Can you grab that nail I just lost?"

"Sure," Soomie said, crouching to the floor. She got up and handed Ariana the nail. "You might want to make that right corner higher. It's crooked."

"Thanks," Ariana said, even though she felt so pent-up and frustrated she wanted to drive the nail through the girl's hand. She turned the hammer around, pulled out the nail she'd just placed, and started over.

"Wow, so I guess you really burned out. I mean, if you've competed so much you can't even remember which events you won and lost," Soomie said, sitting down again.

"Exactly. That's why I'm moving on to tennis," she said, feeling relieved that the conversation had come around to a logical conclusion. "I think it'll be fun to start over."

"I guess," Soomie said. "But when I'm that good at something, I never give it up."

Ariana sighed, wishing Soomie would drop it already. Just then, Tahira walked by the open door of her room. Ariana's whole body tensed at the thought of talking to the girl, but it was better to just put the gears in motion. Besides, it would be a great way to shut Soomie up already.

"Tahira?" she called out, stepping over to the threshold.

The Dubai princess paused with her hand on the doorknob of her own room. "Can I help you with something, *Love?*" she asked with a condescending glance.

Ariana's fingers tightened around the hammer's handle. *Don't kill her. You cannot kill her.*

"Actually, I was hoping to help *you*," Ariana replied, plastering on a smile. She crossed her arms over her chest, letting the hammer dangle from her fingers. "I'd like to volunteer to work the tables at the fundraiser."

Tahira, understandably, looked suspicious. She crossed her arms over her chest as well, and faced Ariana head-on. "Why? You're already doing crew. You've fulfilled your requirement."

"I don't just fulfill requirements," Ariana explained. "I like to do as much as I can."

With a dubious look, Tahira shoved open the door to her room. "All right then. We'd *love* to have you."

"That's going to get old real fast," Ariana told her as the hall phone rang.

"No it's not!" Tahira sang with a huge grin. She slammed the door to her and Zuri's room, and Ariana pressed her lips together to keep from cursing under her breath, which Soomie would undoubtedly hear.

You're doing this for a reason, she reminded herself, tapping the hammer against the open palm of her hand. *You're doing this so you can finally shed your past and move on.*

"Ana!" Brigit shouted, leaning out of the old-school phone booth at the end of the hallway. "There's someone down at the gate for you and he's not on your list of approved visitors. They need to know if they should let him through."

Ariana's vision instantly prickled over with gray spots. She could not have heard that correctly. Someone at the gate for her? For Briana Leigh? Who the hell would drop by unannounced like this? Briana Leigh had very few friends and even fewer who knew she'd be attending APH. Unless it was Téo, Briana Leigh's former fiancé. Ariana backed against the wall of the hallway, her knees weak. The hammer hit the plaster with a dull thud.

Oh, God, please don't let it be Téo.

"Ana? Are you okay?" Soomie said from inside her room.

"Fine. I'm fine," Ariana replied quickly.

"You should really talk to him," Brigit prompted. "The guards don't like us, so they get kind of mean when we keep them waiting. Something about us being overprivileged snobby bitches."

"Okay," Ariana heard herself say. Her voice sounded very far away. Like it was coming through the heating vent beneath her feet after traveling through five stories of pipes. "I'll be right back," she told Soomie. She slowly made her way to the phone, unable to breathe the entire way. This was it. This was how she was going to get caught.

"What's the matter?" Brigit asked, her blue eyes wide as she held out the phone. "Do you think it's an ex-boyfriend or something?"

Ariana didn't answer. Couldn't. She grabbed the phone from Brigit and held it half an inch from her ear, as if it might scald her. Her other hand clung to the hammer.

"This is Briana Leigh Covington," she said.

"Yes, Miss Covington," a clipped male voice replied. "We have an Ashley Hudson here to see you."

Ariana's butt hit the tiny wooden seat in the booth and pain radiated up her spine. Hudson was here? Why the hell would he be coming to see Briana Leigh? And what was he going to do when he saw *her*—the girl he knew as Emma Walsh—instead? This was even worse than Téo. Ariana pressed the butt of the hammer's handle against her forehead and closed her eyes, her mind racing.

This isn't happening. . . . this is not *happening. . . .*

"Miss Covington?"

"One sec," Ariana said.

She was surprised to realize that part of her wanted to see Hudson. Was dying to, actually. A friendly face—the face of a person who actually cared about her—would be a welcome thing right then. But how was she going to explain the fact that she was even here?

"Are you okay?" Brigit asked from outside the booth. "OMG, it *is* an ex-boyfriend, isn't it? Is he hot? Can I meet him?"

Ariana shot Brigit a look of death. She didn't mean to, it just happened. Luckily, Brigit didn't seem to notice. She was probably too busy formulating her next battery of questions.

Questions. She was sure Hudson was going to have thousands of them. But maybe it was better to attempt to answer them now and get rid of him for good. Clearly, ignoring his texts and phone calls was not going to work.

"Fine," she said into the phone, eyeing the hammer as she spoke. "You can let him in."

EMMA, ANA, LOVE

Ariana shoved open the front door of Cornwall Hall and paused when she saw Hudson standing there on the stone patio between the parking lot and the entrance, reading the plaque set in the stone border around a cherry tree. She had a moment—one moment before Hudson saw her—in which to take him in. His floppy blond hair, slightly floppier than the last time she'd seen him, the way he stood with his shoulders just slightly rounded, unaffected and unpretentious, the line of his perfect jaw. She didn't realize until that moment how much she'd come to care for him in those couple of weeks they'd had together. She took that one moment, savored it, then said her own, private good-bye.

He didn't know it yet, but it was time to move on.

Finally, he turned. His face registered total shock, followed quickly by pure glee. Ariana's heart shattered as he raced forward and took her up in his arms.

"Emma! What are you doing here!?" he said into the thick blanket of her hair.

Ariana released herself from his grasp, making sure not to inhale his scent, which might physically hurt her, and looked around. No one in sight, thank goodness. No one had heard him call her "Emma."

"I transferred here over the summer," Ariana explained, sticking to the story she'd made up in the stairwell on her way down. "That's why you couldn't find me at Easton."

Hudson held both her hands in his, a bright smile lighting his handsome features. He was wearing a light blue oxford shirt, open over a faded burgundy Harvard T-shirt, and jeans that had seen better days. There was a small coffee stain on one thigh, and they were wrinkled beyond belief. Had he just driven all the way down here from Connecticut? Ariana was touched by the thought.

But no. She couldn't let herself feel. This was good-bye. Good-bye, good-bye, good-bye.

"Couldn't stay away from Briana Leigh, huh?" he joked.

Ariana smirked at the irony of the question. "Something like that."

"This is unbelievable," he said, squeezing one hand as he released the other. He tugged her toward one of the stone benches on the patio outside the dorm. "I honestly can't believe you're here! I was starting to think I'd never see you again."

If only, Ariana thought. "So . . . why are *you* here?" she asked.

Hudson laughed as he sat down in the sun. "Well, when I didn't find you at Easton I tried to think of how else I might get in touch with you, and Briana Leigh was the only person who came to mind. But I didn't have her number, and the last thing Téo wanted to talk about was Briana Leigh. I couldn't get it from him, so . . ."

"You talked to Téo?" Ariana asked. "How is he?"

Not that she cared. She just wanted to make sure that *he* wouldn't be making any surprise visits anytime soon.

Hudson pressed his lips together as she sat next to him. "He's, um, pissed. He couldn't believe Briana Leigh actually broke up with him by mail, but . . . he's using his anger in constructive ways."

"Such as?" Ariana asked, raising her eyebrows.

"Oh , you know, he's in Ibiza, so . . . you can pretty much use your imagination."

He laughed uncomfortably, and Ariana made a disgusted face. Maybe it was a good thing Briana Leigh never got the chance to marry the guy. She decided to change the subject.

"So you drove all the way down here. From Connecticut."

"School doesn't start until next week for me, so I figured . . . what the hell?" he said, lacing his fingers through hers and holding their hands atop his thigh. "I thought I'd find out where you were, but instead I found *you*."

Ariana looked down at her lap. Did he have to be so damn joyful about the whole thing? It was going to make it that much harder to break his heart. And maybe that much harder to get rid of him if it came to that.

"Is this totally pathetic?" he asked.

With a deep breath, Ariana was about to answer, but at that

moment the door to the dorm was flung open and out strolled Allison and Zuri. Ariana's words died on her tongue and her throat closed over.

If you two say anything that gives me away, I swear I will—

"What's up, *Love?*" Zuri said, throwing Allison into a giggle fit.

Ariana bit her tongue as they walked by without another word. She'd never embraced that nickname more. But her heart was still pounding painfully. Having Hudson here was dangerous, for both of them. She had never been more convinced that he had to go. Fast.

"What was that about?" Hudson asked, watching the girls as they disappeared around the corner.

"Just a stupid nickname," Ariana said with a wave of her hand. "They give them to all the transfers and freshmen. Like a hazing thing."

Wow. Her forked tongue was really on a roll. At that moment her cell phone let out a beep. She knew who it was, what the message would be, and chose to ignore it. It beeped again.

"You need to get that?" Hudson asked.

Ariana rolled her eyes and yanked the phone out, checking the screen. Predictably, the message was from Kaitlynn. This time it read:

Wheres the $$$ BL? tick tick tick . . .

A new wave of frustration and anger and fear crashed over Ariana's shoulders. These people from her past were everywhere. Closing in.

Choking her. Smothering her. She shoved the phone back in her bag and stood up.

"What was that?" Hudson asked.

"Nothing. Come on," she said, pulling him with her. "Let's go somewhere more private where we can talk."

"Wait," Hudson said, clinging to her hand. "Is Briana Leigh coming down? I feel like I should at least say hi."

Ariana looked past him at the door of the dorm, as if Briana Leigh might actually emerge from it. "Uh, no. When security called up, we both figured you'd want to see me, so she went off to lunch with some of the girls. She said to say hi, though."

"Oh. Okay," Hudson said. He didn't seem put out at all. Why would he be? He was holding the hand of the girl he loved. He didn't need Briana Leigh anymore. And hopefully, in about five minutes, he wouldn't need Emma Walsh either.

"Where to?" Hudson asked.

Ariana smiled, though her nerves were as frayed as Allison's split ends. "I know a perfect place."

FAKE BOYFRIEND

"This campus is amazing," Hudson said, looking around as they approached a copse of shade trees near the edge of the pond. Ariana had noticed it during the debate victory party and knew the trees would afford some privacy. Unfortunately, Hudson veered off toward the water before she could lead him to the shade. There were two white swans cutting circles across the surface of the pond, and a warm breeze bent the longer grass along the shoreline. "How do you like it here?"

Ariana's heart contracted. "Hudson, we need to talk," she said, turning her back to the water, which was rippling languidly in the breeze.

"Before you say anything, you're wrong," Hudson said, raising his hands. His eyes twinkled merrily.

"You don't even know what I was going to say," she replied impatiently.

"Yeah. I do," he replied, shoving his hands into his pockets and taking a confident, wide-legged stance. "You were going to say I shouldn't be here. That it's over, blah, blah, blah," he said, pacing past her. "But what you fail to realize is that if it *were* over I *wouldn't* be here, and neither would you."

He paused behind her, forcing her to turn. "How very existential of you," she said.

"Thank you." He gave a modest nod.

Ariana sighed, trying in vain to bite back her smile. No. No smiling. She did not like him anymore. *Could* not like him anymore. This was over. No matter how handsome he looked against the backdrop of the bright blue sky. "Hudson, this is ridiculous. You go to school in Boston, I'm in D.C. I don't want a long-distance relationship."

"We can figure all that out," Hudson said, stepping closer to her. "Emma, all I know is . . . what we had this summer was real. I want to see where it'll go."

From the corner of her eye, Ariana saw a group of people walking toward the pond with picnic blankets and sports equipment. They were headed for the north end, yards and yards away, but the very sight of them made her shoulders tense. She had to get Hudson off the APH campus as quickly as possible, before he had the chance to interact with anyone else. It was time to stop playing nice.

"It's not going anywhere," she said flatly.

Hudson's smile faltered, but just briefly. "I disagree."

"Hudson, I was in Texas all summer, I needed a distraction, you were hot, and you were there," Ariana said, lifting her chin. "That's all it was."

Hudson took a small step back. She could see the doubt and hurt in his eyes, and it pained her heart, but only for a moment. There were far more important things at stake than Hudson's feelings.

"I don't believe you," he said.

Ariana blew out a loud, exasperated sigh. "I have a boyfriend. I told you that. And if you want the brutal truth, I transferred here to be with him, not Briana Leigh."

"He goes *here*?" Hudson blurted.

The group of students were settling in near the edge of the pond. Ariana glanced over and noticed that Palmer was among them—and he was still standing—watching her. Ariana's fingers curled into a fist. This was not good. This was very not good.

"I'm sorry, Hudson, I have to go," Ariana said, turning away. Hoping against hope that he would just let it be. Then she felt his fingers close around her wrist. She whirled around, annoyed, and her own fingers curled instinctively. That was when she saw that Palmer was now approaching, a concerned look on his handsome face. Instantly, a new plan clicked into focus.

"Dammit. Here he comes," Ariana said under her breath, looking past Hudson.

Hudson had just enough time to glance over his shoulder before Palmer was upon them.

"Everything okay over here?" he asked in that proprietary voice. As if anything and everything that happened on this campus was his concern. Of course, to Hudson, it probably sounded as if he was just being possessive of Ariana. Perfect.

"Actually, no," Ariana replied. She made a big show of wrenching her arm out of Hudson's grasp, then grabbed the spot where his fingers had been, as if he'd been hurting her. Which, of course, he had not. Palmer's gaze flicked to Ariana's wrist. He glared at Hudson, clearly appalled.

"Is that really necessary, man?" he asked, crossing his arms over his chest in a way that made his biceps bulge. Ariana felt a thrill of attraction and forced herself to look at the grass beneath her feet.

"I wasn't. . . . I . . ." Hudson stammered.

"Palmer, can you please walk me back to my dorm?" Ariana asked, forcing a tremble into her voice.

"Of course," Palmer said. Then, much to Ariana's delight, he put his arm around her shoulders in a protective way. He was playing his role to perfection and he didn't even know it. "You're gonna want to leave campus before I call security," he warned Hudson.

Ariana and Palmer turned to walk away. They were a few yards off when Palmer took Ariana's fingers in his free hand and studied her wrist. "Are you sure you're all right? Do you *want* me to call security?"

Ariana was overwhelmed by his solicitousness. "No. I'm okay. He was just—"

"You can't end it like this, Emma!" Hudson called after her. "I know you care about me!"

A hot rush of anger overtook Ariana as Palmer paused. He had to freaking call her Emma, didn't he? He couldn't just get a clue and let it go. She turned around and shot him a look that would have killed a weaker guy on the spot. Hudson stopped in his tracks and he paled. If that didn't get the message across, nothing would.

"Why did he just call you Emma?" Palmer asked.

Ariana cleared her throat, buying time. How to explain this one away? "It's kind of embarrassing."

Palmer smirked. "What? Now you have to tell me."

"I . . . I met him when I was out with friends and I could just tell he was creepy, so I gave him a fake name," Ariana lied, looking away as if humiliated by her own behavior. "And sure enough it became this whole big stalker thing. I don't even know how he got on campus."

"Wow. I am *definitely* calling security," Palmer said, reaching for his cell in his back pocket.

"No. No, it's okay," Ariana glanced over at Hudson, who seemed to be debating which way to go—back toward the gate, or toward her and Palmer. "He's harmless. I actually told him you were my boyfriend, so you coming over was pretty perfect. I think he's gotten the picture."

"You told him I was your boyfriend?" Palmer asked with a teasing smile.

"I had to tell the guy *something*," Ariana replied, the color rising in her cheeks.

"Well, then, let's make absolutely *sure* he's gotten the picture," Palmer said.

Then, before Ariana could even absorb his words, he'd grabbed her by the waist and tugged her into him. With his other hand he cupped the back of her head, leaned down, and touched his lips to hers. Ariana was so surprised she just melted into him and let him have his way with her for a good half a minute. Everything about him was so self-assured. The way he held her, the way he kissed her, the way his hand moved across her back. He was in charge, and Ariana felt safe. She felt like she belonged in those arms, as if she could stay there all day.

And then it was over. And along with the air between them, the import of what had just happened rushed over her. Palmer had just kissed her. Lexa's *boyfriend* had just kissed her. Right out here in the open in the middle of campus. Talk about losing control.

But damn, was Lexa a lucky girl.

Ariana's fingers fluttered to her tingling lips. Palmer kept one hand on her waist and glanced toward the pond.

"Yeah, that did it. Stalker boy is on the move," he said.

Ariana blinked. She had forgotten all about Hudson. But sure enough, there he was, hoofing it toward the parking lot. Thank God that was over. And she hadn't been forced to do anything unsavory. He was part of her past, and her past was not welcome here.

"Let's get you back to Cornwall," Palmer said with a Cheshire cat grin.

Ariana took a deep breath. She had to get control of herself here, get control of the situation. The other day Palmer had basically told her that he *couldn't* like her, that he wouldn't do that to Lexa, whom he loved. But now, here he was, kissing her like she was the only girl on Earth. Like Lexa didn't even exist.

Ignoring the fact that her whole body was still responding to his kiss, Ariana managed to take a step back. "What the hell was that?" she demanded.

Palmer's face fell. "What?"

"You just kissed me," Ariana blurted. "I thought you had a girl-friend. I thought you were all in love. You stood there in the boat-house acting all holier-than-thou like you're some perfect, stand-up guy and then you—"

"Whoa, whoa, *whoa*," Palmer said, holding up both hands. "I just did that to help you out. That's all that was."

"Oh, you're such a martyr," she said sarcastically, knowing full well he'd enjoyed the kiss as much as she had. "I'm sure Lexa would see it that way if she found out."

"Wait. You're not going to tell her, are you?" he said, his eyes sud-denly wide.

Ariana sighed. "No. Of course I'm not going to tell her. But it's not going to happen again."

Palmer looked momentarily, gratifyingly, disappointed. Ariana's heart flipped. She knew it. He *had* enjoyed it. Not that it mattered. Palmer was unavailable, untouchable, off limits. Lexa was too impor-tant.

But still. It was nice to be wanted.

"No. It's not gonna happen again," he said finally.

"Good. I think I can make it back to Cornwall on my own now, thanks," she said. "You should probably go find your actual girlfriend."

Then she turned and swiftly walked back to her dorm, already thinking ahead to a cold shower.

WORTHY

"Okay, people, listen up!" Tahira shouted, quieting the relatively boister-ous crowd of gold team members who had gathered around the fountain on Friday morning. Tahira was wearing a red top and red and purple sarong-style skirt with gold embellishments all over. Red, no doubt, because it was a power color, and she clearly lived to remind everyone that she was in charge. "I called this little impromptu meeting because you guys are slacking!" she shouted. "I need at least ten more volunteers to work the event tonight, and you can't slough this off on the freshmen and transfers. They are all accounted for already! So rise to the occasion, juniors and seniors. Show some freaking leadership skills already."

There were general groans and whispers among the crowd where Ariana stood with Brigit, Lexa, Soomie, and Landon.

"Yeah, Soom. Why don't you show some freaking leadership skills already?" Landon joked, running his hand up under Soomie's hair from behind and letting it all slide through his fingers.

Soomie blushed and knocked his hand away in a flirtatious gesture. "God! Quit doing that!"

"Why?" Landon teased, doing it again. "You have the softest damn hair on terra firma."

Soomie scoffed and rolled her eyes. "Because it tickles," she said, shoving him away again. Her blush was so bright she could have directed traffic with it. Ariana wondered what Maria would think if she were there. Then Soomie's BlackBerry beeped and she whipped it out and groaned. "Maria's nine-one-oneing me from the Hill. I'd better go. You girls coming?" she asked the group.

Ariana bit her tongue. She had a feeling that Maria was nowhere near the Hill, but had somehow seen what was going on and stopped it. Nice play.

"She didn't text me," Lexa said, checking her phone. "You go. Let us know if she needs more backup."

"Okay," Soomie said reluctantly, backing away from Landon. "See you later?" she said, raising her eyebrows.

"Actually, I'll come with," Landon said, pushing his hands into the front pockets of his jeans.

Soomie lit up at his words, even though Ariana was sure that Landon's offer was born out of concern for Maria rather than the desire to stay with Soomie. The two of them strolled off together.

"You guys wanna bounce?" Brigit suggested. "I'm sick of listening to this crap already."

Suddenly, Ariana's phone beeped and, against her better judgment, she looked at the screen. The text was from Kaitlynn. It read, simply:

$$$???

Ariana's heart filled with dread for the hundredth time that week. She snapped the phone shut.

"Was that Maria?" Lexa asked.

"No. Just spam," Ariana replied. Then she glanced at Brigit. "You know, you should work the tables with us tonight. It'll be fun," she said with a forced grin.

If the plan that Ariana's brain was slowly forming was going to work, she would need Brigit there tonight.

"Yes! You totally should," Lexa put in.

Ariana smiled. Lexa's support was a helpful surprise.

Brigit scoffed from the back of her throat. "That would be a 'no way,'" she said, toying with a bangle bracelet. "I helped Soomie with the debate research specifically because I did not want to help Tahira."

"Don't think of it as helping Tahira—think of it as helping the team. Right, Lex?" Ariana said, glancing past Brigit at Lexa.

Lexa smiled at having her own words repeated back to her. "Right. Come on, Brigit, keep us company. If nothing else, it'll be fun just to see all those girls screaming all over Landon."

Brigit considered this. "That *would* be amusing. And good stuff for my blog."

"Your blog?" Ariana asked.

Brigit nodded excitedly. "Me and a bunch of other royals all blog on tiaradish.com. It's way fun. You should check it out."

"So you're in?" Lexa asked.

"I'm in," Brigit said. Then she looked up at Tahira and raised her hand. "I'm in!"

Tahira scrunched her nose. "Fine," she said, making a note on her clipboard. "But now I'm really scraping the bottom of the barrel here, people."

A few girls nearby laughed and two pink spots appeared on Brigit's cheeks. She rolled her eyes and turned to walk away. Lexa and Ariana followed, leaving Tahira and her pleas for volunteers behind.

"Don't let her get to you, Bridge," Lexa said, putting her hand on Brigit's back.

"She's not. I just have to go. I have to log my time on the treadmill," Brigit said quickly. "I'll see you guys later."

She took off for the state-of-the-art gymnasium at a speed walk. Ariana and Lexa paused to watch her go. "I don't know what I'm going to do with that girl," Lexa mused.

"What do you mean?" Ariana asked.

"Oh, nothing. It's just that Brigit can be her own worst enemy," Lexa replied. "With the eating thing and the Tahira thing. I mean, she's a junior now, and I've told her a million times that this is her last chance to get into the—"

Lexa abruptly stopped talking. Her gaze flicked to Ariana, and there was actual fear in her eyes. She swallowed hard and coughed, as if she'd just caught a fly with her tongue.

"Last chance to get into the what?" Ariana asked.

"I have to go," Lexa said, turning around and sprint-walking away, her brown hair flying.

Ariana scurried to catch up. Her heart was pounding a mile a minute. Suddenly she felt as if she was on the verge of something huge. Something that might explain away dozens of tiny, niggling little questions that had been biting at her brain for the past few days. Lexa made an abrupt turn and inexplicably headed for the library. The automatic doors slid aside to welcome her in and Ariana followed, shivering as the frigid air hit her bare arms.

"Lexa," Ariana hissed. "You have to tell me what you were about to say. I swear I won't tell anyone."

Lexa's expression was pained as she turned around. But Ariana wasn't about to give up. She hated knowing there was some huge secret out there and that she wasn't in on it. Lexa walked over to a display of information packets on the inside wall of the library and pretended to be engrossed. Ariana stepped up next to her and stared at the cover of a pamphlet about STDs and how to prevent them.

"You know you can trust me, Lex," she said under her breath. Lexa clutched her own arms. Ariana could practically *feel* the girl bursting to tell. "I promise."

"I am so, *so* stupid." Lexa took a deep breath. "Fine," she said, grabbing Ariana's hand.

She glanced around, then tugged Ariana into an alcove just outside a door marked EMPLOYEES ONLY. Once inside, she peeked her head out again and looked around, just to be sure no one had seen them, Ariana assumed. All the cloak and dagger was making her even more excited.

Lexa breathed in again, closed her eyes, and blew out the breath.

She looked Ariana in the eye. "Fine," she said again. "But you have to understand, I'm breaking about a thousand rules just mentioning this to you. If anyone *ever* finds out I told you—"

"I'll take it to the grave," Ariana promised.

"Okay." Lexa held her breath. When she spoke, it was at a whisper so quiet it could barely be heard above the whooshing air conditioner. "There are secret societies here at Atherton-Pryce. Three of them, to be exact. And right now, even as we speak, you're being evaluated."

Ariana's blood ran cold. Suddenly she felt as if someone was watching her from behind, and her spine curled. "*What?*"

"Each of the teams—gold, blue, gray—represents one of the societies," Lexa said in a rush. "You were picked to be on gold because you have some of the traits we—they—look for in a society member. Not everyone on gold is in the society, you understand. Only a select few people are asked to join. But if you're on gold, you're either in the society or you're being considered as a potential member."

Ariana nodded, even though her pulse was racing with terror. A secret society was *watching her every move?* Ariana had heard about these organizations in the past. They were powerful, selective, all-knowing. Suddenly every questionable move Ariana had made since arriving on campus flooded her memory. Stealing Christian's watch, sneaking back to the dorm during the professors' picnic to lift all that jewelry, going into D.C. to pawn the swag, meeting with Kaitlynn at the diner, *going to Kaitlynn's hotel to try to murder her.* Had they been watching her through all of this? Did they know what she was up to? Did they suspect she wasn't actually Briana Leigh?

Suddenly, Ariana felt light-headed. She leaned back against the cool cinder-block wall as waves of heated panic crashed over her.

"Ana? Are you okay?" Lexa asked, grabbing her wrist.

The cool touch of Lexa's fingers brought her back just a bit. Enough to remind herself to breathe.

In, one . . . two . . . three . . .

Out, one . . . two . . . three . . .

In, one . . . two . . . three . . .

Out, one . . . two . . . three . . .

She opened her eyes and focused on Lexa's pretty, pert face and the concern reflected there. Of course the secret society didn't know what she was up to. If someone had figured her out, surely they would have called the police. Ariana breathed in, let out a sigh, and felt much calmer.

"I'm fine," she said. "It's just a lot to take in."

Of course, now that she thought about it, it made perfect sense. Suddenly she understood all of Maria's thinly veiled comments—why she was always warning Ariana to do well, measure up, wear the right things, and contribute to Welcome Week. Why she and Tahira and Palmer knew who Ariana was when she first arrived on campus. They had heard of her because this secret society had decided to check her out for membership. Did that mean that they were all members? Even Tahira? That might better explain why Lexa tried to be nice to the girl. Why Palmer had chosen her to head up the fund-raiser over Brigit.

"Maria's in it, too, isn't she?" Ariana whispered. "And Palmer? Tahira?"

Lexa turned green. "I've already said too much. But listen, I really want you to get in. And I—"

"Am I doing okay?" Ariana asked, feeling suddenly desperate. "How is it decided? I mean, am I *going* to get in?"

Lexa shook her head. "I don't know. I can't tell you anything more."

I really want you to get in, Lexa had said. Was this why she was try-ing to be happy for Ariana over being chosen as cox for the crew race? Was the fact that Palmer had asked her to do something so important a good sign?

Deep breath, Ariana. Control.

"But Brigit's not in yet," Ariana mused. "That's what you started to say."

"No. She's not. And as a junior, this is her last chance," Lexa said sadly.

And I'm a junior, too, Ariana thought. *So this is my one and* only *chance.*

Ariana's mind reeled. If Brigit was having a hard time getting in, this must be a seriously exclusive secret society. The girl was an actual princess, for goodness' sake. If she couldn't get in, what were the requirements? Ariana's blood rushed so swiftly through her veins she started to tremble. She gripped her arm and held on for dear life, trying to keep herself in check. Whatever the requirements were, she would meet them. Lexa was in this society. Maria was too, she was sure. And Palmer, of course. Palmer was obviously some sort of leader. If they were all in, Ariana wanted in, too. *Needed* in. She had to prove that she was worthy.

The library door slid open and a few people walked through, their conversation hushed. Lexa's hand automatically clasped Ariana's shoulder.

"Briana Leigh, I need to know that you understand how important this is," Lexa said firmly, her tone more serious than Ariana had ever heard it before. "You can't tell anyone I told you. If you do I'm done and you'll never get in. Swear you'll never tell a soul."

Ariana looked into her friend's eyes. She felt that this was the most important conversation she'd had since arriving at Atherton-Pryce. Her schedule didn't matter; her friendships with Maria, Brigit, and Soomie didn't matter; everything with Palmer didn't matter. This moment, right here, right now, was going to define Briana Leigh Covington for the remainder of her career at this school. Maybe even beyond.

"I swear I will never tell a soul."

PURPOSE

Ariana strode across campus toward Cornwall, her hand still shaking as she punched in Kaitlynn's cell phone number. Secret societies at Atherton-Pryce Hall? What could be more perfect? The whole thing smacked of tradition and honor and intrigue—three of Ariana's favorite things. This morning, she had woken up wanting nothing more than to get rid of Kaitlynn and pass her last exam. Now all she could think about was this. Who else was in the society other than Lexa? Maria, she was sure. Soomie, most likely. The three of them were probably working hard behind the scenes to get Brigit accepted. Palmer, clearly. He was the president of the school and the captain of Team Gold. He was obviously in. But what about Landon? Maybe, if the fame thing had any cache. Tahira? There was a solid chance. She *had* known who Briana Leigh was before Ariana had introduced herself as such. Maria and Soomie could not like the girl and still be in the same society with her, right? Ariana was sure it happened all the time. God, maybe she would even have to start being nice to Tahira.

A shudder passed through Ariana at the thought. She wished Lexa would have just *told* her whether Tahira was in or not. Getting in would be so much easier if she knew who to focus her attention on. Or did they frown on people who sucked up to them? Ariana's heart felt panicky as she debated the issue. What did she have to do to get in?

Well, not get pegged as an imposter and arrested, for starters, she thought wryly.

She held the phone to her ear with a new sense of purpose coursing through her veins. Kaitlynn picked up on the first ring.

"Why, Briana Leigh!" she sang in her teasing voice. "To what do I owe the honor of—"

"Meet me tonight, the alleyway behind the American Museum of Pop Culture," Ariana said flatly. "Ten o'clock"

"Wow. Someone's just full of demands all of a sudden," Kaitlynn said, her voice much less buoyant. "Do you have the—"

"Trust me, after tonight, we won't be seeing each other again," Ariana said. Then she turned off the phone completely, before Kaitlynn could utter another word.

SMALL VICTORY

Ariana opened the thick wooden door to the Hill and stepped inside. The tall windows were partially obscured by heavy brocade drapes, and after the sunlit quad, it took a moment for her eyes to adjust to the relative darkness. The lounge was dotted with mismatched antique chairs, couches, and tables, and housed a snack bar and coffee counter against the far wall. All around the room students lounged together, read novels, played chess or cards. There wasn't a TV or video game in sight, and just being there made Ariana feel as if she had entered a time warp. If not for the hissing of the cappuccino machine, she could have been a nineteenth-century coed, surrounded by her fellow knowledge-seeking classmates.

She spotted Maria, Soomie, and Landon hanging out in a circle of seats near the windows, Maria on a cushy-looking couch by herself while Landon and Soomie were in separate chairs next to each other. Ariana took a deep breath. Now that she knew that Maria's suggestions and outright directions had been designed to *help* her, she wanted to be the girl's friend more than ever. Not just because it would help her solidify her place at APH, but because she was starting to actually like her. She was no-nonsense, which Ariana appreciated in a girl. Shaking her hair back from her shoulders, she strolled over and dropped down in one of the free chairs.

"Hey," she said, leaning back. "It's so hot out there I thought I was going to melt."

"You should have an iced coffee," Soomie said, taking a sip of her own. "Cools you right off."

Maria simply stretched her arms above her head and yawned, not even bothering to acknowledge her.

"What's up, Ana?" Landon said, tilting his head against the back of his chair and looking at her through his lashes. "I sent you some files this morning. You listened to them yet?"

"Sorry. Haven't had a chance," Ariana replied, lifting her hair from the back of her neck to fan her skin.

"Your loss," he said.

"Well, maybe if you go up there and get me an iced latte I'll give them a try," Ariana replied.

She saw Soomie and Maria exchange a startled look. Ariana was flirting with their boy. Or Soomie's boy, as far as Soomie knew. Landon, oblivious to any games being played, simply smiled.

"I'm on it," he said, rising languidly from his seat. "You ladies need anything?"

"I'm good," Maria said, waving a hand at her espresso.

"I'll come with you," Soomie suggested predictably.

And then, just as Ariana had intended, she and Maria were left alone. Ariana turned her knees toward Maria's couch as Maria reached for her bag and extracted a *W* magazine.

"So, what was the nine-one-one?" Ariana asked.

"It was nothing," Maria said, flipping a page blithely. "I'm in this regional ballet company and I just found out I have to be a marching soldier *again* this year. I was hoping to move up to Sugarplum Fairy, but what are you gonna do?"

"That sucks," Ariana said, crooking her arms over the arm of her chair. "Are you sure it wasn't just that you saw Soomie and Landon flirting and wanted to get her away from him?"

Maria froze, but to her credit, didn't look up. "What is your obsession with me and Landon?"

"I know what it's like," Ariana said, lowering her voice as some senior boys walked by, headed for the coffee counter. "The whole forbidden-love thing. I've done it, believe me."

Her mind lingered for a moment on an image of Thomas Pearson, his blue eyes mischievous as he smiled at her from across the dining hall. She allowed herself one nostalgic pang, then let him disappear into the ether.

Maria started turning pages again, but slowly, and her eyes were unfocused.

"I know it's not your friends who disapprove, because Soomie talks about nothing but him and no one seems to care. So what is it . . . your family?" Ariana asked.

Finally, Maria looked up. Her expression was guarded. Ariana's
heart tap-danced around in her chest. She was getting somewhere.

"Can I tell you something I haven't told anyone?" Ariana breathed,
her fingers gripping the armrest.

"That's your prerogative," Maria said.

"I was engaged. Over the summer, my boyfriend asked me to
marry him and I said yes," Ariana told her, thinking back to Téo's
ever-so-public proposal to Briana Leigh in the middle of a street fair.
"But when my grandmother found out, she freaked. She told me that
if I didn't break up with him, she'd disinherit me."

Maria leaned forward slightly, and Ariana knew she had struck a
nerve. This story sounded familiar to Maria. Very familiar.

"So what'd you do?" Maria asked.

Ariana leaned back in her chair. She sighed and looked down at
her lap, toying with her fingers. "I broke up with him. It was the hard-
est thing I've ever had to do. He was the love of my life."

Maria looked over her shoulder at the coffee counter. Ariana
watched her features tighten, as if the very idea of saying good-bye
to Landon was passing through her consciousness. Then she glanced
back at Ariana.

"You were weak," she said.

Ariana felt defensive and straightened her back. "I don't see it that
way. It might sound terrible, but she won't live forever. And then we'll
get back together."

"If he waits for you," Maria shot back.

"Oh, he'll wait," Ariana lied. If what Hudson had said about Téo was true, the boy had already forgotten about Briana Leigh ten times over.

Maria smirked, closing her magazine and crooking her legs up on the couch. "Well, my father's still pretty young, so if I go with your plan I'll be eighty before Landon and I can be together."

"So it's your dad," Ariana said.

With a deep sigh, Maria turned to check Landon and Soomie's progress once again. They had just reached the front of the line and were placing their order.

"Lexa is the only person who knows this," she said, twisting her hair around her finger. "And I'm only telling you because you trusted me with your story. But I swear to God, Ana, if you tell *anyone*, you will regret it."

Ariana held her breath. She thought of the secret society and wondered if Maria would use it to make good on her threat. Not that Ariana had any intention of spilling whatever secret Maria was about to tell. Not if discretion would get her that much closer to her goals.

"I won't tell yours if you won't tell mine," she replied.

"Fine. Landon and I have been together for over a year. Secretly. Because I'm not allowed to date until I'm in college," Maria told her. "Which is especially cruel considering I don't want to go to college," she added, looking up at the ceiling in frustration. "If Landon were anyone else, we'd just have your standard, secret, only-on-campus romance, but with him, things are tricky."

Ariana nodded. "Because every move he makes is photographed and documented."

"Exactly," Maria said. She curled her hair into a tight twist, then released it. It uncoiled over her shoulder. "If we ever even touched each other in public, word could get out and the tabloids would be all over us. Which means my dad would find out and instantly transfer me to some all-girl school in Bulgaria. Truly."

"But what about Soomie?" Ariana asked, glancing up as Soomie and Landon gathered a couple of napkins and an extra straw. Landon carried a tray full of pastries while Soomie had Ariana's drink.

"Yeah, that's a wrinkle I wasn't expecting," Maria whispered. "I told Landon not to lead her on, but he's a natural flirt, so . . ."

"So when you saw him playing with her hair on the quad, you nine-one-oned her," Ariana said knowingly.

"I was going to come join you guys, but then I saw the look on her face. . . . She was so excited," Maria said quickly. "I feel so—"

"Shh!" Ariana said, noticing that the pair was getting dangerously close.

Maria fell silent. She flipped a page in her magazine, looking for all the world like she hadn't uttered a word, let alone had a tense conversation, while her two friends were gone.

"Anyone up for a sugar rush?" Landon asked, placing the tray on the table.

"Iced latte," Soomie said, handing Ariana her drink with a smile.

"Thanks, Soomie," Ariana said, making sure not to pay any added attention to Landon. She didn't want Soomie to think she was *actually* interested in the guy. That would just make this already messy situation that much messier.

Soomie perched on her chair and looked up at Landon expectantly, but he chose to sit on the empty end of Maria's couch rather than reclaim the chair next to Soomie's. Maria gave him a quick smile and went right back to her reading. Landon reached for a scone, tore off a piece, and handed it to Maria, who popped it right into her mouth without even thinking. Soomie cleared her throat.

"So, Landon, ready to greet your adoring fans tonight?" she asked.

"Guy's gotta do what a guy's gotta do," he said, slumping down in his seat and letting his legs fall open. He leaned forward for a donut, ripped off half, and stuffed it in his mouth. "You coming, Ria? Maybe I'll let you be my personal assistant for the night."

Ariana's heart skipped. Landon was clearly trying to find a way to spend more time with his girlfriend. She relished the fact that she knew this and Soomie didn't. But Maria simply sighed and lifted the magazine to her face, taking a quick whiff of a perfume ad.

"And watch a bunch of pathetic tweeners throw themselves at you? No, thanks. I've already done my duty for gold. I think I'll stay home and get in some time at the barre."

Landon didn't seem surprised or even put out by her rejection. He tore off another piece of the scone and handed it to her. Once again, she ate it. This was an interesting development.

"I can be your assistant for the night," Soomie offered. "I'm very organized."

Maria and Landon exchanged the briefest of looks. There was a warning in Maria's eyes, but Ariana could tell that Landon felt trapped by the offer. Ariana jumped at the chance to make herself useful—even valuable—to Maria. To make her feel confident in her decision to let Ariana in.

"I thought you already told Christian he could be your PA," Ariana said, taking a sip of her coffee. "He was all excited about using his position as your right-hand man to impress the ladies."

Landon looked confused for a split second, but then jumped right onboard Ariana's lie. "That's right. Sorry, Soomie. Gotta help a brother out."

Soomie's disappointment was evident, but she lifted one shoulder and grabbed a donut from the tray. "No biggie. It'll give me more time to help Tahira with the tallies. I know you're going to make tons of cash," she said with a smile.

Ariana felt a surge of fear at the idea that Soomie might be keeping running tallies of the money that night, but she let it pass. It wouldn't change her plan. Because she had no backup.

"Whatever I can do to help the team," Landon said, lifting a palm.

As Soomie became consumed with her BlackBerry, Maria glanced up at Ariana and gave her a grateful look. Ariana smiled in response. This tête-à-tête couldn't have gone more perfectly if she'd written the script herself. She sat back with a contented sigh to savor her latest victory with a side of iced latte.

LANDON MANIA

That night, Ariana fully understood why Soomie and the others had been so shocked that Ariana had never heard of Landon Jacobs. The scene at the Pop Culture Museum looked like something out of a big-budget Hollywood disaster movie where an entire city was trying to evacuate through one gate. But in this case, everyone was crowding *into* the museum and toward Landon. All the girls were screaming. Some of them were crying. Ariana saw at least three of them faint. One girl scratched another girl's face when she tried to cut in line, and someone was carried out on a stretcher, but there were so many bodies between Ariana and the door, she couldn't get a good look at who it was or what had happened to them.

Landon stood on a large stage at the front of the room for his photo ops, backed by about a hundred plasma screens suspended from the wall. Each screen played his latest video, which for some reason featured both cheerleaders and geisha girls. All the waitresses circulating at the event were dressed in the same way as the girls in the video, right down to their elaborate eye shadow and supersprayed hairstyles. They served free hors d'oeuvres and flavored sodas to the kids, and ten-dollars-and-up drinks to the adults, who, as Tahira had predicted, all seemed to be in serious need of a little something to take the edge off. On the screens half a dozen of the geishas and cheerleaders were fawning all over Landon, who was shirtless in the clip. Shirtless and, in Ariana's view, kind of scrawny and unsexy.

"This is ridiculous," Ariana said, shouting to be heard over the din of voices and cries and screams and applause, not to mention the insanely loud rock music that was being pumped through dozens of huge speakers. "I'm sorry, but what's so great about Landon? He seems like a totally average person to me."

"I know, right?" Lexa said, taking a twenty-dollar bill from one of the dozens of girls trying to crowd their table. She quickly made change and handed it over, then stamped the girl's hand. "I wonder if they would be so excited about him if they knew he can literally spend an hour picking his toenails."

"Ew," Ariana said. She glanced over at Landon as he slung his arm around a bawling redheaded girl and smirked for the camera, tilting his head so that his hair fell over his eye just so. "How do *you* know that?"

"We all hit Saint-Tropez together last year for Columbus Day weekend," Lexa said, leaning toward Ariana. "I *saw* him do it right there on the beach."

Ariana bit back a gag.

"Here you go!" a tall, stocky girl with long brown hair appeared in front of the table with a plate full of food. "I got three of each of the passed hors d'oeuvres."

"Thanks, Melanie. I'm starved," Lexa said. "Ana, have you met Melanie?"

Melanie turned to Ariana with a smile. "No. Nice to meet you," Ariana said. "Snack duty, I assume?"

"That's me," Melanie replied. "Let me know if you guys need anything else!"

Then she quickly turned and made her way back into the fray. Lexa picked up the tiniest hamburger Ariana had ever seen and took a bite.

"Tahira outdid herself with the food," she said. "*Très* smart going for finger foods that the masses could recognize instead of getting fancy. Try one!"

Ariana grabbed a teeny grilled cheese wedge and popped it in her mouth, where it melted on her tongue. "Not bad," she conceded.

"Okay! Okay! Get off!" Brigit shouted, elbowing some brace-faced girl aside as she returned from the bathroom. She shuddered, straightened the sparkly cardigan sweater she wore over her black dress, and stepped up to Ariana's side. Without a second thought she grabbed one of the grilled cheese triangles and ate it. "It's a good thing I offered up my security detail to watch the cash tonight. If Rudolpho had been out here with me, he would have flattened that girl!"

"Are you okay?" Lexa asked, checking Brigit over. The second her friends' backs were turned, Ariana slipped a stack of bills out of the cash box and quickly shoved it into her bag at her feet. She'd been doing this all night whenever no one was looking, but every time she did it, she held her breath, which was starting to make her feel light-headed. Still, by the time Brigit and Lexa turned around again, she was sitting up straight, taking another twenty-five dollars from a young girl with pigtails, and stamping the girl's hand with a big purple *L*.

"There you go!" Ariana said brightly. "Just show that stamp to the guy at the front of the line so he knows you've paid for your photo op!"

"Do you *really* go to school with him?" the girl asked, her eyes wide as she clutched a *Seventeen* magazine with Landon on the cover.

"Yeah," Ariana said with a nod. "I really do."

"You are *soooo* lucky," the girl behind her said. "I would *kill* to go to school with him."

And I would kill to get to stay *at that school,* Ariana thought, placing her foot atop the bag that held every cent she had collected for Kait-lynn so far. Inside her suede hobo was a collapsible duffel, and inside that was the money she had earned by pawning off all the things she had stolen—something she hadn't heard about again since that one time in the dining hall, thank the universe for small favors. Every time she felt even the slightest bit of hesitation over what she had to do tonight, she reminded herself of all the risks she had taken already, just to get the piddling amount of money that was in her bag. If she didn't see her plan through, all that would have been for nothing. Besides, after tonight, the money would be out of her hands, and there would be zero evidence that she was the culprit. She just had to get through the event.

"Thanks!" Brigit said to another paying customer. "Grab his butt! He likes that!" she joked.

Ariana and Lexa laughed as Brigit pulled the metal cash box toward her. She checked inside and grinned. "We are *so* going to win."

"I know. We have taken in an obscene amount of cash," Lexa replied.

Suddenly, Adam slid in behind the table and lifted a hand in greeting. "Hey," he said, breathless. "Need me to run anything to the bank room?"

He already had a cash box tucked under one arm and his face was red from the exertion of fighting through the crowd for the millionth time that night. The kid was working harder than anyone else in the museum.

"Yeah. This one's full," Brigit said, slapping the metal box closed and handing it over. "Actually, I think I'll come with you and check on Rudolpho."

"Okay," Adam said with a smile. "You can protect me from the crazies."

"Protect *you*?" Brigit said, turning to look at him. "Is that a crack at my weight?"

Adam's eyes went wide. "No! No! I swear. It's a crack at my total weaklingness," he replied awkwardly.

"Weaklingness, huh?" Brigit narrowed her eyes, but then smiled. "Okay, then. I'll protect you."

The two of them took off together, sidestepping a group of chattering girls. "The bank room" was their nickname for the coatroom area, where Brigit's bodyguard, Rudolpho, had been posted to collect all the money from the various stations and the bar throughout the night and pool it all together into larger bags. Adam had been making runs to the various stations and bringing the cash back to Rudolpho, who didn't seem all that psyched about his reassignment. Brigit had explained that on normal days, inside the protective walls at Atherton-Pryce, she didn't need someone watching over her, but whenever she went out for a big public event like this one, the king and queen insisted she take along a guard. But she had Rudolpho wrapped around her pinky finger, so she was able to convince him not to breathe down her neck all night, and to do a much more important job instead—guard the money with his life.

While the very thought of the many security guards hired by the museum made Ariana sweat in a very unappealing way, the fact that Brigit's own detail was watching the money was actually a boon for Ariana. She had a feeling it was going to make her plan *easier* to execute rather than harder. If she could just get all the pawns to line up as she'd planned.

Unlike Brigit, Tahira had gone for a full security detail—probably because it made her look important. As she circulated the room, she was flanked by two burly bodyguards and turned heads wherever she went as those not-in-the-know wondered who she was and whether she was famous. Ariana had heard more than a few jealous little girls wonder whether Tahira might be Landon's girlfriend, and if he might have hired the bodyguards to take care of her.

Across the room, Ariana saw Tahira pause to talk to some parents, making sure their drinks from the cash bar were full and encouraging them to spend on their daughters. Girl really knew how to glean every last dollar out of these people.

"They'd make a cute couple, wouldn't they?" Lexa mused.

"Who?" Ariana asked, her thoughts still dawdling on Tahira and Landon.

"Brigit and Adam," Lexa said, opening a new cash box and making change for a pair of twin girls. "The princess and the pauper? It's a classic."

Ariana smirked. She didn't bother to point out that *The* Prince *and the Pauper* was not about a romantic couple, but about two guys. "I guess I could see it. They're both so . . . innocent."

"I know, right? Maybe we should hook that up," Lexa said, her eyes bright with possibility.

Ariana's heart fluttered at the very idea of being included in a matchmaking scheme with Lexa. It felt so best-friendy. "Yeah. We definitely should."

Tahira was wending her way closer as she schmoozed, her security detail making sure the masses gave her a wide berth.

"I wonder what it's like to have bodyguards," Ariana said.

"I bet it sucks," Lexa replied. "Imagine having no control over your own life?"

Yeah. I kind of know what that's like, Ariana thought, checking her watch. Her heart skipped a surprised beat. It was already eight-thirty. Time flew when a thousand crazed girls were screaming in one's face.

Kaitlynn would be in the alley outside in exactly an hour and a half. Ariana's stomach clenched and her palms started to sweat. She knew that the money at her feet wasn't nearly enough to pay Kaitlynn off. If she was going to succeed, she was going to have to get into the bank room. This was where Brigit's guard was going to come in handy. The risk was insanely high. And if she was caught . . .

In, one . . . two . . . three . . .

Out, one . . . two . . . three . . .

Ariana breathed in and out through her nose, clutching her forearm under the table. No. She was not going to get caught. This was her one and only chance to hold on to her new life. She had to think positively.

"Blue and gray are so going down," Lexa sang as she continued stamping hands.

Ariana simply smiled and tried to ignore the knot of guilt lodged in her stomach. What if gold lost because of her? What if she got caught? She'd be blackballed from the secret society for sure. But then again, she'd be expelled—or arrested—before that had a chance to happen. She could lose everything as a result of this scheme—her home, her friends, her education, her future. But if she *didn't* steal the money, it wouldn't matter whether or not she got expelled, because it would all be over anyway.

In a way, Ariana had both nothing, and everything, to lose.

If we don't take this event, we can still win the crew race and get into Privilege House, Ariana reasoned with herself. *We only have to win two out of three events. And they won't find out what I've done. They won't. I've been so careful. . . .*

Of course, the next step was going to be messy, but there was nothing she could do about that now. It was her only hope. Ariana glanced back at the bank room, keeping an eye on Brigit's position, then scanned the room to make sure she knew where Tahira was as well. She checked her watch again, took in some cash, stamped a few hands. Another hour or so and it would be on to plan B. She just hoped that no one would be hurt. Unless, of course, they absolutely had to be.

PLAN B

Ariana checked her watch. It was a quarter to ten. Go time. She glanced at Lexa, felt a squeeze of guilt over what she was about to do, and let it pass. Above all, she had to stay at Atherton-Pryce Hall. This was the only way.

"I so have to pee," Ariana announced, bouncing her legs up and down under the table for effect.

"Don't leave me," Lexa said with a laugh, clutching Ariana's arm. "I can't do this alone."

"Okay. I'll wait for Brigit to get back," Ariana replied, trying to sound reluctant. In truth, she was not planning on going anywhere until after Brigit returned from her latest trip with Adam to the cash box—a run that Lexa had suggested they continue to make together. Not until after plan B was in full effect. "Oh, hey. There's Tahira," Ariana said, lifting her head as the Dubai princess passed within a few yards of their table. "Let's see how we're doing." Ariana stood up and shouted over the heads of the thronging girls. "Tahira! Come here a sec!" she shouted, waving her hand.

Tahira looked over with a smile that fell away the moment she saw that it was Ariana who was summoning her. She said something to one of her bodyguards and all three of them moved toward the table, parting the crowd like the Red Sea. As they arrived Ariana glanced out of the corner of her eye and saw Brigit returning. She bit back a triumphant smile. This was going to work. It had to.

"Hey, Lexa," she said in a normal tone of voice. Then she lifted one eyebrow at Ariana and, in a derisive tone added, "*Love.*"

It was interesting that Tahira didn't seem to mind talking down to Lexa's friends right in front of her—and how Lexa didn't often feel the need to defend those friends. It was almost as if they had some kind of unspoken agreement allowing such behavior. Yet another mystery Ariana would have to get to the bottom of, if she managed to pull this plan off and remain at APH.

"What is it?" Tahira asked, crossing her arms over her chest. She and her bodyguards formed a complete wall between the table and the paying customers, causing a pause in the commerce for the moment. "I have guests to attend to."

"I know. I won't keep you long," Ariana said, all sugary sweetness. "We just wanted to get the update. How are we doing?"

Tahira leaned toward the table as Brigit and Adam arrived, her smile totally self-satisfied. "Well, we have already taken in well over a million dollars," she said in a whisper-shout. "That's more money than gold has ever raised in the past, and we're only halfway through the night."

"Whoa. Are you serious?" Adam said, as if it had never occurred to him that they could raise that much.

Ariana froze up a bit, realizing that it was not good that Tahira was so very aware of the dollar amounts raised. But she couldn't think about that now. She had to get on with the plan.

"A million? Really? That's it?" she said, trying to sound both concerned and amused.

Everyone looked at Ariana as if she were speaking in tongues. Even the bodyguards changed expression for a split second before returning to their disinterested glares.

"What do you mean, *that's it?*" Tahira snapped, lifting her palms so that her gold bangles clinked together. "Did you not hear what I just said? We've already broken records."

"Oh," Ariana said faux-innocently. "It just seemed like Brigit's idea would have raised twice as much. Don't you think, Brigit?"

Everyone looked at the Norwegian princess. Her jaw dropped slightly at having been put on the spot, but then she glanced at Tahira and assumed her defiant stance. "Probably," she sniffed. Ariana widened her eyes at Brigit, telling her to be strong. "Definitely, I mean. I definitely would have raised more. And I wouldn't have had to rely on the fame of one of my fellow students to do it."

"Girls," Lexa said in a warning tone. "Do we have to do this here?"

Unfortunately, yes. It has *to be here,* Ariana thought.

"Oh, really?" Tahira said, ignoring Lexa and walking around the table. "So tell me, what were these brilliant ideas that would have raised zillions?" she demanded. "Because apparently Palmer didn't agree that any of them were better than mine."

Ariana bit the inside of her lip. This was going even better than she'd hoped. She picked up her hobo bag from under the table. It weighed a lot more than it had when she'd arrived.

"I still have to go to the bathroom," Ariana whispered to Lexa, a pained expression on her face. "Do you mind?"

"No! Go! Go ahead," Lexa said, shooing her away. "Adam will stay with me and help keep the peace, right, Adam?"

Put on the spot, Adam hesitated. "Uh, sure."

"That's because Palmer thought it would be amusing to put his buddy Landon in the spotlight for a night," Brigit said to Tahira. "All you did was play to the boys'-club mentality. That's why he went with you. Did you have your little boy toy Rob whispering in his ear too? Can you get anything done without a man helping you?"

Tahira let out an indignant gasp. "Take that back!"

"What are you going to do, have your *male* bodyguards beat me up?" Brigit shot back.

As Ariana walked away, total commotion exploded behind her. Lexa grabbed Brigit's arm as Tahira lunged forward. The bodyguards attempted to hold the Dubai princess back, but somehow Brigit and Tahira ended up on the floor, grappling with each other as Adam tried in vain to coax Brigit up. Girls screamed for a whole new reason, and a couple of boyfriends who had been dragged along whipped out their phones to take pictures. Ariana was halfway to the "bathroom," which was conveniently located right near the bank room, when Brigit's security guard came rushing out to help her, leaving the money unattended.

Perfection.

Ariana had known that Brigit's bodyguard was going to come in handy. Any random security guard might have stuck with the money, but Brigit's personal guard couldn't stand by and let his princess get drop-kicked by Tahira. Rudolpho would definitely be occupied for the next few minutes.

Her heart pounding at an insane beat, Ariana slid behind the coat-check counter and paused. At her feet were no fewer than five canvas money bags stuffed to their brims. Part of her wanted to just grab one and run, but if one of the bags went missing it would be way too obvious. Checking to make sure the riot was still in full swing, Ariana dropped to her knees, whipped the collapsible duffel bag from the inside of her hobo, and loosened the strings on the first canvas bag. She reached inside and grabbed fistfuls of cash, stuffing them into her duffel. When she felt like she'd made a dent, she quickly reclosed the bag and opened the next one, following the same pattern. Once she had gotten through three bags, she felt she had done all she could without both screwing Team Gold into the ground, and making it totally obvious that there was money missing. She zipped up her duffel, peeked over the edge of the counter, and froze. Order had been restored. Rudolpho was checking Brigit over to make sure she was unharmed. Any second they were both going to realize that the money was not being watched.

"Damn," Ariana said under her breath.

She slid out from behind the counter and ducked down the hallway just as Brigit pointed toward the coatroom. Ariana didn't wait to see whether Brigit or her guard had noticed her. She simply kept moving, down the hall, through a metal door, down a set of stairs, and out to the alleyway, feeling the whole way that at any moment someone was going to grab her shoulder. It wasn't until she was through the door and it had slammed behind her that she started to breathe again.

Kaitlynn stepped away from the far wall. Ariana was momentarily startled, but she recovered quickly. She didn't even give the girl a chance to speak.

"Here," she said, dropping the duffel at her feet on the silty ground. "Here's your money. Now leave me alone."

Kaitlynn wore black leggings, an oversize flannel shirt, and a torn denim jacket. She nudged the bag with the toe of her clunky black boot as if she was checking to make sure it wasn't full of snakes.

"It's all there?" she said dubiously. "One million dollars."

Ariana sighed in an exasperated way. She could just lie and say that yes, it was all there, but she was sure that Kaitlynn would be calling her up tomorrow, making more threats.

"It's close, okay? It's enough."

Kaitlynn smirked. "Let's see how close."

Then the girl sat down cross-legged, right there on the cold, dirty alley floor, and started to count.

"You're going to do this here?" Ariana demanded, glancing around.

"No. *We* are," Kaitlynn replied. "Sit."

"I can't sit in this dress," Ariana said, looking down at her cream-colored Ralph Lauren. "Besides, I have to get back."

"First you stiff me and now you're bailing? I don't think so," Kaitlynn said. "Sit."

Holding back the fury that was building inside of her, Ariana glanced around and spotted a metal door on the other side of the alley. She walked over and peeked through the cracked glass window. Inside was a set of industrial-looking stairs and a single, flickering lightbulb protruding from the wall. Ariana tried the door, which squealed as it opened.

"In here," she said.

Kaitlynn rolled her eyes, but picked up the bag and strolled over.

"What if someone comes down?" she said.

"Then we'll deal with it," Ariana replied through her teeth. "It's a lot better than being out here in the open where a police car could drive by or a security guard could come out for a cigarette."

Kaitlynn walked inside and dropped down on the bottom step to resume counting. Ariana reluctantly joined her, crouching to the dirty linoleum floor and folding the skirt of her dress up over her thighs to keep it from getting smudged. She reached into the bag, pulled out a handful of cash, and started to count, keeping one ear on the stairs above for the sound of a slamming door or a footfall. Hours seemed to pass. Days. There was a ton of money in smallish bills. But they got through every single dollar. And when they were done, Kaitlynn did the tally.

"Nine hundred thousand twenty dollars," she said, looking up at Ariana. "You were right. It's close."

But was it close enough? Ariana couldn't bring herself to ask the question. Couldn't fathom letting herself sound that desperate. Kaitlynn slowly placed all the stacks of cash into the duffel bag. Then she zipped it up, shouldered the strap, and stood. She offered Ariana her hand, but Ariana ignored her. For a long few moments Kaitlynn just stood there, silently regarding Ariana. With each second that passed, Ariana felt more and more trapped, more and more excruciatingly anxious.

Just go away. Get out of my life, she willed Kaitlynn. *What the hell is the difference between nine hundred K and one million?*

Finally, Kaitlynn spoke. "A hundred thousand dollars is a lot of money, Ariana."

The fury inside Ariana exploded. Her vision clouded over and her fingers curled into fists. She bit down on her tongue so hard she drew blood.

"Just *take it*!" she said through her teeth, her eyes so wide it was painful. "Just take it and get on the freaking plane and go!"

Kaitlynn smiled. She shook her head and tsked softly under her breath. "You just don't get it. We had a deal. And if you don't get me the rest of the money by tomorrow morning, Ariana . . ." She pulled her cell phone out of her pocket, hit a button, and held it up. The screen read *D.C. Police.* "I have them on speed dial."

Ariana shook from head to toe. "I hate you. I hate you more than I've ever hated anyone in my life."

In that moment, Ariana actually felt this was true. She hated Kaitlynn more than she'd hated Dr. Meloni. More than she'd hated Reed Brennan, who had stolen Thomas Pearson from her, and Mel Johnston, who had threatened to take him away. More than she'd hated Thomas in those fleeting moments when she'd allowed his betrayal to burn under her skin.

Kaitlynn's smile widened, as if she was proud to hear it. "Wow. With you, that's really saying something." She patted Ariana twice on the shoulder. It was all Ariana could do not to reach up and twist the girl's arm out of its socket. "Tomorrow morning, *B.L.* Give me a call."

Then she turned and shoved through the door. Ariana stepped into the alley and watched her go. Watched her disappear around the corner, taking with her all of Ariana's hopes for the future. Ariana's shoulders slumped. Every muscle in her body felt weak as she crashed from her adrenaline high, and her eyes welled with desperate tears.

All that work. All that sneaking and stealing and praying that she wouldn't get caught. All of it was going to be for nothing. Because there was absolutely no way she was going to get her hands on a hundred thousand dollars by tomorrow morning.

No way in hell.

PLAN C

By the time the Atherton-Pryce Hall shuttle buses dropped Ariana and her friends off in the parking lot in front of the dorms, Ariana was physically and emotionally exhausted. Everyone around her was in a celebratory mood, telling stories about crazy things the fans had done and projecting the amount of money they'd hauled in, but all Ariana could think about was the fact that at this time tomorrow, her life would be over.

Should she pack up tonight and flee? Wait until first light? And where would she go? She had no one. Not a friendly place on earth. She supposed she could go back to Texas for a few days. Briana Leigh's grandmother had liked "Emma Walsh." Perhaps she would put her up for a little while, but if Kaitlynn told the police everything, wouldn't they look for her there? Ariana suddenly felt exhausted and backbreakingly sad. How could she have failed? All that risk, and her reward was going to be a one-way ticket back to the Brenda T. The very idea of being locked up inside those cinder-block walls again made her blood curdle and her heart pound with desperation.

There was no way she was going back there. She would die first.

But that left only one option. She was going to have to throw herself at Kaitlynn's feet and beg for mercy. The idea brought bile into the back of Ariana's throat, but it was all she had.

"Well, everyone, thanks for all your hard work," Tahira said as the students gathered in the parking lot. "We'll be counting up our take tomorrow, but be assured, we kicked blue and gray's ass tonight!"

Everyone cheered and whooped. Ariana forced a smile for Lexa and Brigit's sake. Brigit was the only one aside from Ariana who wasn't cheering. She just stared Tahira down like she was out for blood. Ariana felt a twinge of guilt over having made the situation between the two princesses even more strained, but it was worth it. Or it would have been worth it if she'd managed to steal another hundred thousand. If only she'd stayed behind that counter for another thirty seconds. Would she have been able to grab enough money to make this all go away?

The regret weighed on her shoulders like the weight of the world was crushing her.

"Come on," Lexa said, slinging her arms around Ariana and Brigit as the crowd broke up. "Let's raid my duty-free snack stash and celebrate."

They were just approaching the alcove outside the door of Cornwall when Tahira and Allison obnoxiously cut in front of them and opened the door. "Thanks for all your help, *Love*," Tahira said sarcastically over her shoulder.

Something inside of Ariana snapped. She did not need this bitch mocking her on top of everything else. And suddenly, it was as if a door opened inside her mind and the perfect idea came popping out with a big "ta-da!" This was it. This was her salvation.

"Okay, *Princess*," she said, extricating herself from Lexa's arm. She stepped up to Tahira in the doorway, facing off with her from mere inches away. "You, me, rematch, tomorrow."

"Sweet!" Brigit said, cheering up considerably.

Tahira laughed in an obnoxious way. "Please. Don't humiliate yourself *again*."

"Forget humiliation," Ariana said as a crowd of Cornwall girls formed on the patio, unable to get inside because she and Tahira were blocking the door. "I'm so confident I'm going to beat you I'll wager . . . let's see . . . a hundred thousand dollars on it."

A hushed whisper skittered through the crowd of onlookers. Lexa's jaw dropped. "Ana, are you sure you want to—"

"You don't have access to that kind of cash," Tahira countered.

Ariana felt a bolt of fear. Tahira was, of course, correct on that score. She didn't even have access to a hundred dollars right then. But this was her last and only hope. The only way to avoid throwing herself at Kaitlynn's mercy. And she could beat Tahira. She knew she could. Especially when the alternative was jail and, potentially, death row.

"Don't I? Do you know who my father was?" Ariana shot back.

For the first time, Tahira broke eye contact, glancing at Allison as if looking for guidance.

She's scared, Ariana thought. *She knows I wouldn't bet that much money unless I knew I could win.* Ariana could practically hear Tahira weighing the pros and cons. The bragging rights and utter triumph if she won. The embarrassment if she lost. For a moment she was sure the girl was going to back down. Lose face now to save face later. But she couldn't let that happen. She *needed* Tahira's money.

"Ana. I don't know if this is such a good idea," Lexa said in her ear. Ariana ignored her. Maybe she would lose the chance to be in the secret society, but she'd get to keep her life.

"Oh, look, Brigit, the Dubai princess is scared!" she teased, earning a satisfying laugh from the crowd. "I thought you were the number one tennis goddess on the eastern seaboard."

"I am," Tahira said through her teeth. Ariana felt a sizzle of excitement and triumph as Tahira stood up straight. "Fine," she said. "Twelve noon on the court. You're on."

Twelve noon would be too late. Kaitlynn was expecting a call in the morning. "Make it eight," Ariana said with a smirk. "I like to get my ego-crushing done before breakfast."

FREEDOM WON

Tahira was sweating. Ariana could see it all the way from the opposite baseline. The fabric of her white tennis tank clung to her skin in unattractive splotches, and big, fat droplets wound their way down her forehead and into her eyes.

Ariana, meanwhile, was as cool as the other side of the pillow. It was Saturday morning, and today, Tahira was Love. And Ariana was more than happy to pass along the nickname. She was up one set to love and five games to one in the second set. All she had to do was close out the next two points, and the money would be hers. Freedom would be hers. Kaitlynn would be history.

"Are you ready? Because you can take a minute if you need to," Ariana said with false concern as she tossed the ball up and down in front of her. Brigit, Lexa, Maria, Soomie, and the rest of their friends laughed. Not Palmer, however. Although she was trying very hard not to care about that.

"Just serve the damn ball," Tahira replied, obviously fed up.

"If you insist."

Ariana tossed the ball up and slammed it across the net as hard as she could. Tahira lunged for it and just got her racket on it. The ball sailed back across the net and Tahira seemed as surprised as Ariana was that she'd had enough power to get it there. Ariana set herself up for a forehand and returned the ball to the opposite corner of the court, sending Tahira sprinting across the baseline. Once again, she managed to get her racket on the ball, but this time there was zero power on it. The ball hit the tape and bounced down on Tahira's side of the net.

"Yes," Ariana said through her teeth as her friends applauded. She looked over at the stands and relished in their cheers. Everyone but Lexa was going nuts. Lexa merely clapped politely, an anomaly that irked Ariana.

"That's forty to fifteen," Ariana called out. "This is match point."

"Thanks for stating the obvious," Tahira replied, her chest heaving as she stood up straight. "How about you just shut up and serve?"

"My pleasure," Ariana replied.

She bounced from foot to foot a few times, her energy mounting as Tahira's plummeted, as if she was somehow sucking the girl dry from across the court. She smiled to herself, relishing the moment. This was it. If she won this point, her life was saved. She tossed the ball up, pulled back, and rocketed it across the court.

Again, Tahira had to lunge. The ball glanced off the top edge of her racket, sailing high and arcing over the net.

"Shit!" Tahira shouted.

The girl knew it was going to go long. *Ariana* knew it was going to go long. Everyone in the *stands* knew it was going to go long. Even Sumit and his roommate Jonathan, who had offered to act as line judges, knew it was going to go long. Ariana's heart leapt with glee, but she jogged backward just in case. If she needed to return, she was going to return it right between the girl's eyes.

"Out!" Sumit shouted as the ball hit the ground at least a foot outside the line.

"Yes!" Ariana cheered as her friends jumped up and raced toward her.

Tahira let out a screech of frustration and slammed her thousand-dollar racket into the ground, breaking the frame in three places. She doubled over on the bench next to the court, hiding her face in her hands. She slapped Rob's hand away when he came to comfort her.

"Oh my God! You did it!" Brigit cried, throwing her arms around Ariana. "I *knew* you could do it!"

"Nice work, Ana," Maria said, nodding as she sipped her large espresso.

Lexa hugged Ariana as Soomie snapped a picture with her Black-Berry. "And the wicked witch goes down," Soomie said with a smile.

Ariana grinned at her friends, who had absolutely no idea how huge this win actually was. She had just saved her own life with a racket and a little green ball.

"Excuse me. I have some business to attend to," Ariana said, strolling away from them and over to Tahira. The girl was still bent at the waist, a towel wrapped around her shoulders, which she was holding against either side of her face. When she saw Ariana's sneakers in front of her, she simply stared at them for a moment, gathering herself.

"Do you have something for me?" Ariana said.

Tahira glared up at her. She reached into her tennis bag and pulled out her iPhone. Her eyes never left Ariana's as she held the phone to her ear.

"Yes, Daddy. It's me," Tahira said into the phone, tucking a stray lock of dark hair behind her ear. "Yes, I need a favor. I need a hundred thousand dollars to settle a bet."

Ariana held her breath. The girl was telling her father she'd wagered all that green? Was she insane? She could have at least come up with a good lie. No parent in his right mind would hand over that much money for a bet. Her skin prickled and already her mind started thinking three steps ahead, to new hair dye and the bus depot and a life on the run.

"Thanks, Daddy. Yes. I know," Tahira said. She held the phone away from her ear and looked at Ariana. "You'll have it tomorrow morning," she whispered, as her father continued to talk on the other end of the call.

Ariana blinked. The images of herself curled up in the back of a Greyhound, fending off smelly passengers on her way to Alabama or some such place disappeared in the wind. She couldn't believe that Tahira could actually get her hands on a hundred thousand dollars so easily. She still hated the girl, but she was impressed.

"In cash," Ariana said, figuring it couldn't hurt to ask.

Tahira rolled her eyes. "In cash, okay, Daddy?" she said into the phone. "Thanks. Love you, too. Kisses to Mom."

She pressed her thumb into the touch pad, then tossed the phone back into her bag and stood up. Face-to-face with Tahira, Ariana could see that the girl was spent. Her hair was soaked with sweat and her eyes were bloodshot. When she walked off this court, there was no doubt in Ariana's mind that the girl would burst into tears over her public humiliation. As long as she was alone. She definitely had too much pride to let anyone see her break down. Oddly enough, another trait Ariana admired.

"My father's man will be here in the morning with a briefcase for you," Tahira said smoothly. "Congratulations. You won the bet."

"Thank you," Ariana replied. "I'm impressed that you're being so gracious about it."

"Yes, well, that's the way I was raised," Tahira replied, reaching back to pick up her bag. "But I wouldn't be too excited about your little win here today," she said, brushing a hand toward the court as if it meant nothing. "There was something much larger at stake, and in that game, you definitely lost."

Ariana's heart slammed into her rib cage as Tahira stared into her eyes, all fire and brimstone. She meant the secret society, didn't she? Now that she had won, she had Briana Leigh's life back. And that life had to be perfect. She needed that secret society. A sizzle of trepidation zipped down Ariana's spine and it was all she could do not to shudder.

"You've just made a serious enemy, Ana," Tahira said with a sniff. "From here on out, I'd watch your back."

With that, Tahira strolled away, followed by Allison, Zuri, and

Rob. Ariana took a deep breath and let it out slowly, telling herself to stay calm. For all she knew, Tahira was throwing out an empty threat to save face. Ariana had dealt with much more formidable enemies in the past. Like Kaitlynn Nottingham. Kaitlynn, whom she now had to convince to wait one more day for her money.

But she knew Kaitlynn would comply. She'd have to. One more day was preferable to both of them going back to the Brenda T. Ariana tilted her head back toward the sun, closed her eyes, and just breathed. This time tomorrow, Kaitlynn would be on her way to the airport. And Ariana would finally be free.

SCREWED

"Good practice, everyone!" Palmer announced later that afternoon, tossing his towel on the bench in front of him. He ran his fingers through his damp hair and a few droplets of water hit his bare shoulders. The guys applauded and cheered, feeling good after their workout on the river. As they started to file out, Ariana gathered her things and followed. Slowly. She hadn't talked to Palmer since that kiss near the pond, and she wanted him to stop her. Wanted him to want to talk to her, too.

There was nothing wrong with wanting to talk to her friend's boyfriend, right? Especially when he might be the leader of the secret society she was dying to be a part of. She needed to make sure she stayed on his radar. Kept his interest. There was an ulterior motive here that had nothing to do with her heart.

"We're screwed," he said.

Ariana froze. She turned to look at him. Did he mean "we" as in the team, or "we" as in him and her?

"What do you mean?" Ariana asked.

"That wasn't a good practice. I just completely lied. Our time was in the tank," he said, running his towel over his hair. "There's no way we're going to beat blue and gray. Their teams are stacked with crew team members and ours is . . . not." He took a deep breath and blew it out as he straddled the bench. "I just hope we won the fund-raiser last night. If we did, we don't even need to worry about the race."

Ariana's heart clenched. This was very not good.

But it was all worth it, remember? Her life had depended on what she'd done last night and on her win against Tahira this morning. She had called Kaitlynn and convinced her to meet up the next day for the final exchange. The very thought of Kaitlynn getting on a plane and winging her way out of Ariana's life made her feel giddier than a girl on her wedding day. But Palmer couldn't know any of this. Would never know any of this.

"Well, they're counting the money from all three fund-raisers right now," she said slowly, trying to hold back the lump of nausea in her throat. "So we should know by the time we get back up to campus if we—"

"Palmer! There you are!" Allison stormed through the outer door of the boathouse, her pale skin flushed. Ariana wanted to reach out and pull the girl's curls for interrupting her alone time with Palmer, but managed to control her impulse. "You'd better come quick. Tahira is freaking out."

Palmer was on his feet in a second, his expression concerned and confused. Ariana, unfortunately, had a feeling she knew exactly what this was about.

"What's the matter?" Palmer asked.

"We lost!" Allison threw her hands up and let them slap down at her sides. "Blue won the fund-raiser event. We came in *third*!"

"What?" Palmer blurted, swinging one leg over the bench as he reached into his bag for a T-shirt. "That's not possible. The Landon thing was a lock!"

"That's what we all thought!" Allison replied, pacing along the wall. "But we didn't make half the amount we projected. It makes no sense! We were taking unofficial tallies all night long, and they were way *higher* than the total amount we just counted."

Ariana's palms prickled with sweat. Her throat was completely dry. Clearly, she'd stolen way too much.

"So where the hell did all that cash go?" Palmer asked, yanking a light blue T-shirt over his head and pulling it down.

"Someone must have stolen it!" Allison replied. "It's the only explanation."

Palmer glanced at Ariana as if he just remembered she was there, and she realized with a start that she should say something. An innocent person would be just as shocked as they were. An innocent person would be indignant and upset.

"Who would have done that?" Ignoring her pounding heart, she infused her voice with shock and anger. "The money was for charity."

"It could have been anyone. The place was a zoo," Palmer said, shouldering his duffel. "But I thought Brigit's guard was on the cash all night. How would someone have gotten by him?"

"Who knows?" Allison said, bringing her hand to her forehead. "Brigit's parents should fire that guy over this."

"This is not good," Palmer said. He pressed his hand against his forehead for a moment, thinking. "You know, between this and Christian's watch and all that other crap that was stolen . . . As much as I hate to say it, maybe it was someone on campus."

"But the only students who were there were on gold. No one on our team would steal. Who needs the money?" Allison said, throwing up a hand.

Ariana felt as if she was going to faint. She forced herself to breathe.

In, one . . . two . . . three . . .

Out, one . . . two . . . three . . .

And suddenly, the answer to Allison's question became clear.

"Adam," she heard herself say. "He was in charge of running the cash to the bank room all night. And he definitely needs the—"

"No." Palmer's voice was so firm and loud, it startled both Ariana and Allison. His jaw was set and his eyes were like pinpricks of anger. "No. I've known him my whole life, and he wouldn't do this."

Ariana's heart felt like it was trying to find a way out of her chest. "Okay."

"But I'm going to make sure there's an investigation," Palmer said. "There's definitely something weird going on around here." He took a deep breath and paced over to the wall, bracing his hand against it above his head as he stared down at the floor. "Shit. This means that if blue wins the crew race on Monday, they get Privilege House. That cannot happen."

"We need to get that money back," Allison said.

"But how?" Ariana said.

Allison looked Ariana up and down like she was dirt. "For starters, you should donate the cash you won from Tahira this morning," she said. "That'll pad the tally."

Ariana's blood stopped cold in her veins. No. No way. She could not give up that money. *Please, God, don't let them actually expect me to—*

"No. That would be cheating," Palmer said, shoving away from the wall. "We're not going to cheat."

Ariana felt a rush of confidence, as if Palmer had just knowingly defended her.

"Besides, there were faculty members presiding over the tallies, right?" she said. "They already have the official numbers."

Allison let out a groan, tipping her head back. "We'd better get back up there. Tahira is beside herself. Between this and what happened this morning," she said, casting another derisive look at Ariana—as if it were *her* fault the girl sucked at tennis. "I don't know. I think she's going to lose it. She wants to apologize to you, Palmer."

"To me? Please. She did her job. This isn't her fault," Palmer said, looking distracted. "I just . . . I don't know what we're going to do now."

"Win the crew race. It's all we can do," Allison said.

Palmer looked at Ariana, a pained expression in his eyes. She knew what he was thinking. And she also knew that as a good leader, he didn't want to say it in front of Allison. But he believed in his heart that the Welcome Week competition was already lost. There was no way they could make a comeback in crew. Just no way.

Ariana had lost Privilege House for her team. She had lost it for Palmer. And he was clearly heartbroken.

"I'd better go talk to Tahira," he said. "She has to know this isn't her fault."

He led Ariana and Allison out the side door and up the pathway to the hill. As Ariana followed behind them, all she could think about was Palmer's devastated face. This wasn't Tahira's fault. It was hers. And she had to find a way to fix it. For the team. For the secret society. But most of all, for Palmer. Maybe she couldn't be with him, but that didn't mean she couldn't help him.

OVER

Sunday morning dawned warm and clear, and Ariana felt hopeful. Even though Privilege House was all but lost, even though Welcome Week was a bust, she had to focus on the positive. After today, there would be no more looking over her shoulder, no more wincing every time her cell phone beeped. Maybe she'd be living in Cornwall with Allison all year long, but at least she'd be alive.

After finding her weekly allowance check from Grandma Covington in her mailbox, she knew for sure it was going to be a good day. The money would help her get off campus, and she had an idea of what she might do with the extra cash if everything worked out. She walked to the bursar's office, signed Briana Leigh's name to the back, and cashed the check. Then she strolled right over to the parking lot in front of Cornwall, where she found a black limousine idling at the curb. Tahira stood next to the driver's door, along with a brick house of a man with a scar across his nose, who was holding a black briefcase.

They both stared Ariana down as she approached, and Ariana couldn't help but feel intimidated. But then she realized that was exactly the point of this charade, so she lifted her chin and calmly stood before them.

"This is her," Tahira said, never taking her eyes off Ariana.

The man wordlessly handed over the briefcase. Heart hammering in her chest, Ariana held it in front of her and popped it open. It was full of crisp one-hundred-dollar bills.

"Don't trust me?" Tahira said snidely.

"I don't trust anyone," Ariana replied.

Tahira narrowed her eyes and for a split second Ariana thought she saw a hint of respect in them. Then a green cab pulled into the parking lot and the driver leaned out the window.

"You Ana Covington?"

"That's me," Ariana replied.

"Where're you going?" Tahira asked.

Ariana's heart caught for a split second. What if Tahira was in the secret society? What if she decided to get in her limo and tail Ariana. But then she felt the weight of the briefcase in her hand and realized there was a perfectly reasonable excuse for her going off campus.

"To the bank. You really think I want to keep this lying around my room?" she asked. She opened the back door of the cab and got inside, feeling guilty. "Later, T. Thanks!"

Then she gave the driver his directions and he turned the car around, leaving Tahira and her scary sidekick behind. All the way to Dupont Circle, Ariana kept glancing behind the car, but there was no sign of Tahira's limousine. She smiled as the driver pulled up in front of the Palomar Hotel. It was almost over.

Inside the air-conditioned lobby of the Palomar Hotel, Ariana spotted Kaitlynn right away. She was sitting in the far corner of the lobby, on a round couch with a high back, dressed in a plain black shift dress and her denim jacket, all the punk jewelry still in place. Ariana took a deep breath and savored the moment before walking over and placing the briefcase on the silver metal table in front of her.

"You can count it, but I'd rather you just go," Ariana said.

Kaitlynn slid the bag toward her and peeked inside. "I trust you."

Ariana's jaw dropped. "Oh, *now* you trust me?"

"I trust that you understand the consequences of failing," Kaitlynn said. She slid the strap of the suede bag up onto her shoulder as she stood, her backpack on the other arm. "Nice work, *B.L.*," she said, sliding a pair of aviator sunglasses onto her nose. "I'll say hi to the kangaroos for you."

As Kaitlynn brushed by, tugging a rolling suitcase behind her, Ariana realized she couldn't move. Didn't want to flinch and risk waking up from what had to be a dream.

"You know, I have to say, I wish it had turned out differently," Kaitlynn said, turning to face her. "You really were the best friend I ever had."

Ariana swallowed back the ten million insults, questions, and accusations that crowded her throat. She did not want to risk angering Kaitlynn now. She did not want to risk the girl lingering here one second longer and deciding she wanted to stay.

"So that's really it," she said. "You're really going."

Kaitlynn smiled a bit sadly. "Yes. This is really it," she said. "Have a nice life, Briana Leigh," she added, saying the name without a hint of sarcasm for the first time.

"You too, whatever your new name is," Ariana replied with a smirk.

Kaitlynn's smile widened for a split second and then she turned and walked away. She strolled through the crowded lobby of the Palomar and shoved the glass door open with the heel of her hand. Ariana stood there, stock still, as she watched the doorman hail a cab. Watched Kaitlynn get inside. Watched her slam the door. Watched the car pull away and disappear into traffic.

The torture was finally over. Really and truly.

And her new life was just about to begin.

LOOKING UP

On the way back to campus, Ariana indulged in a shopping spree. She blew almost all of her five-hundred-dollar allowance on champagne, chocolates, glassware, and a glass platter at an upscale market near Capitol Hill. If she was truly going to start her new life, she intended to do it in style. She was so confident and giddy, the clerk behind the counter barely even glanced at her fake ID. As Ariana got back in the cab and headed toward APH, she took in the sights of Washington for the first time since her arrival. Finally, she felt able to enjoy the historical buildings and stately monuments. Things were very much looking up.

Back at school, Ariana felt as if the universe were smiling down at her. Allison was nowhere to be found, so she had the room all to herself to set up. She laid out the treats on the platter and poured five glasses of bubbly, then slipped handwritten invitations under the doors of her friends' rooms. Within minutes there was a knock on her dorm room door. When she opened it, all four of them were gathered in the hallway.

"What's all this about?" Lexa asked, holding up the invitation.

"Just a little celebration!" Ariana said, lifting a palm. "Come in!"

"Is that champagne?" Soomie asked, her eyes widening. She quickly closed the door behind her, then stayed close to it, as if she wanted to be ready to make her escape in case of a raid. Maria and Brigit, meanwhile, pounced on the glasses. "That is *so* against the rules."

"Come on, Soomie. Live a little," Maria said, handing her a glass. Soomie took it between her thumb and fingers and wrinkled her nose, holding it away from her as if it were a glass of liquid poison.

"So, what are we celebrating?" Lexa asked, holding her glass aloft.

"Whatever you guys want to celebrate," Ariana said. Her heart was so giddy she wanted to giggle. But she had always hated giggling. It was so unsophisticated. She struggled to hold the urge back and pressed her lips together.

"To winning the crew race tomorrow and getting into Privilege House" Lexa said, tipping her glass slightly.

Ariana's heart panged, but she let it go. She was not going to think negative thoughts. Not here. Not now.

"To the start of a new school year," Soomie suggested, finally stepping away from the door.

"To Ana kicking Tahira's ass!" Brigit put in.

"To . . . new friends," Maria said, glancing at Ariana.

Ariana smiled. The giggle finally escaped and she didn't even mind. "To new beginnings."

"Hear, hear," Lexa cheered. Everyone laughed, and together they stepped into a tight circle, clinking their glasses together as one.

REDEMPTION

That evening after dinner, Soomie challenged Ariana to a game of chess and Ariana, ignoring the warnings of her other friends about Soomie's skill, agreed. They all adjourned to the Hill, which was packed with people unwinding after their meal, and Ariana was looking forward to a good battle of wits.

But she should have heeded her friends' warnings. Soomie was beating her. Big-time.

"So I wanted to go to a dance academy, but my father forbade it," Maria said, lounging back with both legs hooked over the leather arm of her chair. "Only if I graduate from APH with a three-point-five or better can I pursue a career in dance. And then I only have one year. If I don't reach some predetermined level of success after one year, it's college."

Ariana sat forward in her comfy suede chair and moved her rook on the chessboard. She was starting to get the feeling that Maria's father was a major dictator. "Who predetermines the level of success you have to reach?"

Without a moment's hesitation, Soomie moved her pawn and sat back again.

"He does, of course," Maria said, sipping her coffee.

"Fathers," Lexa said, rolling her eyes.

"Tell me about it. My dad totally fired Rudolpho," Brigit added, dropping onto the end of the couch where Soomie was seated. "I *liked* Rudolpho. What happened wasn't his fault."

Ariana sucked in a breath through her teeth and her fingers automatically clenched into a fist. Did they have to talk about the missing money every second? Couldn't they all just relax?

"Well, stick a fork in us. We're done," Palmer announced, flopping onto the couch next to Lexa and leaning back into the crook of her arm. Ariana's fist clenched even tighter. Palmer rolled his baseball between his hands and gazed at it in a distracted way.

"What's the matter?" Lexa asked, reaching up to run her fingers over his hair.

He sighed. "I just talked to Elizabeth and Martin and wheedled their crew times out of them. They each have a good five seconds on our best time. There's no way we can win this thing. Hope you girls are comfortable at Cornwall, because it looks like it's where you'll be staying."

"No!" Maria said lifting her head. "I need my river view!"

"Sorry. Get used to staring at the parking lot," Palmer said with a sigh.

"Some captain you are," Brigit said.

Everyone gaped at her.

"Brigit!" Lexa scolded.

"What?" Brigit scooched to the edge of her seat and planted her feet firmly on the floor. "I'm serious! What kind of captain talks like that?"

"A realistic one," Palmer said, sitting up straight and sliding away from Lexa. Ariana's fingers unclenched and she felt the sting of the points where her nails had dug into her palm.

Let it go. You have to let this attraction go, she told herself. *Lexa told you about the secret societies. She has your back. You have to have hers.*

She reached for the board and moved her rook again.

"The blue and gray teams are packed with crew team members, and we only have three: me, Landon, and Rob," Palmer said, bracing his elbows on his thighs as he leaned forward. "And scrawny guys like Adam and Christian are not gonna get it done."

"I say we sabotage their boats," Lexa suggested, glancing at Maria and laughing. "Mess with their rudders or something."

Ariana's heart skipped a beat. Was that possible?

"Why does everyone keep suggesting cheating?" Palmer blurted, dropping back on the couch. "I'd rather lose fairly than cheat."

Lexa's cheeks darkened in embarrassment. "I was just kidding, Palmer," she said, glancing toward the center of the room and away from him. "You know me better than that."

Palmer blew out a sigh. "I know. I'm sorry." He reached up and toyed with her hair on her back. "I'm just pissed off. With that Landon fund-raiser, I really thought this whole thing was in the bag."

"So did we," Maria said sadly.

Soomie smacked her pawn down in front of Ariana's king. "Check-mate!" she announced happily.

Ariana sighed. She hadn't remotely seen that move coming, but she didn't even mind the loss. Her brain was too busy formulating a new plan. One that would assure gold the win and secure Privilege House for her and her friends. One that would redeem her for what she had done.

Maybe Lexa couldn't do this for Palmer—wouldn't do this. But Ariana could.

PLAY IT SAFE

Ariana waited until the digital clock on her desk clicked over to exactly 2 a.m. Then she quietly moved her sheets aside to expose her fully clothed body, sat up, and shoved her feet into her black ballet flats. Before bed she had dressed in a long-sleeved black T-shirt and black cigarette pants, then cuddled under the covers until Allison was finished with her fifteen-minute marathon floss session and went to sleep. During the last four hours of wide-awake waiting, she had reviewed the plan meticulously from start to finish over and over and over again. By now, she was confident and more than ready to get it over with. And more than ready to get away from Allison's snoring for a little while. She tiptoed across the room, opened the door without a sound, and moved swiftly down the hall.

Outside, the air was cool and still, Ariana hesitated for a moment. She had planned to take the direct route and sprint across campus, but now that she was faced with all the glowing pathway lamps and security lights, she wasn't so sure. Maybe it would be better to stick to the shadows and move along the walls of the buildings. Always better to play it safe.

As she raced along the outer walls of the dorms, heading for the hill and the river down below, all she could think about was Palmer's face. The look of shocked glee he'd wear when Team Gold won the race later this morning. He wouldn't know it, but it would all be thanks to her. Maybe one day, when they were old and gray and watching their grandkids play in the front yard of their sprawling desert estate, she would tell him. And he would look at her and smile and say he always knew she would take care of him.

Ariana bit back a giddy laugh just thinking about it. It was a stupid fantasy, she knew, but it was the middle of the night and she felt daring and dangerous. And as long as she kept it to herself, who the hell cared? She scampered down the hill, her long auburn hair trailing behind her. She was racing toward the boathouse, but it felt more like she was racing toward her future.

LITTLE MIRACLE

Ariana stood on the dock before the race Monday morning, surrounded by the rest of her team, her hair pulled back in a tight ponytail. It seemed as if the entire school had gathered either at the starting
point of the race, or near the finish line upriver. Blue, gray, and gold
balloons were tied all along the safety railings on the dock and everyone was dressed up in team colors. The excitement in the air was
palpable as photos were snapped, friendly bets were made and trash
talking abounded. This was it. The final event of Welcome Week.
This race would determine which team got to live in Privilege House.
And which secret society would secure bragging rights for the rest of
the year.

As Palmer geared up for his pre-race speech, Ariana wondered
how long it would be before the true tests of the secret society began.
There had to be more to getting in than being a hard worker during Welcome Week. Whatever it was, Ariana would be ready for the

challenge. Hadn't she already proven that last night, risking her neck so gold would win today? She only wished the society could know the lengths she had gone to. But that could never be.

"All right, team, it all comes down to this," Palmer said, strolling back and forth in front of the crew members. He was wearing a tight black shirt and dark gold APH mesh shorts and looking gorgeous. "We win this, we're in. Privilege House is within our grasp. So dig in, concentrate, and leave it all out there on the water, okay?"

The team cheered and Ariana clapped along with them.

"Ladies! Gentlemen! To the boats!" Headmaster Jansen announced, strolling along the dock.

The air filled with cheers and a bunch of spectators took off and grabbed their bikes, intent on getting to the finish line before the race was over. Palmer stepped over to Ariana and crossed his arms over his chest as the rest of the team filed by, headed for their boat.

"You ready for this?" he asked.

"Definitely," she said, trying to hide the extreme level of her giddiness. "Good speech. You seem a little more confident than you did last night."

"Well, Brigit had a point," Palmer said, looking out at the water. "If I'm going to be a leader, I've got to lead, not bring everyone down. But I can tell *you* the truth," he said under his breath, causing Ariana's face to flush. He was about to take her into his confidence. She was the one person he could be truthful with. In that split second she decided it was okay to pretend that she was Palmer's girlfriend, that Lexa didn't exist. After all, she was the one who was here for him—the one he had *chosen* to be here—while Lexa was out there somewhere in the faceless crowd. She looked up into his eyes and felt that they were the only two people in the world.

"We're going to need a miracle," he said.

"All we can do is go out there and give it everything we have," Ariana said in a soothing voice. "Whatever happens, happens."

Palmer smiled. "Thanks, Ana. Let's go do it."

Ariana bit back a smile as he squeezed her upper arm, then turned to join the others. Little did Palmer know, she was his own little miracle.

GLORY

"Pull! Pull! Come on, you losers, pull!" Ariana shouted, straining her voice to its limit. The wind tore at her face and coaxed tears from the corners of her eyes as the boat zipped across the water. In her peripheral vision, she could see both blue and gray gaining on them. How was this possible? How could they be so close when she had spent the wee hours of the morning sabotaging their boats?

Apparently, Team Gold really *did* suck.

"Dig in, you guys! You've got this! Pull!" Ariana cried, sitting forward.

She could hear the guys grunting, straining for every last ounce of strength. Stray cheers floated across the water now and then, niggling at her nerves. She looked up at the finish line. Almost there.

"This is it, guys. The last stretch! This is Privilege House! Now pull! Pull! Pull!" Ariana screamed. She could see blue's cox now. Their boat was inching up. Inching up to meet gold's. Or were they ahead? Ariana couldn't tell. It was far too close to tell.

"Pull! Pull! Pull!"

And then, they were over the finish line. An air horn blared. There was a suspended moment of silence as the guys dropped their oars and looked up, sweat pouring down their faces and necks. The boat continued to glide away from the crowds as everyone waited for the announcement.

"What the hell happened?" Palmer asked, looking up at Ariana. "Was it just me or did we just—"

"And the winner of the crew race is . . . the gold team!" Headmaster Jansen announced.

"Yes!" Palmer thrust his fists in the air as the rest of the boat celebrated. Ariana would have killed to hug him, but it wasn't possible from where they were both sitting. Back on the shore, the hundred or so members of Team Gold celebrated, jumping up and down and dancing around and screaming their congratulations toward the boat. Ariana laughed and leaned back, looking up at the sun.

Privilege House was hers.

Back on shore a few minutes later, Ariana was greeted by her friends with hugs and backslaps and squeals of joy. Tahira jumped into Rob's sweaty arms, and Landon managed to give Maria a real kiss in all the mayhem, though he followed it up with cheek kisses for several other girls, including Soomie, just to be safe. Adam hugged Brigit for a tad longer than was absolutely necessary, so it seemed as if Lexa's plan was working there. Everyone had someone to celebrate with, except Ariana, but she wasn't going to let it get her down. Her adrenaline was still rushing through her veins as she took this in. All she wanted to do was get moving. Get back to Cornwall and pack her stuff. See what the inside of Privilege House was like. Start taking advantage of those privileges. Start truly showing the members of this secret society what she was all about. She did notice, however, that Lexa did not immediately jump Palmer's bones, but figured it had something to do with the fact that Palmer was down by the edge of the water with the other two team captains and the headmaster.

Headmaster Jansen called the crowd to order, standing near the edge of the water in a short-sleeved button down shirt and khakis. There was a huge gold trophy situated on a table to her left.

"Congratulations to Team Gold for a fantastic win!" she announced. The gold team members exploded in cheers while the rest of the student body applauded politely. "Palmer, why don't you come over here and collect your trophy?"

Palmer acknowledged the cheers with a modest wave as he walked by Elizabeth and Martin, then thrust the trophy overhead with both hands. As the din died down, Headmaster Jansen laughed.

"All right now, it's time to bring the Welcome Week events to a close with the shedding of the colors," she said. All around Ariana, students removed their armbands and tossed them on the ground at their feet. She quickly untied her own and let it fall. "From here on out we are one school with one purpose," Headmaster Jansen announced.

"Yeah, but tonight, gold is gonna party!" Landon shouted, earning hoots and hollers from his teammates.

Ariana grinned. She knew that, in fact, everyone was going to party that night. There was a school-wide soiree scheduled for that evening as the official close of Welcome Week and the official start of the school year. Now Ariana was looking forward to it more than ever. It would be the first event at Atherton-Pryce where she could fully relax. Palmer walked over to join his team with the trophy and everyone gathered around him. Ariana slipped to the front of the crowd.

"Congratulations, Captain," she said.

"Congratulations, Cox," he replied.

Then he reached down and hugged her, all sweaty and smelly and perfect. Ariana closed her eyes and savored the moment. In her heart she felt as if they had both engineered their win. He had led the team in the spotlight, while she had led behind the scenes. This was their moment of glory. A moment she'd remember forever.

"Lexa!" Palmer shouted, suddenly releasing Ariana. His face turned red as he glanced guiltily at Ariana and wiped his free palm on his shorts. "There you are, love of my life!" he crowed. Ariana stepped back, feeling sour. *Way to overcompensate, Palmer.*

Lexa jogged over and jumped into Palmer's arms, planting her lips on his. He held her tightly in his arms, the trophy still clutched in one hand behind her back. Team Gold cheered for the couple as if *they* were the ones who had won the competition for them. As if Lexa had anything to do with anything. Ariana had to take another step back to keep from being smacked in the head by the trophy. Her entire body flushed with anger and searing jealousy from head to toe. That was her moment— hers and Palmer's—and Lexa had just ripped it away from her.

Why does she have to be here? If she weren't here, Palmer would be mine. I know it, Ariana thought. *If only she could just disappear.*

Suddenly, Ariana felt something snap inside her mind. She had not just thought that. No. Lexa was not expendable. Lexa was her friend. And she wasn't about to do anything to jeopardize her new life.

Nothing, she told herself as Palmer kissed the tip of Lexa's adorable nose. *Nothing, nothing, nothing.*

THE GREATER GOOD

"Well, Miss Covington, I must say . . . I'm amazed," Mr. Pitt said, folding his hands on his desk in front of him. Outside the sun was just starting to go down and Ariana could hear the shouts and laughter coming from the quad. The party to mark the end of Welcome Week was just beginning, and she longed to be there.

"Amazed?" Ariana repeated.

"Your test scores went up by an average of twenty-four percent," he said, handing over a printout of her grades. "If that's not amazing, I don't know what is."

Ariana's chest inflated with pride as she reached for the paper. She knew she had done well, but she was pleased by how *very* well. "Does this mean I have a new schedule?" she asked hopefully.

"Done and done," Mr. Pitt said, handing over a schedule card as well.

Ariana bit her bottom lip as she looked it over. Honors English, honors American history, honors chemistry, honors French, calculus, and her two electives, creative writing and modern literature.

"I hate to get ahead of myself, but if you manage to ace that curriculum, Princeton is going to *have* to accept you," he said.

"Thank you," Ariana replied, beaming. "Thank you so much for everything, Mr. Pitt."

She knew that he was not responsible for this. That it was her own determination and talent and drive that had gotten her to this place. But at that moment her heart was so full, she felt she should share the wealth with someone.

"You're welcome, Miss Covington," he said, reaching for a book that he had open facedown on his desk. "Now, I believe you have a party to attend."

"I do," Ariana said, standing up and tucking the two pieces of paper—the evidence of her triumph—into her bag. "Goodnight, Mr. Pitt!"

"Good luck, Miss Covington."

Ariana closed the door behind her and covered her mouth with both hands, squeezing her eyes closed with joy. She was on her way. On her way to straight A's and Princeton and the life she'd always wanted. As she stepped outside into the cool evening air, she felt a sense of absolute peace. She was going to get everything she wanted. She was certain of it.

In the distance she saw the twinkle lights that had been strung all around the quad flicker on, and the student body cheered. Music wafted across campus and happy voices filled the air. Ariana smiled and turned her steps toward the party, feeling as if it was being thrown just for her.

She had only taken two steps when Palmer came around the side of the building and nearly slammed right into her.

"Sorry, I—"

"Oh my gosh, Palmer. You scared me!" she exclaimed, hand to her chest. She was about to suggest they walk to the party together when she got a good look at his face. His distressed, panicked face. "What's wrong?"

"Nothing. Everything. I . . ." He looked at her curiously, as if he was deciding whether or not to trust her. Ariana's heart skipped a beat. There was nothing she wanted more in that moment than for Palmer to trust her. "I have to go talk to the headmaster," he said finally.

"About what?" Ariana asked, stopping him with her hand to his arm.

Palmer blew out a frustrated sigh. "I just came from the boat-house." He took a step closer to her and looked around, then lowered his voice. "Lexa did it. She cheated. The rudders on the other two boats were all screwed up."

All of the breath rushed from Ariana's lungs. This was not happening. Why would Palmer have gone back and inspected the boats? Why couldn't he have just left it alone? But then, a little flame of hope sparked in her mind. He was blaming Lexa. He was automatically blaming Lexa.

This was something she could use to her advantage.

"How do you know it was Lexa?" she asked.

"Who else could it have been?" Palmer asked, palms to the sky. "You were there. It was her idea."

Ariana had to play this perfectly. She had to say what a friend would say in this moment.

"Well, if she did it . . . she did it for you," Ariana said. "For the team."

"Yeah, but I *told* her not to," Palmer fumed, blotches of anger coloring his cheeks. "She knows that cheaters make me sick. She *knows* that. How could she do this?"

"Palmer. Calm down," Ariana said in a soothing voice.

"I can't," he said, looking off toward the quad and the party. "We can't do this. I have to tell Headmaster Jansen, and gold has to forfeit their win."

"What? No!" Ariana breathed. "You can't do that."

"Why not? I don't see any other choice," Palmer replied.

"Just wait. Think about this for a second," Ariana said, her mind reeling. She could not lose Privilege House now. Not after all the ups and downs of the last week. Not after everything she'd risked. "If you . . . if you tell the headmaster, Lexa's going to get in trouble. She'll be humiliated in front of the entire school. She might even get expelled."

"Well, she should have thought about that before she did something this stupid," he spat.

Wow. This guy was really serious about his values. Apparently they meant more to him than his girlfriend, a thought that made Ariana's heart flutter with hope.

"Okay, but what about the rest of the team?" Ariana said. "They'll be so disappointed. Everyone worked their butts off. And we should have won the fund-raiser. We would have if some idiot hadn't made off with half the money."

Palmer glanced at her. For the first time she saw something shift in his eyes. He was considering this. He was listening to her.

"True," he said finally.

"And if we'd won the fund-raiser, we would have won the whole thing," Ariana continued. "So technically, we should be in Privilege House. Should the whole team be punished because one person cheated?"

Palmer dropped his head forward and pinched the top of his nose with his thumb and forefinger. "You may have a point."

Ariana smiled to herself. She was so good at this. So good for him. Feeling emboldened by her day of successes, she stepped forward and placed her hand on his forearm. He lifted his head and gazed at her fingers.

"Besides," she said, sliding her fingers down his wrist and into his hand, pulling his arm down straight as she did. "If you report this, we won't get to live in the same dorm."

They were holding hands now, the two of them alone in the oncoming darkness. And Palmer made no move to change this. He slowly moved his gaze from their entwined fingers, up Ariana's torso and neck and chin and nose, until he was staring into her eyes. The surge of attraction between them was so strong at that moment, Ariana was certain he felt it too.

"This goes against everything I believe in," he said softly.

"Sometimes you have to sacrifice yourself . . . sacrifice your beliefs . . . for the greater good," she said. It was a lesson she'd learned time and again over the past few years. The lesson that had gotten her to this place.

Palmer let out a sigh. "Come on," he said wearily, squeezing her hand. "Let's go party."

PERFECT

"So when do we move into Privilege House?" Ariana asked Landon. She was standing with him and Adam near the snack table, watching as the rest of the student body mingled and danced. Lexa, Maria, and Soomie had gone off to the bathroom together fifteen minutes ago, and Palmer had spent most of the night with a group of guys from the crew team, avoiding both her and Lexa. She hadn't seen Brigit all night and wondered if she was off in the gym, working on the diet plan.

"Tonight," Landon said, tossing up a piece of popcorn and catching it in his mouth.

"In the dark?" Ariana asked.

"Yeah. It's actually kind of fun," Landon replied, looking her up and down.

"Sounds needlessly difficult to me," Ariana replied, sipping her iced tea.

Adam took a bite of a chocolate chip cookie and spoke with his mouth full. "I'll second that." Ariana tried not to cringe at his lack of manners. He was Palmer's friend, after all.

"So, Ana, did you listen to those songs yet?" Landon asked, grabbing some more popcorn.

"Not yet," Ariana said. She had seen them sitting in her in-box, but downloading them hadn't exactly been a priority with everything else going on. Landon put his popcorn-filled fists to his heart as if she'd just speared him, and Ariana laughed. "I will, I will. I should have a little more time on my hands now."

"Now," Landon said dubiously. "Now that classes are gonna start you'll have *more* time."

Ariana shrugged. "It's been a busy week."

"Seriously. And I still can't believe we won today," Adam said. "How is that possible?"

"Maybe Ana, here, is just good at her job," Landon said, nudging Ariana with his elbow before tossing and catching another kernel. "Dude, I'm so glad Palmer picked you instead of Lexa. Girl's probably never raised her voice in her life."

"Looks like she's doing that right now," Adam put in, lifting his chin.

Ariana glanced across the dance floor and saw Lexa and Palmer engaged in a heated conversation on the outskirts of the party. Maria and Soomie stood a few feet off to the side, looking tense and uncomfortable. Ariana's heart skipped ten thousand beats. Apparently, Palmer had intercepted Lexa on her way back from the bathroom, but what was he saying to her? Was he accusing her? Were they breaking up? Why, why, why had Ariana turned down their invite to the bathroom? She should be over there with them right now, overhearing every word.

"Uh oh," Landon said, crunching away. "Looks like APH's numero uno couple have uncoupled."

Sure enough, Lexa was rushing off in tears, Soomie and Maria trailing behind her. Ariana took a step to follow, but stopped the second Palmer turned around. He looked right at her with an expression so full of meaning it made her feel weightless.

He had done this for her. He had broken up with Lexa to be with her.

Slowly, Palmer broke eye contact and returned to Robert and Christian. Ariana got it. He couldn't come right over to her after breaking Lexa's heart. That would be too gauche. In fact, for the next few days at least, they would probably need to steer clear of each other. Until Lexa got over him. Until the appropriate mourning period had passed. But as soon as that happened, Palmer would be hers.

Ariana felt as if she had just been granted her every wish. Kaitlynn was well on her way to Australia, Palmer was single, she had her dream schedule, and she would be living in Privilege House as of tonight. Yes, Lexa was upset, but she would get over it. People broke up all the time. Soon everything would be fine. Perfect, actually.

"Ana! Hey!" Brigit grabbed Ariana's arm and spun her around.

"Hey, where have you been?" Ariana asked Brigit. "Everyone's been looking for you."

"I know. I was at the student affairs office. The headmaster asked me to welcome a new transfer," Brigit said, all excited. "She seems pretty cool, so I thought maybe you guys could bond, since both of you are new and all."

She looked over her shoulder and Ariana followed her gaze. A tall girl in a pink cable-knit sweater and khaki shorts was making her way through the crowd, drawing the interested glances of the students as she passed by. Christian stopped her to introduce himself and her face was in shadow, but Ariana saw that her brown hair was cut short in a preppy do. Ariana was just about to plaster on her best welcoming smile when the girl looked up and caught her eye.

Ariana's heart completely stopped.

"Hi! I'm Lillian Oswald," the girl announced, stepping forward. "You must be Ana. Brigit already told me *all* about you. We are going to have *so* much fun this year!"

Then she reached out her arms and, much to Brigit's obvious delight, pulled Ariana toward her. Every inch of Ariana's body wanted to recoil in horror, but she couldn't. Not with Brigit right there and all these people around. All she could do was close her eyes, grit her teeth, and allow herself to be embraced by the girl she hated most in the world.

Kaitlynn Nottingham.

Visit the official home of

PRI⛨ILEGE

WWW.PRIVATENOVELS.COM

Where Kate Brian fans chat, win prizes, *and*
find out what happens next!

Yachts, premieres, couture . . .

When you're this big,

those are the little things in life.

The Girl series

Girl Stays in the Picture
June 2009

Check out the first book in the new series
from the bestselling author of
The Au Pairs and *Blue Bloods.*